ABOUT THE AUTHOR

Dave Rigby, who lives in West Yorkshire, started writing after he retired twelve years ago.

His first book, *Darkstone*, was published in 2015.

Shoreline, the first Harry Vos Investigation, followed in 2016 with the second, *Redline*, joining in 2018.

End of the Line is the third of the Harry Vos books.

End of the Line

A Harry Vos Investigation

Dave Rigby

Matador
9 Priory Business Park,
Wistow Road, Kibworth Beauchamp,
Leicestershire. LE8 0RX
Tel: 0116 279 2299
Email: books@troubador.co.uk
Web: www.troubador.co.uk/matador
Twitter: @matadorbooks

ISBN 978 1800465 725

British Library Cataloguing in Publication Data.
A catalogue record for this book is available from the British Library.

Printed and bound by CPI Group (UK) Ltd, Croydon, CR0 4YY
Typeset in 11pt Minion Pro by Troubador Publishing Ltd, Leicester, UK

Matador is an imprint of Troubador Publishing Ltd

For Harry, Mary & Jo

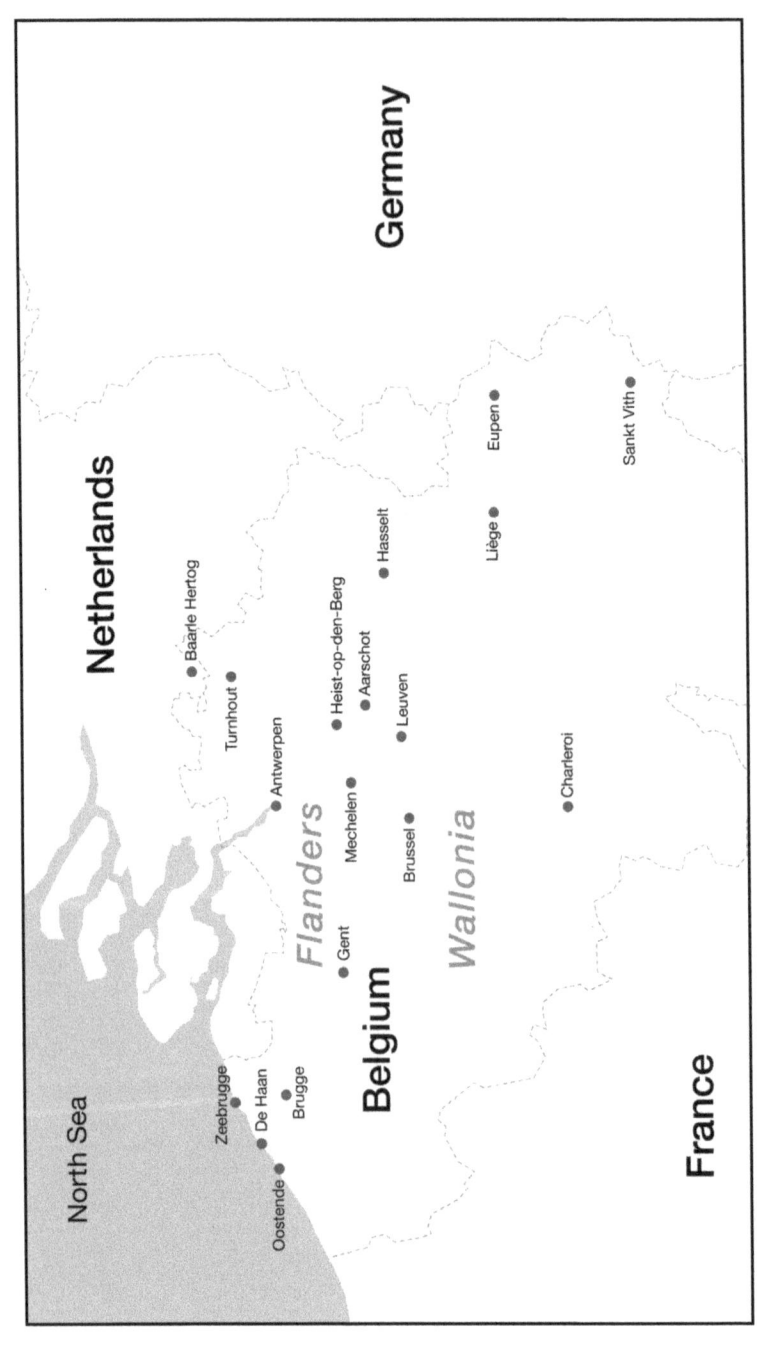

One

The sound of a car pulling up, low voices, a door opening and closing. A dream.

Marc was suddenly awake. Midnight. Nothing to be heard. Nothing.

Not even the radio, which was usually on all night in the bedroom through the party wall – news or classical music. Not loud enough for him to be able to pick out individual words or particular tunes, but a low buzz, vaguely reassuring, letting him know that his neighbour, Kurt, was around.

In contrast, the only other house in the little terrace of three was frequently empty for weeks on end, the owner working away. Even when it was occupied, there was barely a sound to be heard.

Should he tap on Kurt's front door, to check he was alright? It wouldn't be that cold outside. He'd just need to slip on a pair of joggers and a fleece. But then he'd feel foolish if everything was OK. Which it probably was.

He turned over.

Next thing – his alarm clock said 7:00am.

Seven hours had flashed by just like that. The sun was demanding attention through his too-thin curtains. Surely, he'd bought a thicker pair to hang, but where had he put them? Still quiet next door. He'd check on Kurt, just as soon as he'd woken up properly with a coffee. Downstairs, mug in hand, he watched the birds swooping in search of breakfast only to be met with the disappointment of empty feeders.

Outside, with only his pyjama top underneath the old paint-stained fleece, it was colder than he'd expected. Even with the stick, his joints complained as they always did first thing. It hadn't been like that in the old days though, roped up, leading the way, feeling on top of the world.

There was no response to his knocking. He unzipped the back pocket of his joggers and removed the just-in-case spare key that Kurt had given him a couple of years back.

Once inside, he flicked on the light in the dark hallway and manoeuvred his way around the boxes stacked up against one wall. It was definitely getting worse. In the living room, Kurt was fast asleep in the big chair to one side of the fireplace, no heat, a heap of ash and a little charred wood. At least the fireguard was in place. More boxes, pictures leaning up against the wall, a radiogram in a walnut-veneered cabinet, piles of hardback books, a shelf-full of 78 rpm records. As Marc pulled back the heavy, dust-laden curtains, light streamed in through the grubby window. Kurt didn't stir.

His stirring days were over.

Two

"Marc, what a nice surprise, everything OK? How's the arthritis?"

"It's a bugger, Harry. I need a stick to get most places these days – just like you. How's the new Mrs?"

"Good thanks. We're both good. Katherine usually works part time now and I'm mainly pottering around. I'm intrigued to know why you're calling though. You've never been a social caller – always have a reason. Don't tell me you've got plans for a trek in the Andes!"

Harry Vos thought back to his mountaineering days and that last fateful climb in the Dolomites, the fall, the serious knee injury, the permanent limp he'd been left with. Marc had been the hero of the day, climbing down and fetching help.

"If only! I dream about the mountains all the time. No, I'm phoning because I've got a job for you – if you're interested."

Vos wasn't sure if he wanted a job. He'd grown to like not doing too much, keeping the garden going, walking Barto, his Irish wolfhound, weekend trips away with Katerine and the occasional minor investigation.

"How would you fancy becoming an heir hunter?"

"A what?"

Marc explained.

Kurt Baumer, his next-door neighbour had just died. Eighty-six years old, no will, something of a recluse, no known relatives, an estate which included the house and some investments. His lawyer had no record of any living relatives and had neither the time nor the inclination to make further enquiries himself. He'd asked for submissions of interest from anyone who was immediately available and had appropriate experience in the field of people-tracing. In other words, to find out if there were any surviving relatives who might have an interest in the estate.

Marc thought Harry was the man for the job.

"Think about it. Let me know by tomorrow if you can. You'd be more than welcome to stay here."

Vos didn't much like staying in other people's homes. Marc had been a good friend, still was up to a point, but they'd never had that much in common apart from the mountaineering. And his friend had always been too much of a drinker.

Vos knew there was a map of Marc's local area somewhere in the house. It wasn't in any of the bookcases, the desk in the hallway, the kitchen cupboard or the living room dresser. He was about to give up the search when he noticed a few maps stuck between CDs on shelving to the side of the cooker. There it was – 1:25000 Sankt Vith and Schoenberg.

Clearing the breakfast crockery off the kitchen table and into the sink, he spread the map out and found Marc's village, which was about five kilometres from St Vith.

A reluctance to disturb his current well-balanced lifestyle wasn't the only reason for some hesitancy about taking on the job. His mother's death had affected him far more than he'd expected. Katerine, his son Eddie and daughters Kim and Josina had all been very supportive. Weeks had passed by with him staying solidly inside his comfort zone. It had been hard to think about taking on anything new.

But maybe it was time to start venturing outside the zone, particularly as Katerine was working away for a few weeks.

A little bell rang in his head. Josina had family connections somewhere in the Ost Kantonen – the German-speaking area in the far east of Belgium. It would be worth having a word with her.

+ + +

The Vectra had made its final journey.

Ryck removed a black beanie hat and scratched the top of his head.

"What kind of vehicle do you want me to look for, Uncle?"

Vos still hadn't got used to the fact that his nephew was effectively running the Berchem garage. Two years previously he'd started a nursing course, full of enthusiasm. Part-time work at the garage had helped him to pay his way as a student. But enthusiasm for the course hadn't lasted. Being under a car bonnet was far more his thing than studying in a classroom. And, as a mechanic, he'd proved a fast learner. The garage had been owned by two brothers ever since Vos could remember. One had recently and very reluctantly retired due to ill-health. The other, Gaston, who was only marginally fitter, was gradually reducing his working week and 'keeping an eye on the place'.

"Well, I got to like that Berlingo I borrowed. Wouldn't mind one of those, but I don't want to spend too much."

"Right you are, I'll see what I can find. What about work? Anything interesting happening?"

Vos felt himself getting quite enthusiastic telling Ryck about the call from Marc in St Vith and the new job hunting for an heir to Kurt Baumer's estate.

"That sounds just right for you, Uncle. How are you going to get down there?"

"Well Josina's got family near St Vith. When I spoke to her about the job, she sounded keen to come with me and visit her relatives. We're going by train, changing at Liege and getting off at a small place called Gouvy. That's where her folks are. I'll get a bus from there to St Vith. Marc lives just outside the town. He's offered me the use of his car to get around."

"Glad to hear you'll have a travelling companion. Makes me wish I could come along as well, get the old team back on the road again. But a family man like me has responsibilities you know." The way Ryck smiled made it difficult for Vos to tell whether his nephew was being serious or not. "Anyway, it's good to see you taking this on. Me and Magda were getting a bit worried about you, after Grandma and everything."

Vos felt it was ironic that he'd be working on behalf of a dead man as a way of helping cope with his grief.

+ + +

Vos boarded the train in Brussels. Josina joined him at Leuven. She'd moved back there to be near her mum, whose health wasn't good. It was working out well.

"My place is close to hers but not too close, so we can each get on with our own lives."

Vos enjoyed talking to her, but after a while, he knew it was time for a nap. Ever since the mini-stroke, he could tire quite quickly.

Although his eyes were closed, he wasn't actually asleep. The voice of the priest at his mother's funeral echoed around his head, sonorous, mournful. Her death had come as a complete shock. Birthday celebrations one day and the next she'd gone. Really, that's how he'd always wanted it to be, but it was difficult to cope with her not being around. There'd always been this guilty feeling of not being quite dutiful enough as a son. After confiding in Katerine, she'd told him that wasn't how his mother had seen it. But it was still difficult to shake off that regret. Mr Wouters, his mother's partner, had been an example to everyone at the funeral, clearly grieving but upright and dignified.

The train rumbled into Liege-Guillemins, where they had time for a coffee before boarding the connection to Gouvy. Josina told him about the hairdressing business, her three assistants and the possibility of taking on another salon. As ever she was upbeat and it helped him shake off his own gloomy thoughts.

"Dad was born in Gouvy, you know."

He hadn't known. She called her step-father 'dad' and him, her biological father, Harry. Vos thought back to the day when Josina had turned up on his doorstep out of the blue, with the news that she was his daughter. She'd not had much to go on but had managed to track him down. Although things had been very difficult for a while, there'd been an instant bond between them.

"I'll be staying with Dad's sister and her husband. We've always been very close. I used to stay with them during the summer holidays when I was in my teens, loved every minute of it and it gave Mum a bit of a break. Haven't seen them for a while, so it'll be good to catch up. Will you be staying with Marc?"

Two nights maximum, Vos had decided. Then he'd find somewhere else to stay.

Josina's aunt was there at Gouvy station to meet her. She offered Vos a lift to St Vith. He thanked her but declined the offer, preferring to take the local bus and have some time on his own to think about the new job. There was apparently a stack of paperwork in Kurt Baumer's house which might reveal some clues as to possible family links. Then there'd be local people who might know something.

The other bus passengers all seemed to know each other and Vos listened in to snatches of their conversation. His German wasn't good but he could pick up the gist of it, a mix of complaints about the weather and the government. The same as most places probably. He texted Marc to arrange for a lift from St. Vith.

When they reached the town, he took his bag down from the rack and left the bus. Just before it pulled away, he realised he'd left his walking stick on board and tapped on the door to attract the driver's attention. Given his dependency on the stick, forgetting it was a rare occurrence. Having retrieved it, he waited in the bus shelter for the arrival of his old mountaineering companion.

+ + +

A familiar sight. Bottles everywhere, empties discarded in large, red plastic boxes, full ones awaiting consumption, piled high in crates. Despite Vos' protests, Marc hauled his bag up the staircase, left hand on the rail for support and into the low-ceilinged back bedroom, a roof-light part-opened to air the place.

An hour with his feet up, willing himself not to go to sleep but inevitably succumbing. A funeral dream again, tossing shovel after shovel of earth into a bottomless grave.

Surprisingly refreshed by his siesta, despite the dream, he sat on an uncomfortably hard chair at the kitchen table, sipping hesitantly at a mug of herbal tea. Not his thing at all but he made an effort.

"How much do you know about your neighbour then?"

"Not that much really, considering I saw him most days and we'd usually exchange a few words. He generally kept himself to himself. Something of a hoarder, to put it mildly, as you'll soon find out. Worked as a colonial administrator in the Congo years ago up till independence and always wished he'd never left. Spent his career in different diplomatic jobs, all fairly junior from what I could gather. Oh, and he was keen on paintings and sculptures. That's about it really. His lawyer, the guy you'll be dealing with, doesn't seem to know much about him either. Holds the deeds for the house, which was owned outright and has details of some investments."

"What about friends?"

"Not sure Kurt had any really. Acquaintances, yes, but not

many of those. Few visitors apart from me, of course, and his doctor. Over the last few years, I've kept an eye on him, helped him with jobs he could no longer manage, fetched medicine from the pharmacy when he was ill – that sort of thing. Anyway, that's enough about Kurt for the time being. We can pick it up later. What about you and Katerine, you lucky man!"

Vos indulged his friend. He rarely talked about his wife, but chatting away, he knew Marc was right. He was a lucky man.

Talking about his mother's death proved difficult ground and he was relieved when his host moved the conversation on to their shared love of mountaineering. They worked their way through some wonderful Alpine photographs in a large, glossy coffee-table book. As they talked, Vos realised how hard it must have been for Marc to come to terms with the disabling effect of his arthritis.

"How are you managing here with the stairs? Must be getting more difficult," Vos said.

"It is. I've thought about moving to an apartment in town – even looked at one or two. But I like it here, don't really want to move. Anyway, it's probably time to go next door so you can get to work, Harry and build up an appetite for dinner!"

As they entered Kurt Baumer's house, it was the smell, or rather smells, that hit Vos: a mustiness despite the house having only been empty for a few days, the legacy of years of cigarette smoke hanging in the air and something that hinted at recent death. Or was that just his imagination working overtime? Then there were the numerous boxes stacked around the place giving off their own distinctive dusty aroma. They gave an appearance of chaos, but Marc mentioned Kurt's insistence that everything in the boxes was there for a purpose and that he knew, down to the last piece of paper, where each item was.

Vos wondered whether there really was some sort of order in the very apparent disorder in the house.

He was drawn to a box of old 78 records and flicked through a mix of classical works, some spread over three or four discs, Paul Robeson, Frank Sinatra and several rarities on a Congolese label. After a few minutes, Marc guided him away from the discs to what he called Kurt's study.

"This is where you're most likely to find something useful, although I wouldn't raise your hopes too high. He used to spend time in here, bashing away on that old typewriter there. Don't think he ever came to terms with the computer age. I'll leave you to it. If you haven't returned by seven, I'll come and drag you back for a drink or two before dinner."

Vos sat down in the wooden, heavily-cushioned swivel chair, swinging himself gently left and right and taking in the press cuttings pinned to the corkboard in front of him, the books on the shelves higher up, the dried-up plants on the windowsill and a single photograph, framed in what looked like ebony, of an old man.

In his search through Kurt's belongings, he'd need to stop himself getting distracted. The 78s were a magnet, but were unlikely to lead him to an heir and would have to wait. He'd start with the correspondence and photographs, particularly the older ones. With a bit of luck some of them might be annotated with the names of those captured on film years ago.

Desk drawers came first. Vos opened his notebook and took a fountain pen from the breast pocket of his jacket. It was a habit he'd got into in his factory days. Just a biro back then, but there'd always been one in the top pocket of his overalls, leaking ink, more often than not. His first wife, Margriet, used to complain about the difficulties this caused her when washing his workwear. Having brought her to mind, he took some time musing on the happy times they'd had together, before telling himself to get on with the job in hand.

Most of the letters were deadly dull. When Vos had made

his decision to take on the job, he'd imagined making a sudden magical discovery – unlocking a door to an estranged family member who would return to claim his or her rightful inheritance. But this correspondence was not inspiring, carbon copies of letters sent to the press complaining about all manner of issues of seemingly little importance, incoming mail from pompous-sounding gallery managers containing obscure details about this painting or that artefact, bills and bank statements going back years.

The castors on the chair squeaked as he pushed himself backwards to stretch his legs and he almost missed the sound of the doorbell. Had Marc forgotten his key?

The man standing on the doorstep looked confident, almost cocky. Mid-fifties Vos reckoned, short greying hair, overweight, well-dressed, a white panama hat in his hand.

"My name's Elias Kirchner. I've come in response to the newspaper advert!"

"I'm sorry," Vos replied. There was something about the man he didn't like. An air of superiority perhaps. "What advert would that be?"

"The notice in the local paper. *Would anyone who has a family connection with Herr Kurt Baumer, or might know of someone with such a connection please contact* …whatsisname, the lawyer. As I haven't yet had a reply from his office, I thought I'd come straight to Uncle Kurt's house. And you are?" The condescension in his voice reinforced Vos' original opinion of the man. He ignored the question.

"I'm afraid you'll need to follow the procedure detailed in the press notice and go through Ahrendt the lawyer before anything else can happen. You say you're a nephew. Was your father a brother of Kurt Baumer?"

"On the contrary, my late mother, Ursula, was his sister. But as the two siblings had not spoken to each other for over forty years, it may well be the case that there is no reference to me or my mother in any current documentation the lawyer may have. However, I can assure you that I have the necessary proof of family connection." Vos wondered why the supposed nephew spoke in such a formal and stilted manner. But he found curiosity was getting the better of him.

"Look, I've been hired to find out whether Kurt Baumer has any living relatives. If you give me the necessary details, I can check them out. You'll appreciate why I need to do this. After all it's not unheard of for people to turn up unexpectedly to claim an inheritance that's not actually theirs."

"Hired by who?"

"By Ahrendt."

The nephew hesitated, twisting the brim of his hat round and round in his hands. Finally, he put the panama back on his head, pulled an envelope out of an inside jacket pocket and handed it to Vos.

"You and the lawyer will find everything you need in there, including my contact details. I'm renting a house out in the sticks, on the way to Bullingen."

With that, he walked down the garden path, unlatched and re-latched the gate, climbed into a small white hatchback and drove off.

Three

Ryck stood in the pit. The lamp clipped to the underside of the Audi above him, was positioned to illuminate the exhaust system. He loved being in the garage, had picked up a great deal from the elderly brothers over the previous two years and couldn't wait to take on full responsibility.

"Ryck!" A shout from Gaston, the brother who was still working. "You've got a visitor."

He walked up the worn, stone steps built in to one end of the pit and instinctively rubbed his hands on one of the oily rags that filled his overall pockets.

The visitor was alert, youngish, casually dressed and not someone he recognised.

"I'm sorry to bother you at work, Mr Vos. You don't know me but your uncle might have mentioned my name – Maes, Eden Maes."

The name was indeed familiar to Ryck and he was immediately worried. Maes had been a central figure in the Redline case his uncle had worked on a couple of years back. It had all got very messy, not to say dangerous.

"Harry did mention your name. But how did you know I worked here?"

"I remember him telling me you worked in a garage in the city and it wasn't hard to track you down from there. Finding things out is something I'm particularly good at. There's been a recent development which I think he should know about but I was worried about his current state of health. I mean he had that mini-stroke and the last thing I want to do is to create stress for him. So, I thought I'd come and test the water with you."

"Didn't you leave the country – like somewhere far away?"

"The Azores! Absolutely beautiful, but very little chance of finding work especially as my Portuguese was limited to asking for a beer, so when my savings ran out, I decided to take a chance and come back. Not to Antwerp. Needed a change of scene. Anyway … this development. How familiar are you with what happened back then with the Redline company?"

Ryck said he could remember quite a bit of the stuff Harry had told him at the time.

"OK, then you may recall the name Webers."

Ryck remembered. A dangerous man.

"He was sent down, but only for four years. They never managed to pin a straight murder charge on him. It was all 'attempted' this and 'conspiracy' that. Good behaviour, early parole hearing and the long and the short of it is that he's back on the streets."

"Shit!" Ryck said

"Exactly. I'm really glad I didn't go back to my old haunts. It would have been too easy for him to find me."

Ryck hadn't paid that much attention to the Redline-related trials, being too tied up at the time pursuing his new career as a car mechanic. So, he'd no idea that Webers had received such a light sentence.

"Well, thank you for taking the trouble to come and tell me about it and for not going to my uncle directly. I mean he's doing OK health-wise but this news will be difficult for him. Webers could be a real threat to Harry – and his wife."

"I didn't know he was married!"

"Oh no, I suppose you wouldn't. It happened after you headed off for the sunshine."

"Ryck!" Gaston called out. "A customer needs to speak to you."

"Just coming," he shouted in reply. "What's your mobile number, Eden?" Ryck tapped the digits into his own phone. "I'm sure Harry will want to speak to you at some point. Do you know where Webers lives now?"

"Not yet. I did a check and found he'd sold his house in Brussels. But I'll find him and let Harry know."

+ + +

Crossing the Boulevard de L'Empereur in central Brussels, a parcel under his arm, Claus Eyckmans removed his sunglasses from their perch on top of his head and used them to shield his eyes from the bright sun as he made his way to his office close to Notre Dame au Sablon.

The entrance was at the end of a short alleyway. Beyond a front door in need of at least two coats of paint, an ornate wrought iron staircase twisted up to the second floor. A single window let in very little light. It was a strange location for a man with a lot of money behind him and a complete contrast to his country house.

The office was anonymous and quite hard to find and yet it was virtually on the Mont Des Arts. So, he was simultaneously both at the centre of things and safely hidden away.

He unwrapped the parcel and removed the protective covering carefully. Inside was a Yaka mask, exquisite in its detail. There was also a brief handwritten note informing him of the source of the artefact and its ultimate destination. This was the part of the job he loved, partly because it was the riskiest stage. Outwardly, when at work, he was unremarkable, chainstore clothes in fawn or pale grey, short well-trimmed hair, slim, wiry. Nobody ever gave him a second glance. A very different man from the one who went out and about socially.

He'd got involved in African artefacts quite by chance, a conversation with a man in Le Perroquet, the two of them standing at the bar studying the beer menu, an art magazine on the counter open at a page featuring Congolese masks and figurines. A shared obsession had emerged and they'd agreed to meet again. The business had developed from there.

His immediate task was to arrange delivery of the mask. All couriers were vetted. By him if they were Belgium-based and by one or two trusted lieutenants for those based in Africa. It was essential to reduce the risk of infiltration to a minimum. There were those who would do whatever it took to try and disrupt his business.

He re-wrapped the mask in its protective covering, removed a small section of flooring, and placed the package in the safe beneath. As yet no one had gained unauthorised access to his office but it was best to try and minimise risks.

+ + +

The envelope handed over by Elias Kirchner contained four documents. His own birth certificate, which detailed that he was born in Hamburg in 1965 and named his mother as Ursula Kirchner and his father as Berthold Kirchner. The parents' marriage certificate, issued in 1963, gave Ursula's maiden name as Baumer. Her own birth certificate, issued in 1936, recorded that her father was Heinrich Baumer. Vos made a note to check that Heinrich was also Kurt's father.

Frustratingly, he'd be unable to speak to Ursula, as the final certificate confirmed she'd died in 2018.

Vos realised that he'd need to put his instinctive dislike of Elias Kirchner to one side. As long as the sibling link between Kurt and Ursula was confirmed, then a combination of this paperwork, backed up by ID in the form of the nephew's passport or driving licence, would surely be enough for him to lodge a claim to Kurt Baumer's estate.

Over a pre-dinner beer, Marc commented on how easy the heir-hunting lark seemed to be. Just put an ad in the local paper and hey presto, someone turns up on the doorstep. Vos shrugged. Although his friend was right, he couldn't quite sign up to Elias the nephew just yet.

After the seabass had disappeared, they loaded large chunks of Roquefort onto oatcakes which were far too small and sipped away at a particularly good port which Marc found at the dusty rear of one of his drinks' cupboards.

With the pair of them relaxing in easy chairs, Marc explained the history of the Ost Kantonen – German then Belgian, then German again during the second world war before reverting back to Belgian immediately post-war.

"We have our own parliament up at Eupen. There are some demands for full regional autonomy," Marc said, "but given the population of the whole area is only about 75,000, it's unlikely to become a reality. You'll hear German spoken a lot around here. Do you remember much about the place from your previous visits, Harry?"

"Very little," Vos said. "Must be well over twenty years since I was last here. But one of the things that struck me then – and again when I arrived today – was that there's nothing left of the old town."

"No. The place was virtually destroyed in the 1944 battle – you'll remember about that, part of the Battle of the Bulge." Vos nodded. "The old Buchel Tower is about the only thing still around. If you search online for St Vith, most of the stuff you'll find is all about the battle and the destruction."

"During my previous visits, we spent quite a bit of time in the village bar here. I didn't notice it when we drove past earlier. Presumably it's gone?"

"Years ago, unfortunately, but I'm pretty well stocked. Just can't serve the beer on draught. What do you fancy once we've finished the port?"

They decided to go for Trappist beers, sampling ever stronger versions as the evening wore on. Although Vos had told himself to take it easy, his early resolve slipped away all too rapidly.

Later, flat out in the bedroom, the ceiling seemed far too low and threatening to get even lower. He got up, opened the roof-light so that the cold night air could help to clear his head a little. Gazing out across the moonlit valley, he wondered whether he'd be able to survive another of Marc's boozy evenings.

Four

Rain and a low mist greeted him at breakfast time. Vos felt far better than he should have done but declined Marc's offer of pork chops and fried potatoes. Coffee, toast, muesli and fruit juice met the needs of his stomach far better.

Having allowed time for his alcohol level to drop, Marc suggested a trip to St Vith in his Renault 4, which although virtually an antique, was in surprisingly good condition. As it rattled along the back road at a fair old lick, Vos couldn't help thinking about all the modern safety features that the car didn't possess.

Marc dropped him off outside the lawyer's office, which was in a small 1970's block in the centre of town. They agreed to meet up later in the Schloss bar.

Ahrendt was a large man gone to seed. Probably too many good lunches and dinners and too little exercise, Vos thought. He was affable enough and pleased that Vos had agreed to take on the heir-hunting role, but it was clear that the appearance of a nephew was completely unexpected.

Although he admitted that his knowledge of Kurt Baumer was distinctly limited, he said that he'd never before heard mention of a sister, let alone a nephew. Vos showed him the paperwork.

"Can I just check with you that Kurt's father's name was Heinrich?" he asked.

"It was. And will you be getting this Kirchner fellow to come up with some ID?" Ahrendt asked.

"My next task," Vos said. "Will you need some additional form of corroboration?"

"Well, given that I've no prior knowledge of a sister or a nephew, that would be best. See what you can come up with. Maybe a conversation with someone who knew the Kirchner family and can confirm certain key details."

Vos said he'd follow it up.

"Do you have any information about Kurt himself?"

Ahrendt gave him a slim file and cleared a space on a table next to the window.

Vos opened the file and started reading from the earliest entries. The first letter, received in 1960 was to Ahrendt's father, with instructions to purchase the house near St Vith. Baumer, still a young man, had been working in the colonial administration in Leopoldville (now Kinshasa). He'd wanted the house as a base for when, with independence, his role in the Congo came to an end. It was clear from the letter how reluctant he was to move back to the old country. But from the content of later letters in the file it was apparent that Baumer hadn't returned permanently to Belgium until the mid-90s after a long, but not particularly distinguished career in the diplomatic service. Ahrendt commented dryly that in his opinion, Baumer had peaked too early.

Vos studied the remaining few documents hoping to find a clue, however small, that might lead him to any other still-living family member. But the letters were silent on this point. There'd been only a small number of legal matters arising over the years. He noticed, with amusement, that one of these had been a neighbour dispute ... with his friend Marc! He wondered how long it had taken to patch things up between the two men.

Near the front of the file was a copy of a letter from a Brussels-based lawyer called Lindner, a specialist opinion on an issue to do with a proposed housing development in a field behind Baumer's property which never materialised. The letter was unremarkable except for the fact that it was headed *My Dear Kurt* and concluded with the words *Yours Affectionately, Oskar.* In his, admittedly limited, contact with the legal profession, Vos had generally come across stuffiness and formality. The tone of this letter was quite different and hinted at a more personal link than simply lawyer to client. He made a note of the relevant contact details.

Just before leaving, he asked Ahrendt about the funeral arrangements and was informed that these were in hand. But given that the body had not yet been released and that it would be sensible to wait a few days in case any still-living family members surfaced, the funeral date wouldn't be fixed just yet. He added that Baumer's temporary resting place in the morgue cold-storage unit wasn't currently in high demand.

Marc was already in the Schloss when Vos arrived, an open bottle of Riesling and a nearly empty glass in front of him. He looked pleased with himself.

"You've either just purchased a real bargain or you've got a good woman on your mind," Vos said, helping himself to wine.

"Whatever makes you think that?" Marc said, looking affronted. But the look lasted only a few seconds. "Her name's Astrid. Now let's have a look at this menu."

They both opted for the venison casserole. Vos was unused to anything more than a bowl of soup and a sandwich at lunchtime but his suddenly expanded appetite coped admirably with the huge portion that arrived from the kitchen.

When Marc suggested a second bottle, Vos asked how they'd get back to the house, hoping his friend wasn't proposing to drive.

"Oh, I often leave the car in town and get Rainer to drive me home. He runs as much of a social service as a taxi service and, what's more, is a reliable source of up-to-date local gossip. Relax! A good lunch should never be shorter than two hours."

Vos' phone rang just as the dessert arrived, a fruits-of-the-forest crumble. It was his daughter.

"Hi Josina. Everything OK?"

"Oh yes, fine. I just wondered if you needed any help tomorrow, you know, going through all those boxes you mentioned. Only I'm free if you need me."

His initial instinct was to say no, as he liked working at his own pace and in his own way. But then Josina was very organised and he could maybe do with some of that.

"That would be very helpful. Thank you. Do you need a lift here?"

"No, I can borrow a car. Remind me where you're staying and I'll be there at ten if that's OK."

It sounded a bit too early to Vos, particularly if he and Marc continued at the drinking pace already established. But he agreed anyway.

+ + +

Luka Rainer got the two older men and their sticks into the back of his Passat, made sure they were strapped in and set off for Marc's house.

When he learnt that Vos was hunting for relatives of Kurt Baumer, he rubbed the stubble on his chin and looked pensive.

"My dad knew him when he first arrived. Didn't fit in at all, thought himself a cut above us locals. Not that he was here that much until the 90's. He mellowed over time, but you had to know his quirks, never gave much away and could be quick to take offence."

"Have you ever heard mention of any relatives who are still around?" Vos asked.

"Afraid not, Harry. And not many visitors either. He was a bit of a loner. I think he preferred it that way. But from time to time

I'd ferry someone out to his place and have a chat on the way. Most of them seemed to have something to do with the African art world – collectors maybe."

"That's useful. Any other little gems you can offer me, skeletons in the closet, secret women?"

"Not with Kurt! Now with most other characters around here I could help you out. Take Marc for example. What I don't know about him isn't worth knowing, but it would cost you to get the full gen."

"I couldn't possibly afford that," Vos said, smiling. "But here's something. This feller turned up yesterday claiming to be Kurt's nephew, his sister's boy. Could that be the case?"

"Never heard anything about a nephew. But there's something niggling at me about your mention of a sister. Something I overheard my parents arguing about years and years ago. Mum claimed Kurt had a sister but dad poo-pooed the idea. I seem to remember her saying the sister moved to somewhere in Germany, when she was barely out of her teens. Of course, this so-called nephew might be just a chancer who's read about the death in the paper."

Rainer dropped them off and refused payment.

"Next time I need a favour, Marc, I'll know where to come. You take care, Harry!"

He turned the Passat and pulled away, but just before the bend in the road, the brake-lights came on and the vehicle reversed at speed back to the house.

"Just remembered something that might help. Years ago, I gave Kurt a lift back from Gouvy station. Unusually for him he'd had a lot to drink and was rambling on about how much he missed the Congo – which wasn't at all unusual – but then he added something about an aunt out there. She was the lucky one, she'd stayed on in Kinshasa. Granted, must be dead herself by now but I thought it was worth mentioning."

Vos watched the taxi drive off for a second time. This felt like progress. From a standing start of having no Baumer relatives, there could now be a nephew, a sister and an aunt. The fact that he had some niggling doubts about one, that another was dead and that the third might have also gone the same way was not sufficient to dampen his newfound optimism.

+ + +

The doorbell rang. Vos checked his watch: it was 10:00am. Josina, who'd borrowed her aunt's car for the trip from Gouvy, was right on time.

She didn't bat an eyelid at the sight of the cardboard boxes littering each room as they toured the house. In the kitchen, he poured her a coffee. She asked him what the plan was.

He didn't really have one. She was prepared, pen and clipboard at the ready.

"Why don't we bring each of the boxes in here, go through the contents on the table and sort them into not important, maybe worth looking at again and definitely interesting. We can do the same with the boxes upstairs once we're finished down here."

Vos, realising that two nights of over-drinking had dulled his ability to plan ahead, was grateful for her suggestion.

"I'm assuming there's not a cellar or an attic," she said. "Wouldn't want to discover even more boxes!" Vos assured her it was just the two storeys.

They made surprisingly rapid progress. A lot of the stuff tipped out onto the table was *junk* as Josina put it.

"I've had another idea," she said. "Why don't we make some more space for ourselves by putting the junk boxes into the garage? Have you got the key for it?"

He was about to say no when he remembered there were

three keys on the ring Marc had handed over. Front door, back door and more than likely garage door.

"There's a car in there," she said on her return, "old but in very good condition. It's a big garage, so there'll still be plenty of room for the boxes. If you carry on with the sifting, I'll start carting them over there." She had a way of directing him which he was comfortable with.

About to restart the sorting, he was suddenly curious about the car and followed Josina out to the garage.

Around thirty years old he reckoned, a beauty, an Opel Rekord that had been very well looked after. Josina was right. There was plenty of storage room, even with the Opel in place.

As he returned to the house, his phone rang. It was Ryck. His news was a shock.

Over the past two years, he'd managed to put Webers right to the back of his mind and yet here was his nephew telling him that the thug was on the street again – even if he didn't know which particular street.

"Is there anything I can do to help?" Ryck asked. "I know things are OK at present with you over there and Katerine working away. But if she's due back in Heist before you ... well, she could always come and stay with me and Magda rather than be at home on her own."

"Thanks, Ryck, that's really thoughtful of you, but she'll be away for a while yet." Vos wondered how his wife would react to the news. "How did Maes sound – I mean apart from the news about Webers?"

"Quite upbeat. He's got some kind of investigative job now. I'll text you his number. Don't try and take on Webers by yourself and let me know if you want anything done."

Vos knew Ryck was playing the guardian, but he didn't want to drag his nephew into anything to do with Webers.

The man was a nasty piece of work and the news that he was

back in circulation was very worrying. He'd need to speak to Eden Maes.

+ + +

By the end of their afternoon shift, the pile of 'interesting' papers was disappointingly small. But there were two letters from Lindner, the lawyer in Brussels, both couched in the same friendly, first name language. One of them made reference to an enclosed gift, a book about the Hautes Fagnes marshlands a few kilometres north of St Vith. For some reason the book title seemed familiar to Vos.

When he mentioned this to Josina, she pointed to it on the top shelf of the bookcase which ran down one wall of the living room.

"The font size used on the spine is quite large," she said, walking across the room to fetch the book. "That's why it caught my attention. I went to the marshlands once on a school field trip, but unfortunately the weather was so miserable and visibility so poor, that we didn't see a single bird."

Vos flicked through the book. The text was quite dense but it was very well illustrated with pen and ink drawings of marshland birds. Perhaps birding had been another of Kurt's interests. He only spotted the handwritten note on the first page of the book by chance. *To Kurt, many happy returns, Uncle Oskar.*

"Wow! That's real progress, Harry. You should give him a ring."

The call went to voicemail. It wasn't a machine-voice that spoke to him, but a personally-recorded message from someone who sounded very elderly and spoke old-fashioned French with a distinctly German accent.

"If he's an uncle he's got to be at least 100 surely!" Vos said. "He certainly sounds that old. I just hope he gets back to me. In the meantime, I'd better get on with checking out our self-proclaimed nephew."

"I could try and make some enquiries about the mother – Kurt's sister. That might lead to evidence of a son," Josina said.

"Are you able to do that sort of tracing?" Vos asked.

"Yes, I've done a fair bit of research into my own family history. It started when I was a teenager. Over the years I've got to know my way around the relevant websites. You mentioned that the sister lived in the Hamburg area, so I'll start off there. Most of the sites have a translation facility, but my German's not bad anyway. Dad and I used to speak it together. Won't be able to start doing it until I get back to my aunt's place though. Don't know if you've noticed, but this place seems to be a computer and wi-fi free zone and I haven't got much data left on my phone."

He had noticed and figured that Baumer would have retired before computerisation hit the workplace. He knew a number of over-seventies who'd remained computer illiterate, but there were others, like himself, who'd picked up the necessary skills at computer classes. And some had younger relatives to steer them in the right direction.

"It might also be worth me looking to see if there's anything online about the aunt in Kinshasa. We haven't got much to go on but I could give it a try."

"Well, that would be a real help, Josina. How about we call it a day now? Marc and me are going out for a meal in the town. Would you like to join us?"

The three of them went in a two-car convoy to an Italian in St Vith. After the meal, Josina drove back to her relatives for the night and the two men returned to Marc's house for more drinks.

Later, it was hard to get to sleep and Vos vowed that he'd start looking for accommodation in the town. There was a limit to his ability to keep up the pace of consumption from Marc's extensive alcohol menu.

Five

The phone woke him up.

"This is Lindner. You left a message." The voice was elderly, ponderous, with more than a hint of unfriendliness.

"Thank you for calling me back. This is a little awkward. I'm afraid I have some bad news concerning Kurt Baumer."

A long silence.

"Who are you exactly?"

"As I said in my message, my name is Harry Vos. Unfortunately, Kurt died very recently. I have been appointed by his lawyer to try and trace any surviving relatives. During my enquiries I came across a reference to you as Kurt's uncle and I wanted to confirm that this is the case." Another long silence.

"This isn't one of those hoax calls, is it? You know, where you draw me in with talk of what I'm due in the way of inheritance, ask for my bank details and then clear out my account?" Lindner was talking more quickly and his tone had become decidedly more unfriendly.

Vos did his best to reassure him that the call was nothing of the sort and offered some substantive facts, details about Baumer, his lawyer, his house and the contents of the letter from Lindner that had led to the phone call being made.

Lindner sounded somewhat mollified.

"Are you ever in Brussels?" he asked.

"I do visit the city from time to time."

"Then come and see me in person, so I can size you up and then we'll see where we are. My office is in the Palais de Justice. You'll know it presumably. Let's say tomorrow at noon." Vos confirmed he'd be there.

Before he had time to digest the strange conversation, his phone rang again.

"Hello this is Doctor Vermeulen, Kurt Baumer's doctor. Ahrendt said you wanted to talk to me. I'm just back from a short holiday and am catching up with what's happened in my absence. I was very sorry to hear about Kurt's death. When and where can we meet?"

It was agreed that she would drive out to Baumer's house straightaway.

Vos rushed through his ablutions, made himself scrambled eggs and a pot of coffee and glanced through Kurt's book on the Hautes Fagnes. Josina arrived promptly for her second day's work and told him about the fruits of her early morning online research.

He was amazed to hear she'd already found online references to Baumer's late sister! No trace of her son as yet, but it was early days.

As he prepared more eggs, Vos asked how she traced people. Josina told him about the various online sites she used: general registers maintained by the state and the local authorities, paid-for ancestry sites, those operated by churches, electoral rolls and newspaper birth, marriage and death columns. Any of them might turn out to be useful depending on what information you were after and how far back you needed to go. He was impressed.

Just as he finished telling her about his phone call with Lindner, Dr Vermeulen arrived.

She turned out to be a friendly, well-dressed, middle-aged woman, who asked if it would be alright to have a look around the house. Vos and Josina left her to it and started on their box-sifting routine.

On her return to the kitchen, the doctor looked puzzled.

"Have you worked on the boxes in his bedroom yet?" Vos told her they'd had more than enough to occupy them so far in the downstairs rooms. "That's what I thought. I've visited the house a few times in connection with Kurt's various ailments. I probably shouldn't say this – Hippocratic oath and all that – but he was something of a hypochondriac. Some days he'd refuse to get up, so there were bedside consultations which means I know that room quite well. Anyway, to get to the point, his boxes were always filled and stacked in a particular way. Kurt was more than a little obsessive about matters like that. The thing is, I'm certain someone must have been through the boxes in his bedroom and then put the contents back any old how. So, if it wasn't you, who was it and when was it done?"

+ + +

Vos couldn't remember the last time he'd been on a bike, although as a youngster he'd been a very keen cyclist.

It had been Marc's idea to get some fresh air, scenery and exercise. And despite their respective disabilities, they both found cycling was manageable. Josina hadn't been tempted to join them as she'd be driving back to Gouvy once her box-sifting had finished.

"What did you say the old railway line was called?" Vos shouted to his friend, a few metres in front.

"The Vennbahn. It connected Aachen to Luxembourg and carried coal and iron. Once that stopped it was used by tourists. But the end of the line came about ten years ago when they ripped up the track. Still, it makes a very good cycleway now. You're on Astrid's bike, by the way."

"Whose bike?"

"Astrid, the girlfriend I told you about. I bought it for her, otherwise she wouldn't get any exercise at all. Listen, there's something I need to tell you. The theory the doc had about someone going through Kurt's boxes. At the time I thought it was a dream, but maybe it wasn't."

"Thought what was a dream?" Vos asked, interested and frustrated in equal measure. Why couldn't his friend be clearer?

"That night, the night he died, well I'd had a bit to drink. Had this dream, the sound of a car, voices, doors opening and closing. But what if it wasn't a dream?"

Vos was in two minds. He knew Marc could be unreliable when he'd had a few. But what if he was right? What if it hadn't been a dream and there really had been visitors to Kurt's house that night?

"Is there anyone we could ask locally, you know, whether they saw a car on the road up to your place? I've noticed there's very little traffic through the village at night. Somebody might have seen something."

"The only one who might know is Ella, the old woman on the corner. Lives just where the lane turns off the main road. Whether she'd tell us is another matter. We can but try."

Marc explained how she'd terrified him as a ten-year-old, how old Ella would force any passing youngster to fetch her cigarettes from the nearest shop in the town, how to this day, she kept watch on comings and goings.

On the return leg of their bike ride, they turned off the Vennbahn and cycled through St Vith and onwards. At the corner in question, they dismounted and leant the bikes against the old woman's garden wall. As the front door was boarded over, they walked around the side of the house to the rear gate. A woman's voice could be heard in the back garden. It gradually became clear to Vos that she was talking to herself which didn't fill him with confidence about her reliability as a witness.

But she surprised them both.

"Oh yes, it would have been after eleven, as I was having my bedtime cocoa. No alcohol at that time of night. Anyway, I was standing at the front window and this car came round the corner too fast and had to brake all of a sudden, thought they were going to hit the bank but they didn't. Streetlight on the corner so I could see it was a big old Datsun, not many of them about these days. Couldn't see clear enough to get the number plate though. Two middle-aged fellers inside, baseball caps but didn't know how to wear them proper. Shame about Baumer, bit of an oddball but he was alright really. You got anything for me?"

Marc whispered to Vos that he always travelled with a little something for emergency use, fetched a small bottle of scotch from his saddlebag and handed it to Ella. She took it across to an ancient dresser, opened a door and stashed the whisky next to several other bottles.

Back on the bike, Vos thought about Marc's dream, Ella's story about two late-night visitors and the doctor's comments about the disturbed bedroom boxes. What had happened that night? And would it be necessary to say something to the police?

+ + +

The following day, Josina joined Vos at Gouvy on his train journey to Brussels, saying goodbye at Leuven with a promise that she'd continue her online research from home.

He called Eden Maes.

"Thanks for the forewarning about Webers. I really appreciate it. Have you managed to find out where he lives?"

"No, not yet, but things are looking promising."

Vos mentioned he was working in St Vith.

"Well, as it happens, I'm not that far away. Once I've discovered Webers' whereabouts, perhaps we could meet and have a catch up." Vos agreed to the suggestion.

On arrival in the capital, he stepped out from the darkness of Centraal station into the sunshine, made his way to Hoogstraat and cut through to the glass elevator that took him up to Gallows Hill and the Palais de Justice. He'd never liked the huge building, the way it dominated everything, a real symbol of power. Inside it felt like something from a Kafka story. A uniformed usher led him to room 232 just as he heard a clock striking twelve.

Barely visible above large piles of paper, Lindner was a tiny man with wispy remnants of hair on both pate and chin. Vos remembered Katerine telling him about academics who never retired and felt the same might be true of lawyers. Lindner, who looked to be at least 90, poured thick, dark coffee from a silver pot into two delicate porcelain cups on matching saucers and gestured for Vos to take one. Each saucer held a tiny wafer biscuit.

"I'm sorry to have been the bearer of sad news," Vos said. "I appreciate this must be a difficult time for you. There are a number of issues I'd like to discuss with you – as Kurt's uncle – if that would be satisfactory." Vos felt the wrong words were tumbling out of his mouth and that he was being far too deferential. Perhaps it was the building that did it, the way it reinforced the realities of power.

"Well, let's not get ahead of ourselves," the old man said. "The reason I wanted to see you face to face was to be able to assess your character and motivation. It is plain to me that you are an honest man and not one driven by money. Since we last spoke, I have been in contact with Ahrendt and he has vouched for you. And so now it is possible to proceed with a conversation regarding Kurt. You see, although he always called me 'uncle', it was an ironic title. Although there were only a few years between us, I used to give him advice, which wasn't always wanted! So, I was very much a Dutch uncle. But that means of course that there is no blood tie between us."

Vos tried to mask his frustration. He'd been dragged to the capital only to be informed of a fact that would have taken less than a minute to explain over the phone. He held his tongue, hoping that there might be a little more to come.

"But I may be able to help a little," Lindner continued. Vos was relieved that he hadn't let his annoyance show. "You may have already picked up that Kurt was a man with few friends and even fewer relatives. His parents passed away sometime in the late1950s, before I knew him. But there is a sister." Ah, that's very welcome corroboration, Vos thought. "However, this is difficult for me," Lindner said. "You see, I promised Kurt never to tell a soul about his secret. Given the circumstances though, I feel it would be justifiable to reveal what I am about to reveal."

Vos was glad he didn't have to deal with such a glacial pace of conversation on a daily basis. He wondered whether a top up coffee might be in the offing but didn't want to distract the lawyer and risk lowering the speed of their discussion even further.

"I recall the conversation with him very clearly, which took place during one of my rare visits to his house near Sankt Vith. I'm pleased the area became part of Belgium again. Do you know much about the history of the place?" Beneath the table, Vos gripped the top of his thighs tightly and stifled a gasp of exasperation. Despite his efforts, perhaps sufficient of his frustration leaked through to make Lindner refocus. "But I digress. It was 1965, a rather cold February evening, if I remember rightly. Kurt was both angry and upset. The cause of his concern was his sister, Ursula. It transpired that she was unexpectedly pregnant. By the way, would you like more coffee?"

Vos decided, after all, to risk further delay and thanked Lindner. The story was taking a turn for the better. He watched the old man's slow deliberate movements feeling sure that at any moment he would drop the delicate cup and saucer and its fresh contents. But the drink survived the journey back to the table. Lindner then took an inordinate amount of time blowing his nose noisily into a very large white handkerchief, before resuming his tale.

"Her husband wasn't earning much and she asked Kurt for financial help. Well, that was like a red rag to him. The two siblings had never got on. Kurt told her he disliked her husband, had never approved of the marriage and wasn't in a position to help. Then I'm afraid he told her to get a termination. Ursula was aghast. Although the pregnancy had not been planned, she'd always wished for a child. Following their heated and acrimonious conversation, they never saw or spoke to each other again."

"Do you know whether she had the baby?" Vos asked.

"No," the lawyer said. "I tried but failed to track her down, not helped by Kurt's refusal to have anything to do with my quest."

Vos told Lindner about Elias Kirchner. The old man stared at him for a while.

"I'm flabbergasted," he said. "After all these years, the child surfaces! I appreciate you may not yet know if this fellow's claim is genuine, but he could well be telling the truth."

+ + +

Arriving back in St Vith, tired and hungry, the last thing Vos felt like doing was calling into the police station. But he needed to pass on the information old Ella had given him.

The officer on duty took down details of the Datsun and its two occupants and noted that the car's destination could have been Kurt Baumer's house. She thanked Vos for his statement and assured him it would be forwarded to the appropriate officer.

Six

Despite the privileges he'd been able to buy, Jos Webers had hated every minute of his time inside. To save their own skins, the company had thrown him to the wolves. At least, that's how it had seemed until the day he'd been called into the prison governor's office to be informed of his early release. Somebody had finally managed to pull some strings for which he was very grateful.

Redline, the company he'd worked for, had disappeared as part of the penance paid for guilty verdicts and illegal activity. But they'd been part of a group and most of the company's activity and operatives had found ways of migrating to other parts of the structure. There'd been some public hand-wringing and a few heads had rolled, but by and large the big ship had continued on its voyage.

Thoughts of revenge had kept Webers going through the long days and even longer nights inside, but on release he felt, strangely, that he didn't need to rush things. The call from his old boss Mertens had been unexpected. He had a new venture underway. Webers was wanted onboard.

In reality it was a lot like the old venture, but it had been cleaned up and repainted in attractive new colours. Naturally he wouldn't have a public-facing role in the company but his undoubted skills would be put to good use. Having been forced to sell off his house to pay his legal bills and to fund the purchase of a few extras to enhance the otherwise miserable prison regime, he needed a reliable income.

The rented apartment didn't provide anything like the level of comfort he'd become used to in his previous residence, but it would do for the interim until money started flowing again. Over a glass or two of wine, he ran through his list of revenge targets.

The tattooist had said far too much at the trial but then, given the lengthy sentence handed to him, the drive to 'make him pay' was weak. His name only appeared on the list out of a sense of completeness.

Having escaped scot-free, Eden Maes was much more in need of retribution. But he'd disappeared. Still there was no hurry. He'd be bound to pop up again somewhere.

But the one who'd really annoyed him was Harry Vos, the interfering, moralistic amateur who'd proved to be a real nuisance. And Webers knew exactly where he was. He just needed to give some thought to an appropriate way of getting his own back on the PI.

+ + +

Barto stopped to sniff a particularly interesting shrub, before cocking his leg and moving on. Ryck had been in two minds as to whether to say yes to his uncle's request to provide a temporary dog-kennelling service. After all there were the two little ones to consider, the lack of space in their small house and the need to walk the dog at least twice a day.

But with Harry off in the far east of the country, Katerine working away and his grandma no longer there to step into the breach, Ryck knew he was the obvious candidate. Not only that, but the truth was he liked having the dog around and luckily Magda was just as keen. As long as they could hand him back.

Barto led the way to the park, a complete circuit, a treat from the woman in the pink tracksuit, her cockapoo, as ever, straining at the leash, a brief stop tied up outside the convenience store and on back to the house.

A glance at his phone revealed a message, a date for a meet up. A group of mates – nursing students and former students like himself – who got together from time to time for a few drinks and, in his case, an escape from the kids. He'd look forward to it.

Sometimes he regretted the way his adult life had zig-zagged. For several years he'd had either a paintbrush or a pastebrush in his hand. The decision to become a nursing student had felt like a real turning point at the time, the possibility of a new career mapped out before him, but hour after hour of trying to cram facts into his head eventually took its toll. The overalls in the workshop and the constantly oil-stained hands were much more him. As for the family-man part of his life? How exactly had that happened? One moment a carefree singleton and seemingly the next, both step-father and father. But it turned out that he loved being a dad.

Back home, sitting on the bottom stair, with one slipper on and one trainer yet to be removed, his phone rang – Harry wanting to know whether he had a view on twenty-year-old Opel Rekords, as he'd just unearthed one. Ryck had an instant view which was that he should drive down to St Vith at the weekend, with the family and give the vehicle the once-over. After a slight pause at the other end of the line, this was agreed. When he asked about the Opel's purchase price, there was a second pause before his uncle told him that it all depended.

+ + +

Vos had made the move into St Vith. Although Marc had taken it as something of a personal slight, the deed was done and he felt the better for it.

His new temporary home was a small bed and breakfast, not far from the railway museum. Helga, his landlady, informed him over breakfast, that the museum had previously been the railway station and that, in her opinion, the line should never had been closed.

As he tucked into a large ham and cheese omelette, feeling all the better for having escaped yet another of Marc's drinks evenings, his phone rang. Dr Vermeulen wanting him to call into the surgery. Something she'd discovered.

Lindner had turned out to be something of a character. In recognition of his status as one of the oldest practising lawyers in Brussels, he'd managed to persuade the authorities to let him use a room in the Palais as his office. He told Vos that it had acquired the name of the Palace of Scaffolding, because it was hard to remember a time when it hadn't been shrouded in that way. But having seen the highly decorative interior, with its huge statues, Vos had responded that perhaps it was the inside that mattered, not the outside.

At the end of their discussion, the old lawyer had advised him to put his reservations about Elias Kirchner to one side and just complete the due diligence.

But first he had an appointment with Doctor Vermeulen. A further advantage of staying in the town was that he could reach everywhere on foot. After a wait of only ten minutes, he was called in to see her. She moved from behind her desk, shook hands and motioned him across to two seats by a small table with a garden view. In addition to the expected flowerbeds, there were also rows of vegetables.

"We have some volunteers who keep the garden trim. In return we've let them take over part of it to grow whatever they want. Works very well." The doctor pushed a stray lock of greying hair behind her ear. "There have been some developments," she continued. "Three factors set me thinking. Firstly, although cause of death was a heart attack, Kurt hadn't experienced any previous problems with his heart. Secondly the realisation that the boxes in Kurt's bedroom had been disturbed. And thirdly your phone call informing me about the men who may have paid him a visit on the night of his death. Admittedly the information about the visitors in the Datsun came from our resident *wahrsagerin*, but she's usually fairly reliable on everyday matters."

"Sorry you've lost me. What was that word?"

"'It means fortune-teller. She doesn't do a lot of it now, but years ago her services were much sought after. Anyway, it seems to me unlikely to have been pure coincidence that Kurt's heart attack occurred around the time he had nocturnal visitors. More likely it was triggered by something, such as shock arising from a threat or even the administration of some sort of drug or poison. That's why I decided to carry out an autopsy."

The quietly-spoken doctor's mention of an autopsy really caught him by surprise. He asked how it had been possible to move so quickly.

"Well, it helps if you're not only a GP but also the local pathologist. I used to do the job full-time up in Liege, but after ten years of it, I decided to return here for a somewhat slower pace of life."

"And did you find anything?"

"I did, but not at all what I expected. No trace of a drug or a poison in his system, but I did find these in Kurt's stomach."

The doctor pulled a small black bag from the pocket of her white coat, loosened a drawstring and tipped four, sparkling objects onto the tabletop. Vos stared at the diamonds.

He found he couldn't stop staring.

+ + +

He'd arranged to meet Kirchner in the guests' living room of his B&B. As the only guest in residence, he had sole use of it.

"I've checked the certificates you gave me and they seem to be in order, thanks. There are one or two additional matters I'd like to raise." Kirchner looked annoyed.

"I'd thought the paperwork I gave you would be sufficient," he said. "What else do you need?"

"Well, firstly some form of ID."

Kirchner immediately pulled out his wallet and extracted his driving licence. Vos took a photo of the document with his phone and emailed it to Ahrendt.

"And just to clarify the position regarding your father. Is he still alive?"

"No, he died some years back. We didn't get on and had virtually no contact. My mother was informed of his death by a mutual friend."

"Would it be possible for me to speak to this friend? You see it would be useful for me to be able to speak to someone who knew your father and your mother and who also, presumably, knows you."

"Why would you want to do that?"

"Just corroboration really. The certificates and your ID are solid enough evidence of your relationship to Kurt, but it would give me additional reassurance if I could speak to someone who was acquainted with the three of you."

"Well unfortunately the friend in question has also passed on. Mother had very few friends and most of them were older than her. There's only one who's still alive. I could ask Herr Schultz whether he'd be willing to speak to you."

All Vos really wanted was someone who could say to him *I know this person and he's definitely Elias Kirchner, son of Ursula and Berthold.* Hopefully this Schultz would be able to come up with the goods.

There was now written evidence to show firstly that Elias was Ursula's son and secondly, from the document Lindner had given him, that Ursula and Kurt were siblings. At the end of the day, it would be up to Ahrendt to decide whether any further corroboration was required – over and above any declaration from Schultz.

He thanked Kirchner for answering his questions and confirmed that he'd arrange a meeting with the lawyer.

As the nephew got into his car, Marc arrived.

"Was that Kirchner?" he asked.

"Yes – how did you know?"

"Well, I've seen him before. He was at Kurt's house recently, twice maybe. I assumed he was an insurance man. Has that look, don't you think?"

"You're right. An old-fashioned model perhaps. It must be nearly all done online these days. So did Kurt tell you anything about him?"

"No. And apart from nosiness, there was really no reason for me to ask."

"Hm! Puzzling. As far as I'd been led to believe, since the big bust-up years ago, there'd never been any contact between Kurt on the one hand and either sister or nephew on the other. I'll have to ask Kirchner about this."

"So, this looks like a nice place," Marc said. "You seem really settled in already. Fancy a bite to eat in the town – my treat?"

"That's a good idea. I'll just get my things."

In the bedroom, changing his shirt and exchanging slippers for shoes, his phone rang. It was Josina, with good news which wasn't really good news. She'd managed to track down Baumer's aunt, the one who'd annoyed Kurt by staying on in the Congo when he'd returned home. Name of Ada. But they'd missed her by three months. Her death certificate had been issued in Kinshasa. And there was no sign of any other surviving relatives over there. Josina had discovered from a newspaper article that the aunt's estate had been left to a charity which was now responsible for running her animal sanctuary. Another dead end – literally this time.

Seven

After another hearty breakfast, Vos phoned Ahrendt to arrange a meeting where they could start to formalise Kirchner's inheritance claim.

Over another cup of coffee, he reflected on how the discovery of the diamonds had changed his whole image of Kurt Baumer. The ageing hoarder who'd longed to return to his colonial days had suddenly been transformed into a man of mystery.

With a bit of added guesswork, it was now possible for Vos to piece together the events of Kurt's last evening. A microwaved meal of macaroni cheese, a glass or two of red, a small portion of chocolate mousse. The menu for what turned out to be his last meal had been established clearly enough. There'd been papers out on the table. Perhaps he was in the habit of eating and reading. And making notes it seemed, as one of the pages in his notebook was stained with chocolate. But what he'd written was not of any importance, merely reflections on the weather and musings over a possible trip to Liege.

So, meal finished, as evidenced by the empty plates, note-making finished as evidenced by the closed notebook. At some point the radio had been turned off. Marc had said definitely by midnight, but maybe earlier than that. Old Ella had told them that the visitors' car had sped past her house sometime after eleven.

Vos speculated on what had happened subsequently at the house.

It had to be assumed that, given the lateness of the hour, the visitors hadn't been paying a social call. But why would Baumer have let them in? It didn't make sense. Assumption number two was that they must have been after the diamonds – otherwise, why would Baumer have swallowed them? And the third assumption was that the two men had threatened him in some way in order to find out where the diamonds were...and that these threats triggered the heart attack.

And afterwards? Well, as old Ella hadn't observed the Datsun making a return journey, it had probably left on the road towards Amel. Thoughts about the car reminded him that he'd heard nothing from the police since making a statement about the Datsun. He'd need to chase it up.

His mind ticked over slowly. It seemed to happen more frequently as he got older, that ideas would hide in the shadows, reluctant to emerge into the open. In fact, sometimes they were so well hidden that he'd miss them completely. But this time the idea crept into view.

His primary focus had to be on the hunt for Baumer relatives – given that's what he'd been hired to do. But with the emergence of Kurt's late-night visitors, not to mention the diamonds, there was now also a police enquiry underway. During the course of his own searches, he might come across information which could assist the police in their investigations. Was there anything he'd *already* come across that could throw some light on Kurt's activities and help explain why he was in possession of the diamonds? It struck him that there'd been several letters from gallery managers and he'd mentally filed them as mundane correspondence, alongside Kurt's pernickety enquiries and his bees-in-bonnets campaigns. But what if the gallery letters had some significance?

As Helga, his landlady, cleared away the breakfast things, he called Rainer.

The taxi driver arrived within minutes. Vos wondered whether he'd struck lucky getting a ride so quickly or whether customers were not so plentiful. They set off for Baumer's house.

"So, you've left your friend on his own," Rainer said. "Couldn't keep up the pace eh?" The man was quick on the uptake.

"You're right. It's a long while since I've put away as much in two consecutive evenings. Time to slow down! Anyway, I was interested in what you told me the other day about some of Kurt's visitors, the ones you reckoned were art collectors. I was wondering whether he might have been an art dealer."

"Look, normally I'd be morally obliged not to respond to such an enquiry." Vos was initially taken aback by the reference to morals. Then he noticed the smile. "You see it can be a bit like the confessional in here. People tell me things they wouldn't want spread around, so I have a reputation to consider. Not your average taxi driver perhaps! But given poor Kurt's no longer with us and you're a good friend of Marc's, then I could perhaps stretch a point. Let me give you a little potted history."

"That would be most helpful."

"Although he was generally reticent, over the years Kurt told me quite a bit about his interest in art. According to him, at school, he showed a lot of promise as an artist. But his father refused to go along with the idea of him progressing to art college and had other ideas. So, instead of messing about with canvases and tubes of paint, the young Kurt was forced into a respectable profession. A degree in classics, followed by diplomatic corps training and eventually a posting to Leopoldville"

"But that wasn't the end of his interest in art?" Vos interjected.

"Well guessed! He developed his painting. His wild African landscapes were apparently well regarded. In addition to creating his own artwork, he developed a real interest in Congolese artefacts, travelling to different parts of the country on the hunt for masks, statues in wood, ivory carvings, woven arts, all that sort of thing and talked to local carvers, sculptors and weavers about their work. He bought pieces from them now and then and they told him about the illegal trade that went on, with older and more valuable items being smuggled out of the country. Lots of them ended up here in Belgium of course. Kurt told me that over time he built up quite an extensive knowledge of artefacts from the Congo."

"So, what about after he came to live here full time? Did he still paint? I haven't seen much evidence of it, apart from a stack of dusty canvases in the spare bedroom."

"Up until recently he'd usually have a canvas on the go, but he got slower and slower. Although occasionally he managed to sell one, generally, as you've spotted, they ended up in the bedroom. I don't think he painted anything over the last couple of years," Rainer said.

"Did he still buy Congolese artefacts?"

"Occasionally, but my guess is that he didn't have much spare cash for that sort of purchase."

"And the collectors who came to see him. What did they want?" Vos asked.

"I never managed to get much out of them and the few times I asked Kurt, he just clammed up. But, given the extent of his knowledge, I'm sure they'd have been wanting to tap into his expertise." Vos thought about the art-related correspondence he'd come across in one of Kurt's boxes – a reflection of this expertise perhaps. He'd need to take a second look at these documents. "Whether it went any further than that, I don't know," Rainer said. "Kurt may have had links to dealers. There was something a bit cloak and dagger about him. But maybe that was just an image he wanted to project. Like you Harry – the mysterious private eye!"

Vos grinned and expressed surprise that Rainer had managed

to get as much as he had out of Baumer, who wasn't known for his conversation.

"Ah! That's just the magic of the cab. People tell me all sorts of things in here."

+ + +

Vos needed to do some re-reading. It had been another of Josina's ideas to number the boxes as they went along and to make a list of the contents of each one, in order to make retrieval easier. The art-related correspondence had been stapled together in box eleven. There were ten documents in total.

He made a coffee and sat down in Kurt's armchair to read them more carefully. They were all carbon copies of documents produced, he assumed, on Kurt's own typewriter, lists of artefacts, giving details of type, condition, estimated price, location and 'availability'. Although his knowledge of the geography of the Democratic Republic of the Congo was limited, each list seemed to relate to a different area of the country. In light of his second reading of these documents, Vos began to wonder whether, rather than just slipping into a quiet retirement, Baumer had developed some kind of role in the art world.

What might that have been? And could it have been linked in any way to the arrival of Baumer's late night visitors, or the presence of the diamonds in his stomach? Or both!

What should he tell the police about his newly emerging suspicions – and when? He was trying to get an appointment with a Chief Inspector Neumann to discuss his statement about the two men in the Datsun. If he succeeded, maybe the conversation could be extended to include these other matters.

He realised somebody else might also have concerns about issues swirling around the late Kurt Baumer. Dr Vermeulen might decide that she needed to talk to the police herself.

Perhaps he should get in first and earn himself some credit with the chief inspector.

+ + +

It struck him as a strange coincidence. Here he was uncovering issues relating to African artefacts in St Vith, whilst, simultaneously, Katerine was in Luxembourg City, taking part in a joint international project on African art and colonialism. But then they'd only met in the first place when he'd found that amulet on the beach at De Haan – which led to his involvement in the people-smuggling case – and had picked her name at random from a list of university artefact specialists.

It was his turn to phone her. Since their marriage two years ago, they'd only spent the odd night away from each other, so they were still firming up the protocol of how much to keep in touch over a period of a few weeks. Too little and it could send out the wrong signals. Too much and it might feel like they were trying to keep tabs on each other. A call each evening, lasting around twenty minutes felt about right.

She told him her paper on the repatriation of cultural artefacts had been well received. Her next task would be to assist her boss, who was due to present his own paper the following day. Vos had always thought that for a head of department, her boss seemed surprisingly lacking in confidence.

As they'd been unable to catch each other the previous evening, this was the first opportunity he'd had to tell her about Webers.

"Oh god, that's awful news. What are we going to do about it?" Although Vos was well aware just how much of a threat Webers could be, he hadn't so far given much thought to what action they might take. She picked up on his hesitancy.

"Come on, Harry, we shouldn't be putting this off. You need

to take the initiative and work out the best way of dealing with him." She was right. But he didn't yet have any ideas.

"How do you mean – *dealing with him*?"

"I don't know! Witness protection of some kind, maybe? Or perhaps we should head him off at the pass!"

"What?"

"You know, like they did in the Westerns." Ah! Get your retaliation in first.

You need to be more proactive, Harry. How many times had he heard that phrase thrown at him? He suddenly thought of Leo Rodenbach, the original villain of the people-smuggling case who'd eventually turned into a bit of a hero. He'd be good at the pass, surely.

"You're absolutely right, love. At least neither of us is at home at present which is a relief. Remind me again when you're due back home? Two weeks on Saturday. OK, that gives me a timescale to work to. We can speak about it again tomorrow evening."

It wouldn't have been wise to have mentioned his idea about Rodenbach just yet. She'd never really trusted the boatman, despite the fact that he'd turned out to be a good man to have on your side.

After finishing the call, he remembered that Ryck was due in St Vith for the weekend – to give the Rekord the once-over. So why didn't he suggest to Katerine that she could join them? It would be easy enough for her to get from Luxembourg to St Vith. When he called her back, she seemed pleased with the idea.

His proactivity was already working.

Just as he was settling down with a beer in the guest lounge, which he still had exclusive use of, his phone rang. Elias Kirchner, responding to the three voicemails Vos had left during the course of the day.

"My apologies for not responding earlier. I mislaid my phone. Have you been able to arrange a meeting with the lawyer?"

"Yes. 2:00pm tomorrow if that's convenient for you," Vos said. Kirchner confirmed he'd be there.

"Did you get to speak to Herr Schultz?" he asked.

"Yes, thank you and he was able to answer all my questions." Although this had been the case, Vos couldn't help thinking that he'd like more. After all the man might have been coached in advance by Kirchner to come up with the right answers. Still, maybe now wasn't the time to raise such suspicions.

"I understand you visited Kurt Baumer shortly before his death."

"How do you know that?" Kirchner asked sounding suspicious.

"Never mind that. I'd been under the impression that neither you nor your mother had any contact with him."

"That certainly used to be the case. But after Mother's death I began to re-evaluate things and concluded that I should establish a link. So, I wrote to him and was very pleasantly surprised when my uncle responded, saying he shared my view. The estrangement had continued for far too long. Since then, I met him a few times and we got on remarkably well. That's why I was so devastated by this death."

This was an entirely different side to Kirchner. It was the first time Vos could recall the nephew showing any signs of sensitivity. Perhaps he should cut him some slack.

Eight

Chief Inspector Magnus Neumann's phone rang, just as he was about to leave the police station. Having been up since five that morning, the last thing he wanted to do was answer it. His mind was filled only with the idea of going home to sleep. There'd been no progress on the three arson attacks and the murder case was still stuck where it had been a month ago.

But he could never ignore a ringing phone.

"Dr Vermeulen! What a pleasant surprise." They'd only been in each other's company a handful of times, all but one of those, official occasions. But that one had been interesting.

Distracted by a mental image of her in a tight white blouse, stethoscope dangling around her neck, he struggled to concentrate until he heard the word *diamonds*! Suddenly he was all ears. He and jewels had seldom crossed paths before. Having more than a touch of OCD in relation to matters of personal hygiene, he couldn't help wondering about what germs the gems might have picked up in their journey through the dead man's digestive system. As he agreed to meet the doctor in the Schloss right away, all thoughts of an early night flew out of the window.

He said good night to a couple of colleagues who were still at their desks and, most unusually, left his briefcase behind. A definite spring in his step had replaced an earlier shuffle across to the filing cabinets.

As a policeman with twenty-five years' experience, he could

usually predict most people's behaviour. But now and then someone really surprised him. If he'd had to draw up a shortlist of local people who would turn up with diamonds about their person, Kurt Baumer wouldn't even have made the top hundred. From what people said, he'd been a man of few words, very intelligent, but dry as dust. It wasn't against the law to ingest valuable gems, but it was likely that some kind of illegal activity had precipitated such an unusual meal. Although he didn't have either the time or the energy for yet another case, he certainly had both for the doctor.

She was standing at the bar when he walked in, nearly his height, a quizzical almost amused look on her face. That was one of the things he really liked about her. Unlike a lot of people, including himself, she didn't take herself too seriously.

They chose a table at the rear of the bar which offered a degree of privacy and ordered glasses of the local beer which, given that the Schloss was a brewery tap, hadn't travelled far. He watched as she checked her phone.

"Never ceases to amaze me what some people define as an emergency." She texted a response to the non-emergency enquiry. "Now, do I have to make any kind of official report about the contents of Herr Baumer's stomach?" She placed her phone face down on the table and took a mouthful from her glass, swallowing slowly.

He could watch her all night.

"Who else knows about this?"

"Well, the detail's in my autopsy report which will be available for a few approved eyes to scan. And a man called Harry Vos who is some kind of private investigator, appointed by Baumer's lawyer to find out if there are any living heirs to his estate."

Neumann felt as if there was a short piece of loose thread dangling before him. If he left well alone, nothing of any consequence would happen. Whereas if he started pulling … who knows what might unravel.

"Where can I find this PI?"

The doctor mentioned the B&B and gave him Vos' phone number.

"Thanks. We'll need to get the diamonds checked. There's always a risk that they come with a problem. OK if I call round to your surgery? In fact, thinking about it, they should be in our police safe. Your place won't be all that secure. Sorry about this. I should have thought of it earlier."

"No problem. Let's do the necessary and we can return here. If you're up for it, that is."

+ + +

The diamonds were a distraction. Pursuing them wouldn't help in the slightest in his heir-hunting role. But they held the promise of intrigue. It was his duty as a citizen to tell the police about them, so that they could investigate. But he didn't want to rule out the possibility of making his own enquiries, in parallel with theirs – taking care, of course, not to get in their way.

Unable to get comfortable in bed and still too mentally active, he got up and used the kit on the table by the window to make himself a hot drink.

How to respond to Webers was the other issue buzzing around his head. He had to come up with a plan – and quickly. A search through his phone failed to reveal Rodenbach's number. Had he changed mobiles since his last call to him? Not as far as he could remember. Maybe he'd used an old school form of recording, a number written down on a piece of paper, normally to be found in his wallet. When he checked – there it was. The system worked.

The number rang and rang. Just as he was about to hang up, a woman answered.

"Yes?"

He could picture her immediately, very attractive, a woman who'd make mincemeat of him and who managed somehow to keep her difficult partner more or less in line. But he couldn't recall her name.

"I've got better things to do than hang around waiting for you to talk!"

Sabina – that was it.

"You probably won't remember me. My name's Harry Vos ..."

"Oh, I remember alright. It generally means trouble when you call. But you're out of luck. He's been laid up in hospital, had an argument with an anchor chain on the boat. I'll tell him you called but don't expect a reply any time soon. What did you want from him?"

"I thought he might be able to deliver a warning to someone I don't like."

"Well, just now, he's not even able to handle a glass of De Koninck, let alone some bruiser you've got the wrong side of." She cut the call.

Given he was made of tough stuff, maybe Rodenbach would be back in action before too long, despite what his Mrs had said. And by then, with a bit of luck, Eden Maes might have come up with an address for Webers.

+ + +

The successful completion of an auction was the kind of moment Eyckmans relished. The proceeds had exceeded his expectations.

The courier had arrived the previous day by train from Paris. The syndicate used varied routes and modes of transport to shift goods from a number of African countries to Brussels. It was best to keep ringing the changes.

Three potential buyers had been lined up, all eager to become the owner of a Ndop statue, fine work by one of the Kuba people.

There'd been a bidding process. Each participant was anonymous, but able to monitor and contribute to the closed-access online auction. Eyckmans had built up the group of bidders over a number of years, based on the three pillars of trust, anonymity and confidentiality. Members of the group were kept sweet with access to inside information about new opportunities to extend their portfolios.

But it was a constant battle trying to keep one step ahead of the government cultural watchdogs, customs services, the tax revenue boys and the self-appointed guardians of African cultural heritage.

The government watchdogs were easier to handle, their constant games of cat and mouse generally predictable. And jobsworth individuals often became more amenable when straightforward bribes were offered. It was the moralistic guardians who got up Eyckman's nose, particularly the air of self-righteousness they brought to their mission. From time to time he'd attempted to infiltrate their ranks, not directly, but by using trusted lieutenants, but had never been able to make much progress.

His career could have been so different. He'd spent twenty years making his way up the greasy pole of the Brussels Mont des Arts establishment and had been poised to take a very senior position. But he'd been careless, an affair of the heart and a pillow-talk indiscretion. Nothing official happened, as too many powerful people would have been implicated, but the word was put around and the senior appointment never materialised. He'd had some involvement in unofficial trading prior to his fall and was able to use that experience and the contacts he'd made to establish the syndicate that controlled the business – four 'investors' in total. Once that was in place, they'd developed a network of interested potential bidders.

His alternative career path had turned out to be far more lucrative than the world of arts bureaucracy and had also enabled him metaphorically to stick two fingers up to the establishment.

And there was no shortage of bidders. The improvement in the fortunes of the country's very-well-off and beyond them, the super-rich, was apparently unstoppable. But, poor things, they needed outlets for their wealth. They already had their grand houses and big cars were so passé. A high cultural profile could help to put them into a different league. If the process of getting there involved paying out larger sums of money than in previous days – then so be it. They were very worthwhile investments.

A small private room in the *Guillaume* in the Sablon area was the perfect place for a syndicate celebration.

Eyckmans ordered two more bottles of Veuve Clicquot. The talk was all about new finds discovered by their field operatives who reported in on a regular basis, tantalising titbits to whet appetites and help build up a head of steam for the next bidding round. Two qualifications were required to become a syndicate member – a finger on the pulse through good contacts in the art world and an ability to hold one's tongue and one's drink. The risk of careless talk undermining the syndicate had to be avoided. Occasionally he'd recruited badly and been forced to ease out a non-compliant member, but over the years, his ability to assess the required qualities had been honed almost to perfection.

Nine

Morning rain was teeming down. Vos, already tetchy because of a lack of sleep, felt his mood lowering further. And the previous evening's phone call to Katerine had not gone well, mainly because he hadn't been able to report any progress on how to tackle Webers. Luckily, Helga's breakfast perked him up. Smoked mackerel on toast, topped with two poached eggs of exactly the right consistency.

He glanced through the local freesheet which was ninety-percent adverts. The remaining ten consisted of short quirky reflections on local life, which were quite entertaining. It was with some amusement that he spotted his taxi driver as one of the contributors.

Through the window, he noticed the arrival of a tall thin man, under a large black umbrella, a policeman through and through, despite the plain clothes.

He hadn't expected the chief inspector to choose the B&B rather than the police station as the location for their appointment. Perhaps he liked getting out of the office.

As Vos filled two cups with coffee from the fresh pot his landlady had brought in, Neumann introduced himself and announced he'd been briefed on Baumer – and his diamonds. There would be an investigation.

So, the doctor had beaten him to the policeman with news of the diamonds, Vos thought. Neumann asked him what he'd found out so far about Baumer.

He gave a quick summary of the key points and mentioned Baumer's connections with the art world.

"It occurs to me that there might be a link between those connections, the suspected late-night visitors in the Datsun and the diamonds. Has there been any progress in tracing the car?"

"We haven't found it yet," Neumann said. "But we did speak to a nocturnal dog-walking villager who confirmed seeing two men leaving Baumer's house around midnight. He was some distance away from them and so wasn't able to give us a description, but confirmed they drove off in an old Datsun."

"That's real progress," Vos said. "Do *you* think there's likely to be a link between the visitors, the diamonds and Baumer's death?" Vos asked, unsure whether he'd get an answer. "I mean it's speculation at this stage as there's not much actual evidence to go on."

The policeman hesitated before replying, perhaps unsure quite how far to trust the PI with his own thoughts.

"I'd say that was highly likely. But let's not get ahead of ourselves. There are two things I need from you. The first is a commitment to let me know about any information you come across in your work for Ahrendt, that might be useful to my investigation."

"Agreed," Vos said. "What's your second request?"

Neumann pulled a face as if to indicate that *request* was the wrong choice of word.

"That you avoid any temptation to make your own enquiries about Baumer's visitors or the diamonds. These are strictly matters for the police!"

"Also agreed," Vos said, knowing that he might be tempted, but not wanting to antagonize Neumann.

The two men shook hands before the policeman left, once more under the protection of his brolly.

By noon the rain had stopped. Helga prepared him a soup

and sandwich lunch which he ate in the garden, sitting beneath the conservatory awning.

"Didn't you say you were meeting the lawyer at two o'clock, Harry? It's a quarter to already."

Helga's voice roused him. Annoyed with himself for falling asleep, he thanked her and hurried off to Ahrendt's. To the frustration of both men, Kirchner didn't turn up or answer his phone.

Walking back to the B&B, his lingering doubts about the nephew's claims reinforced by the exasperating no-show, Vos wondered whether he should request a DNA test to confirm his blood link to Kurt.

+ + +

Jules Fontaine ran a brand agency in Antwerp which handled PR for a number of firms in the fashion trade. That was her publicly-known role. The fact she was also the co-ordinator of Circle 10, was known to few.

She was worried. Kurt Baumer had been out of contact for over two weeks. The old man was usually as regular as clockwork, touching base every Friday. She'd left messages on his phone, but there'd been no response. It was possible he'd been threatened and was lying low. She'd received threats herself, but as the co-ordinator, that was only to be expected.

They had no physical HQ. Members were scattered geographically and kept in touch via texts on basic, difficult-to-trace phones. The group's effectiveness was dependent on the kind of high-quality intelligence that Baumer and others provided. This in turn was dependent on developing and maintaining contacts with the right people in the right institutions both at home and in central Africa; in particular, the Democratic Republic of the Congo. Over time they'd established an early warning system in order to flag up proposed movements of valuable artefacts. Baumer was a key part of this system.

Fontaine decided to leave things for a few more days. If by then there'd still been no response from him, she'd have to send one of the team to St Vith to try and find out what had happened.

+ + +

As the voice was little more than a croak, it took a while for Vos to work out that it was Leo Rodenbach. For all her unhelpfulness over the phone, Sabina must, after all, have passed the message on to her partner.

He sounded in a bad way but insisted that Vos should tell him about the job in hand. He'd need a few more days' recuperation at home, but would then be available to assist.

That might fit in well enough, Vos thought, given that they didn't yet have a location for Webers and that Katerine wasn't due back home for another two weeks.

He struggled to explain exactly what he wanted from his old adversary. A warning of some kind, strong enough to deter Webers from any revenge activity. But he didn't want things to get out of hand and for Webers to end up in hospital or worse. Rodenbach said he'd have a think about it and come up with a proposal. A difficult conversation with Katerine lay just round the corner. He could report on progress, but she'd no doubt have strong reservations about his choice of operative.

Call finished, Vos noticed a text from Ryck, announcing that he and the family would be arriving in St Vith a day earlier than originally planned. Vos slowly cottoned on to the fact that this meant later that afternoon. A second text informed him that they'd all be staying in *his* B&B. It had been planned as a surprise, which was why his landlady hadn't mentioned it.

Vos was both pleased and a little disgruntled. It would of

course be nice to see them, but he'd grown accustomed to having the place to himself, and the two youngsters, whilst close to his heart, always left him feeling exhausted. Still, with Katerine arriving the following day, at least their impact could be halved.

+ + +

Not long after the family's arrival, Ryck drove Vos out to Baumer's place, leaving the children in the B&B garden sandpit and Magda talking away to Helga, as if they'd known each other for years.

Vos opened up the garage and they stood together gazing at the Opel Rekord, casting admiring glances at the bodywork.

"This is in such good nick!" Ryck said. "I presume you've got the keys."

"Yes, I found them in a kitchen drawer. Here – fire her up."

The engine started first time and purred away.

"Looks good and sounds good," Ryck said. He switched off, released the bonnet catch and went to inspect. "Look at the condition of this engine, Uncle. I noticed there's only 50k on the clock, which given her age is nothing. I guess he must have just pottered around locally."

Closing the bonnet, he walked to the back of the car and noticed that the rear offside tyre was flat.

"Can't have that!" he said. "We might want to take the car out for a spin. I'll get it changed."

"Do you really want to bother with that now?" his uncle asked.

"Oh, it's no bother. Better just check out the spare first though, make sure that's not flat as well!"

It looked to be fully inflated. Ryck unscrewed the fixing and lifted up the wheel.

"Hang about – there's something underneath it."

Ryck pulled out a leather bag and handed it to his uncle.

"I think you should be the one to open this!"

Vos pulled a green A4 file from the bag and removed a number of papers.

"There's not enough light in here for me to read these. Let's take them outside."

"No need, Uncle," Ryck said, yanking a pull-switch and bathing the garage's interior with fluorescent light.

"So, let's see what we've got here." Vos flicked through each page. "Well, well! These go nicely together with some papers I've just been looking at. Lists drawn up by Kurt of African artwork – you know, like masks, small statues, pottery, that kind of thing. These seem to be recent letters to Kurt from dealers, confirming availability of various items. The interesting thing is that both sets of papers have been typed – on actual typewriters – real old school. So, the question is why – two whys actually."

"Why were they typed and why were they hidden away under the spare tyre?" Ryck responded.

"Exactly! Either they don't have access to computers, which seems highly unlikely or, these documents are sensitive and they wanted to avoid any risk of being hacked."

"Or being found in any search of the house," Ryck added. "Why don't you go and have a proper look at them while I get this wheel changed?"

"Good idea. I can also have a think about whether to try and buy the Rekord. My sort of car really."

Ryck watched his uncle walk up the garden path and in through the front door, pleased that Harry had found something to get his teeth into. He always seemed like a different man, a younger one, when fully absorbed in a case. There was a risk of investigations getting out of hand, but Ryck thought it unlikely with this one.

Once he'd replaced the wheel, he eased the Rekord out onto the driveway, opened the bonnet again and poked around for a while, more than satisfied with what he saw. Even though it hadn't been driven much, Baumer had clearly looked after the vehicle. Ryck knew it wouldn't get the same degree of care and attention if his uncle were to get his hands on it. There was also the question of how much he'd end up having to pay for it. Probably too much, given its near-mint condition.

Satisfied that the car had a very clean bill of health, he reversed it back into the garage and locked up.

Vos was at the kitchen table studying the newly discovered information intently.

"What's the verdict then, Uncle? Something or nothing?" Getting no response, Ryck asked again.

"Sorry, I was miles away. I think my first assumptions were right, that they're all from dealers, who are identified by reference numbers, rather than names. And they've been sent through the post. Look, a couple of them still have their envelopes attached. Again, that would be a security thing. Although mail can go missing, it's not at risk of being hacked. All this reinforces what I've been told so far, which is that as well as being an artworks expert, Kurt was also involved in some kind of dealing. And I have a feeling that some of it may not have been legit."

Vos felt himself being drawn in. Were these documents linked to activities which might have led to Kurt's death – or the presence of the diamonds?

"Are you going to tell your copper about this?" Ryck asked. "What's his name again?"

"Neumann," Vos replied. "Not yet. I'll wait and see if anything else turns up. It's still speculative at this stage."

"I just wish I'd got time to get involved," Ryck said, "but one way or another I'm pretty fully booked. All this art stuff's a bit of a distraction for you though, isn't it? Aren't you meant to be concentrating on finding a Baumer heir?"

"You're right of course Ryck. But it's difficult not to be interested...and if I can find out anything that relates to Kurt's death…well it seems the right thing to do…in my own time of course. It's not as if I'm hunting for surviving members of the Baumer family 24/7. So, what's your verdict on the car then?"

"It's a real gem," Ryck said. "The thing is though, wouldn't it have to be valued as part of Baumer's estate, if that's the right word? It might be worth a fair bit, given it's in such good condition and is quite a rarity. E2s were common enough but this one's early 90s with a V6 engine which means it must have been made in South Africa."

"How do you know all this, Ryck?"

"Don't forget I'm in the trade, Harry, and I have a smart phone which gives me instant access to all sorts of specialist rubbish. Anyway, the point I was trying to get across is that it's likely to be something of a collector's item which might put it outside your price range."

"Just when I was imagining myself behind the wheel, driving down to the flea market in Heist! Anyway, it's probably too big for my modest needs and I don't suppose it'd be very economical. Would have been nice to take it for a spin though."

"Well, given that I'm covered to drive any car, why don't I take us all out for a ride sometime over the weekend? We can get the flat tyre sorted out in St Vith beforehand. You'll have to be content to stay in the passenger seat though! Oh, and while we're on the subject of cars, I'm on the trail for a suitable Berlingo. Don't want you to be stuck without wheels once you're back in Heist."

Ten

A clipboard held the paperwork which showed that the load in the back of the big Citroen van was legit. What it didn't show was the large wheelie suitcase buried under the sacks of coffee.

The van's occupants watched the Nyiragongo volcano smoking threateningly to their left as they bumped along the potholed road away from Goma, towards the Rwandan border.

The driver stopped suddenly.

"Need a piss," he said.

"Should've gone before we set off," Skip shouted at him. "Get a fucking move on!"

The driver walked a few metres away from the road, stopped on an area of marshy ground and unzipped. Suddenly he collapsed in a heap.

"Mazuku!" Kela shouted. She grabbed the oxygen cylinder from behind the passenger seat and leapt out of the van, Skip close behind. The two of them dragged the driver away from the marshy hollow. Kela fixed the mask over his nose and waited for him to recover.

"What the fuck happened?" he asked, coughing and spluttering.

"Of course – not from round here, are you?" Kela said. "We call it Mazuku, toxic carbon dioxide, bubbles up from the ground. It can kill you. That's why we try and have oxygen handy. It's the kids who are most at risk. By the way you need to zip up your flies."

It took a while before the driver felt well enough to get back behind the wheel.

The DRC border check was the riskiest part of their journey. Normally, the guards were only interested in guns or drugs but occasionally there'd be a crackdown on smuggled artworks.

They were in luck. Papers were checked cursorily, van doors opened briefly, a quick rummage around a couple of coffee sacks within arms' reach, cash handed over. Before they knew it, the van was waved through. The Rwandan guards were even less interested – except in the money.

Four hours to Kigali.

At the airport, Kela removed the wheelie from the back of the van and waved the other two off. The forged export permits weren't particularly good, but Kela knew it would be better to use them and declare the artefacts, rather than risk their discovery by the airport baggage scanner. Another payment and she was through.

Having previously used other 'export' routes, it was Kela's first time on the Kigali-to-Amsterdam flight. She slept or dozed for most of the eight hours.

+ + +

Marc had invited the extended Vos family round to his place for tea.

He lifted Sun up so that she could hang the re-filled bird feeder back on its hook. Next up was half a coconut that she fixed by its string to the other hook. The shell had been deprived of its original contents and filled with … well nobody was quite sure exactly what it now contained.

Vos was aware that Marc had no young relatives, yet there he was looking like a natural kindergarten teacher. Little Freddie tugged at the bottom of Marc's jeans, keen to get in on the bird-feeding act.

With Ryck and Magda out on a short walk, Vos took full advantage of his friend's presence to delegate grand-uncle duties. Stretched out on a sun-lounger, taking occasional sips from his glass of orange juice, he allowed himself to close his eyes and forget about everything. He could just hear Josina, who'd joined them for the weekend, talking away on her phone at the end of the garden. Katerine, who'd arrived that morning with tales of conference gossip, was taking a nap inside.

Once everyone was back in the garden, Marc ordered pizzas and they spent delivery time drinking chilled wine and expensive artisan lemonade, eating nibbles, basking in the sun and chatting.

The food, which vanished all too quickly, was followed by garden games which became increasingly raucous. Ryck drove his family back to the B&B as dusk fell. The remaining four retired to the kitchen and sat around the table in candlelight. The wine continued to flow and the cards came out. Josina hadn't played pinochle before and Vos was impressed by how quickly she picked it up. When they switched to the cutthroat version, she proved to be a natural.

"What was that noise?" Katerine asked, just as she was about to bid and out. None of the others had heard anything. "Something from next door," she said. "Listen, there it is again, quite faint but it sounds like someone or something moving around."

"I think you're imagining it," Marc said.

"No, she isn't," Josina butted in. "I heard it that time."

"I'll go and have a look," Vos said.

"We'll both go," Katerine said, swiftly.

Vos unlocked the front door to Baumer's house and they walked in. Not a sound. He flicked on the light switch. Nothing happened.

"Probably just a bulb that's gone," he said.

Hearing sudden footsteps, he flinched before realising that the noise was moving away from them. The back door opened. He rushed through the house and into the garden. The side gate was wide open. A car started up. Two figures in it, silhouetted by the security light on the gable end. Vos just managed to glimpse the number plate of the old Peugeot 406, before the vehicle sped away.

"What do you think they were up to, Harry?" Katerine held on to his arm, a little breathless.

His immediate assumption was that the intruders would have been interested in the diamonds, but as they spelt trouble, he didn't want to mention them yet. At some point he'd have to tell his wife, but wanted to prepare the ground for that discussion. Since his mini-stroke, she'd been wary about his involvement in anything that might become too stressful. He didn't want her understandable concern to lead to him having to drop his new found interest in diamonds.

"Opportunist burglars I'd have thought, maybe read about Kurt's death and thought they'd try their luck in an empty house. As we didn't have any lights on next door, they probably assumed there was nobody around there either and that it was OK to make a bit of noise."

"How do you think they got in?"

"Don't know. Let's have a look."

The front door hadn't been damaged in any way. At first sight that back door seemed to be intact as well. But on closer examination he found the lock was no longer functioning.

"This was their route in," Vos said. "Do you want to go back to Marc's and I'll secure this temporarily. There are some tools in the cupboard under the kitchen sink."

"OK. Don't be long."

A couple of well-placed screws did the job. He'd ask Marc to fit a decent mortice in the morning. Before returning next door, he made a call to St Vith police station to tell them about the break-in and the Peugeot.

A thought occurred to him. Had he used the back door at all

since he'd been working in the house? No. In which case, maybe the lock had been damaged by Baumer's visitors on the night of his death. He'd been puzzled why Kurt would have let anyone in, so late in the evening. But what if they'd made their own way in to the house?

Back at Marc's he played it all down. Their card game was resumed.

But he was worried.

+ + +

At Schipol, Kela Mpenda retrieved the wheelie from the carousel and waited in line. She was hoping the Dutch customs guys would be unfamiliar with DRC export permits and would find it difficult to spot a forgery. The queue was long and she was tired, hungry and hot. *Behave naturally* was a key message drilled into all team members. She struck up a conversation with the woman next to her in the queue, an everyday sort of chat about the weather, the problems of flying and the prospect of some decent food after a diet of airline meals.

Much to her relief, Kela was waved through without a check or a single question. Glancing back, she noticed the woman she'd been talking to had been pulled to one side and was being led into an interview cubicle. There was always that danger.

The train to Antwerp was jam-packed and she stood in one of the vestibules, case by her side. A snatched coffee, croissant and chocolate bar at the airport had staved off immediate hunger pangs. The train stopped for what seemed like an age just outside Antwerp. She worried that the stoppage might be for a customs spot-check. These happened occasionally at the border. But nobody appeared and eventually the train crept slowly forwards into the city.

Outside the station, a Mercedes van was waiting for her. They sped out along the A1 towards Mechelen and took the N26 towards Leuven, as she'd expected, before turning off and slowing along country lanes. The ornate wrought iron double gates opened automatically on approach and they swept up the long drive to an imposing house.

The driver rang the bell. Kela was surprised when Eyckmans himself opened the door. Not that they'd ever met, but she'd seen his photo. He spoke to the driver but barely acknowledged her presence. The suitcase was taken away for the contents to be checked prior to payment being made.

"Would it be possible for me to have a quick look at your gallery?" Kela asked. "Skip told me about it and as a sculptor myself, I would love a chance to see a few of the pieces."

Eyckmans hesitated, perhaps unsure about how to respond to the delivery girl who might be a little more than that.

"Very well. I'll get the caretaker to escort you. Just a brief look and no photography."

Kela moved from exhibit to exhibit taking it all in. Although Skip had made some casual comments about the gallery, his only interest in art was how to make money out of it and his few words hadn't conveyed how impressive it was. The caretaker dogged her footsteps as they passed through each of the four rooms.

At the end of her over-guided tour, she was taken to a small room at the back of the house and told to wait for Eyckman's return. It wasn't difficult for her to mentally retrace her steps around the gallery, recall key pieces and note details of them on her phone. Some of the exhibits she was already aware of. Others were a complete surprise.

+ + +

It was a glorious Sunday morning, perfect for the picnic Ryck and Magda had planned down by the river Our.

They were all in full relaxation mode, with picnic blankets and camping chairs spread out over the riverbank, enough sandwiches to feed an army, not to mention the fruit juices, cakes and biscuits.

Vos found he couldn't stop eating. Eventually, *full to bursting* as he told the kids, he placed his cap over his eyes and snoozed, a faint buzz of conversation floating around on the light breeze, the river burbling by, the ping of shuttlecock on racket as Josina took the lead against Ryck.

Vos was content and wanted the afternoon to roll on as slowly as possible. At last, he felt he was coming to terms with his mother's death. Maybe he finally could stop blaming himself for not having been more attentive during the last few years of her life.

The sudden torrential rain caught everyone by surprise and there was an almighty rush to get everything back into the cars. The kids squealed at the thunder and lightning. But after a short while, the weather changed just as quickly in the opposite direction, the sky suddenly blue again. All the kit, apart from the blankets, was hauled back out of the vehicles and repositioned on the wet gleaming grass.

Vos sat next to Katerine and talked about nothing very much. It really was peaceful on the riverside.

On their return to the B&B, Ryck suggested a ride out along the backroads in the Rekord. It was the sort of trip you normally paid good money for, Katerine said, swanning about the countryside in an unusual motor.

After a teatime snack, the rest of the family left for home and Vos and his wife took advantage of the early evening sun in the B&B garden. Their conversation earlier that day about Rodenbach had gone better than he'd expected. Although still having some reservations about his choice of operative, she was pleased he was taking the threat seriously. They'd also talked a little over the weekend about the search for Kurt's heirs and she was aware of his need for more information about the Baumer family.

She suggested he approach a few key locals again, on the off-chance that somebody might, perhaps without realising it, know something useful about Kurt Baumer. Good advice, he thought and decided to start, there and then, with old Ella. Katerine was keen to accompany him.

It was a very pleasant evening for a walk and they took turns with her binoculars to study the marshland birds.

The woman was suspicious about Vos' return visit, but Katerine managed to break the ice by asking about her herb garden. As the two women poked about in the greenery, he took the chance to sit down on an old bench and close his eyes.

The next thing he took in was Katerine thanking Ella and saying goodbye. It was a surprise to be told that during the time he'd been dozing, his wife had managed to prise some very unexpected information from the herb gardener. As they walked a little further along the cycle track, Vos shouted at a head-down cyclist who tore past them without warning. But his comments were lost on the ear-podded man who was clearly oblivious to his surroundings.

"So, you're telling me that she knew Kurt's Aunt Ada!"

"Well, it only came out after a while. Although she takes pride in her memory, I had to prod a bit, wait a while and then try again. Ada was staying temporarily at her brother's house outside St Vith and attended Ella's school for a term. They were aged about fifteen, very different, but both viewed by other pupils as oddballs. As a result, they stuck together for mutual protection. The two of them also shared a fascination with plants and animals. Ella remembered Ada inviting her to the house where she was staying. Her brother – Kurt's father of course – was renting it and living there with his young family. A rambling place in poor condition. Apparently, he was much better at talking about money than keeping hold of it."

Like father like son, Vos thought.

"Anyway, listen to this!" Katerine continued. "Ella swore blind that there were three young children in the house."

"Three? How can that be?"

"Well, Kurt who must have been about eight, his sister who was three years younger and then an even younger brother."

"That's a real turn up! Another possible claimant to Kurt's estate. You did well getting that out of Ella. Strange though that nobody else has mentioned a brother. I wonder how reliable her memory is. She must be over ninety."

"I guess so, Harry, but she sounded convinced. When I asked if she could remember the young boy's name she went into a sort of trance, complete with rolling eyes. Then, all of a sudden, she was back and telling me he was called Sebastien. She wasn't invited to the house again and shortly afterwards the Baumer family moved away from St Vith. A new line of enquiry for you, Detective Vos, and it hasn't cost you a cent!"

"Well, it's certainly earned you a kiss," he said, grinning.

On the walk back to the B&B, his phone rang. It was Eden Maes wanting to know if he'd be free to meet up the following morning.

+ + +

That evening Vos and his wife joined Rainer for a drink in the Ost Bar. They started with glasses of Bellevaux Malmedy Tripel

Vos mentioned the name Sebastien to the taxi driver and one or two other locals in the bar, but none of them had heard of a Kurt Baumer brother. The general view was one of scepticism. Either the old woman's memory was unreliable or she'd just made up the story. Only Rainer gave her story any credibility. He'd found her information to be helpful in the past.

And he had some new information of his own that might be useful to Vos.

"A pal of mine was on his way to shoot wild fowl and saw a car parked up near Kurt's house. Must have been the day before his death. Feller sat in the driving seat, looking across at the property and talking into his phone. When I told my mate about your interest in Kurt, he gave me more. Said he remembered the car's number plate."

"Really," Vos asked. "That's a bit unusual."

"Oh, he's a bit nerdy like that but it helped that it was similar to the plate on one of his dad's cars. This is the interesting bit though. The car was an old Datsun!"

"Well, well, just like the one used by Kurt's visitors. Must have been scoping the place. Just the one guy in the car though?" Vos said.

"That's right. Unfortunately, my pal wasn't able to see his face, so couldn't give me a description, but he was wearing a baseball cap! Anyway, I did my public duty and phoned Neumann, who was his usual dour self. I'm assuming he'll check it out, but you might want to chase him up."

"Do I pick up a hint that you and the chief inspector don't get on?"

"You could say that. He's got his suspicions about me. Completely groundless of course."

As the Vosses found the Tripel to be far too strong, they switched to a more moderate brew, leaving Rainer to continue with the hard stuff. When the session finally came to an end, he told them he'd be walking home and would pick the taxi up in the morning.

After their own short walk to the B&B, they decided to take advantage of the rest of the family having flown the nest and enjoy an early night.

Eleven

After providing an early morning taxi service so that Katerine could catch her train from Gouvy back to Luxembourg, Vos returned to St Vith for his rendezvous with Maes.

He failed to recognise the man who arrived on the B&B doorstep.

"Don't worry! It *is* me," Maes said with a smile. "When I got back from the Azores, I decided to change both my location and my appearance. Hence the shaved head and the specs. Although, to be honest, I do actually need the glasses these days. It's good to see you, Harry."

Vos led him through to the garden. It was a very pleasant morning made even better by Helga's arrival with a tray bearing coffee and cakes.

"So, have you found Webers?" Vos asked, unable to contain his curiosity any longer.

"I have – with some help from two ex-Redline mates. He's still in the capital and has an apartment up near the Atomium."

"That's brilliant!" Vos said, thinking that with a location he now had a chance to be proactive – he was getting to like the word – rather than sit around worrying about when his adversary might strike.

"Here's his address and an up-to-date photograph of him. What are you planning to do?"

Vos told him about Rodenbach.

"You will take care, won't you, Harry? Webers is a nasty piece of work."

"Yes. Don't worry. Katerine, my wife, will keep me in line. And Leo's a good man to have on board." Vos hoped that he really was the man for the job – whatever the job turned out to be. "Anyway, tell me about yourself. What are you up to?"

The conversation flowed. An hour flashed by.

As soon as Maes had driven off, Vos phoned Rodenbach.

"I'm just about good to go," he said. "Do we have a location yet?"

Vos gave him the details and said he'd forward a photograph of Webers.

"And what level of warning do you want me to give?"

Vos wasn't sure.

"Enough to make him realise it won't be worth pursuing some sort of vendetta, I suppose. Do you have any ideas yourself, Leo?"

There was a sharp intake of breath at the other end of the line.

"That wasn't a response to your question," Rodenbach said, "just my reaction to turning too quickly. Some things are still a bit painful. But I'm a quick healer." Vos heard the click of a lighter and could almost smell the tobacco smoke. "Look – I don't know this guy, but from what you've told me, he's not stupid. And having been inside, he probably won't want to return anytime soon. Strikes me he's a bit like an annoying wasp. Hit him with a rolled-up newspaper and he'll definitely come after you. You might be surprised to hear this, but my advice would be for us to be a bit cleverer than that. Why don't we arrange to meet him for a nice little conversation? Don't get me wrong, I'm quite prepared to go much further than that, but I don't think it would be in your best interests. Or Katerine's!"

It wasn't at all what Vos had expected, but maybe Rodenbach's suggestion of a 'conversation' was a good one. Would Webers listen, though?

"How about we pay him a visit tomorrow?" Vos asked, keen to get on with things.

"That's good for me. I'll make sure he's going to be there. Don't worry, he won't have a clue that I'm checking up on him. If I find out he's not going to be around, I'll let you know and we can rearrange."

+ + +

With Rainer unusually unavailable, Vos got a ride out to Baumer's house in another taxi with a driver who didn't want to talk.

Despite what had happened there, he liked being in the house. There seemed to be no lingering spirits associated with Kurt's death. And now that a lot of the storage boxes had been shifted to the garage, the place felt a lot airier. After spending some time on box-sifting and wanting some variety, he decided to search the house and garage more thoroughly. So far, he and Josina had found neither a mobile phone nor a computer. Given the nature of Kurt's involvement in the art world, it was hard to believe that he'd operated entirely without either.

It took him about an hour to go through the upstairs rooms. There were a number of things that caught his attention but turned out on closer inspection not to be important. He moved to the garage for a further change of scene.

There was something about the building which reminded him of the stable at the rear of his maternal grandparents' house in Mons which he'd visited frequently during school holidays. It had been one of his play areas and he had a clear memory of discovering a hidey-hole behind a loose brick in the inner garage wall. The secret space had been put to good use as a store for 'valuables' such as his best set of crayons and his catapult.

Might a search of Kurt's old garage reveal a secret compartment of its own?

The front wall was mainly taken up by the garage doors and an examination of the two side walls revealed nothing that hinted at a hiding place behind. With the exception of the bottom metre or so, the internal rear wall of the garage was covered in shelving fixed to timber boarding. He removed the contents of the shelves in order to check the boarding behind, tapping each section with the head of a large screwdriver. Just as he was beginning to think the search was futile, a different sound answered back. A hollowness! On closer examination, it looked as if a section was removable. The business end of the screwdriver was then put to good use to prise open a half metre length of boarding, revealing a gap just wide and deep enough for a bit of storage.

When Vos shone a torch into the gap it revealed evidence that Kurt Baumer might well have been computer literate after all.

Back in the house, he had a quick scout around for anything that looked like a password which would get him into the laptop. Nothing caught his eye. It was time for a lunchbreak. He'd made some purchases that morning from the deli in St Vith.

Mackerel pate, now spread across four slices of toast, tomatoes, neatly sliced, a banana, cut up into small pieces and a glass of milk. Just the job, he thought. The open laptop sat next to this mini-feast. Before he could make a start on the meal, his phone rang. It was Neumann.

"You need to come to the station, within the next hour," he said. "I've got a very busy day and haven't got time to hang around."

As it happened, the summons suited Vos as he needed to talk to the chief inspector. But, not wanting to miss out on his lunch, he wasn't going to rush there. After a call to Rainer, who this time was available, he began to eat with his left hand and test out passwords on Baumer's laptop with his right. He was sure it wouldn't be totally random, more likely something unusual to everyone else, but very familiar to the old man. Maybe with a DRC connection?

He tapped away at the keys, trying to avoid smearing pate over the keyboard. The more obvious DRC place names, rivers and lakes got him nowhere, but then there was also the question of what additional characters might get added to words such as *Kinshasa* or *Goma*. Perhaps part of his date of birth?

The pate really was good. He'd definitely use the deli again. Halfway through the sliced banana, Rainer's Passat arrived. Vos stuffed the remaining pieces in his mouth, drained his glass and stacked things by the side of the sink.

As he was about to leave, the laptop caught his eye. Given the possible risk of another break in, he decided to take it with him. Having locked up, he jumped into the taxi.

"I'm just off to see the chief inspector. I know you two don't get on, but what can you tell me about him?"

"Not that much," Rainer said. "He's divorced, had to sell the house as part of the settlement and now rents a place in town, likes his food and is a very good squash player by all accounts. Rumour has it that he and the good doctor Vermeulen are more than just acquaintances."

Vos was intrigued by this particular bit of news, but didn't want to get distracted by it.

"Anything particular you're after?" Rainer asked.

"Not really. It's just that I seem to be coming across him more than I'd anticipated and always like to know who I'm dealing with."

"Well, what I can tell you is that something's really bugging him today. Saw him crossing the road earlier, with a takeout coffee in his hand and a face like thunder. Forewarned and all that …"

At the police station reception Vos was ushered immediately into an interview room. Neumann arrived within a minute.

"You took your time! Take a seat please. I'm recording this interview." The machine made a slight whirring sound. Neumann gave details of the date and time and who was present. "Have you found out any more about Elias Kirchner?"

Vos hadn't expected him to be on the agenda.

"Nothing, but then he hasn't been responding to my messages."

"Hm ... interesting," Neumann said. "He was abducted by two men from the house he was renting off the Bullingen road. Happened this morning. The witness has provided a description of the abductors and the registration number of the car – a Toyota."

Vos was completely thrown by this news. Granted he'd had some reservations about Kirchner, but couldn't imagine why someone would have carted him off. What had he done to deserve that sort of treatment?

"Please tell me everything you know about him."

Vos told the chief inspector what he'd found out. Only half his mind was focused on this task while the other half drifted off, trying to work out how Kirchner's abduction would affect his own investigation. The discussion with Ahrendt about Kirchner's status as a likely heir would have to be put on hold as would the idea of requesting a DNA test. At least the delay would give him a chance to try and track down someone other than Schultz who'd known both Elias and his mother. Someone who hadn't been hand-picked by the nephew!

The buzz of the mobile in his jacket pocket brought him back to full concentration. It was in his hand before he'd really considered whether it was the right thing to do in the middle of a police interview. A quick glance showed that it was a text from Rodenbach which would have to wait.

"Do you have any idea why Kirchner might have been abducted?" Neumann asked.

"Not a clue. Let's hope you'll be able to trace the abductors' car."

"That would certainly help."

"Talking of cars," Vos said, "has there been any progress finding the Datsun used by Kurt Baumer's visitors? I understand a new witness was able to provide you with the registration number."

"How did you know about that?" Neumann asked looking annoyed. But the look lasted only a moment. "Never mind. I know how quickly some news travels locally. No progress so far, not helped by the fact that there are no cameras on the route we think they used after leaving Baumer's place. We have managed to track down the Peugeot you reported, but, as it turned out to be a stolen vehicle, it hasn't got us very far. We have some prints off it but no matches."

"So, are your enquiries about Baumer's death, his visitors and the diamonds interlinked now?" Vos asked. Again, a brief look of annoyance from Neumann.

"Yes – not that it's really any of your business. Given that the autopsy showed Baumer died of a heart attack, we're not currently treating his death as murder. But it's possible the actions of the visitors precipitated the heart attack and that those actions were driven by a desire to get hold of the diamonds. If this series of assumptions is correct, then the subsequent break in at Baumer's house – the one you interrupted – was almost certainly aimed at trying to find and remove the diamonds. We're pursuing enquiries as to how Baumer acquired them. That includes talking to people who knew him, to see if they can shed any light on this. Although you never actually met him, you probably know more about him than most. So, if you've come across anything that might explain how he got the diamonds in the first place I need to know."

"Well, he was something of an expert on art, or to be more precise, on African, mainly Congolese, artefacts. There's not a lot to go on, but I've come across documents that indicate he had some involvement in dealing."

"Interesting! Do you think this might link to the diamonds?"

"There's no evidence to back this up, but I suppose it's possible he acquired them as a form of payment."

"That's most helpful, Vos. I should stress that this is entirely a police matter and I don't want you stumbling around making your own enquiries. Apart from anything else, it could be dangerous."

The chief inspector's phone rang.

"Hello, Doctor." Vos wasn't surprised to see Neumann's face reddening. "Yes indeed. 8:00pm that'll be fine. I am. It's Vos, the PI. He's assisting with my enquiries. I do indeed have a valuation but as you'll understand, I can't reveal such detail. Eight o'clock then. Thank you. Goodbye."

Neumann poured out two glasses of water and handed one to Vos.

"Now, where were we? Ah yes, I was warning you of the dangers. You may not be aware, but the art world can be pretty murky, what with smuggling, bribery, disguising works of art so they can be exported 'legitimately' and even the laundering of drug money and other illicit gains through the art trade. You get the picture." Vos nodded. Neumann couldn't have been clearer about warning him off. "Let's assume for a moment that there is a link between his dealing and the diamonds, that they were some form of payment. We'll follow up this possibility, but progress may be slow simply because there aren't enough specialist officers available to get much beyond the tip of the iceberg. Still, be that as it may, I'd be obliged if you could let me have copies of those Baumer documents you mentioned and keep me informed of any other relevant information you might come across during the course of your enquiries."

"I'll certainly do that," Vos said, knowing that he'd be the one to decide what exactly was 'relevant'.

An officer came into the room and whispered in Neumann's ear.

"I have to go, Vos. Don't forget what I told you."

+ + +

On the walk back to his lodgings, he thought about the policeman and the doctor. They seemed to be two very different characters, but then wasn't that often the case with couples? Whatever was going on between them – and like Rainer, he was fairly certain there was something – it appeared to be in its early stages.

Although such musings were both harmless and enjoyable, they were yet another distraction. He needed to concentrate on finding out whether Sebastien really existed and texted Josina, hoping she'd be able to assist in the search.

By the time he got to Kurt's house, she'd already responded and confirmed that Sebastien would be her next priority.

What about Lindner? He hadn't said anything about a Baumer brother – just a sister. But it would be worth checking with him. Message left.

It occurred to Vos that there was another way of trying to find out about Sebastien. Although Aunt Ada was no longer around, there might be someone working at her animal sanctuary in Kinshasa who could, at the least, confirm Sebastien's existence? He suspected it would be difficult trying to make such enquiries by phone or email. What was needed was a more personal approach. Would his friend Jalloh be able to help? The two of them had worked together on the people-smuggling case and built up a good rapport. He lived in Brussels, but had grown up in Kinshasa, still had relatives in the city and was involved in twinning activities between the two Matonges, one in Brussels, the other in the DRC capital. Perhaps, armed with an official authorization from Ahrendt, Jalloh could pay a visit to the sanctuary on his next trip to the city and ask a few discreet questions about Kurt and a possible brother.

And one other avenue was worth trying.

Vos hadn't come across any evidence in Kurt's paperwork or photographs that suggested he had a brother. This might be because there was no brother, or that there had been, but he'd died young, or that he'd turned out to be the black sheep of the family and had subsequently been expunged from the family records. The other possible explanation, Vos thought, was that he just hadn't been diligent enough in his search of Kurt's records.

A second trawl through some of the information might prove worthwhile. Thanks to Josina's clear labelling, it was a straightforward task to find the two relevant boxes in the garage and bring them back to the house. With one of Kurt's old jazz LPs playing softly and a glass of whisky by his side, he looked at each item in turn. It was a harder task second time around, because nothing was likely to be new and yet he still had to concentrate. Needles and haystacks sprang to mind.

He found nothing useful in the first box. The second was full of photographs, which were mostly in albums, dated and annotated in Kurt's distinctive script. But some were loose. Vos realised he must have been less than thorough in his first search when he came across a few photos he definitely hadn't seen before. One of them was a picture of a large family group. A magnifying glass, retrieved from the bureau in the study enabled him to pick out the distinctive features of Kurt in his late teens – long nose, curly hair and a slightly quizzical look – standing next to a young woman, very probably his sister Ursula. Next to her was a younger boy, tall and gangly. Could this be Sebastien? He could always ask old Ella.

The Charlie Parker came to an end. He selected a TPOK Jazz album from the pile and lowered the stylus onto the disc. It crackled just like the first one. Perhaps Baumer hadn't taken much care of his records.

The idea that there might be a younger brother began to feel more substantial.

At the very bottom of the second box, he found a thin plastic wallet stuck under one of the cardboard flaps which he'd completely missed first time around. Inside was a small collection of Kinshasa memorabilia – tickets, a few postcards, leaflets, restaurant and bar receipts. He assumed these must have been collected by Kurt on visits to Aunt Ada. It had puzzled him that, given how much Kurt had apparently liked the place, up till now, there'd been no evidence in the boxes that he'd ever gone back to the DRC.

His phone rang. It was Lindner – a brief conversation. He'd never heard any mention of a younger brother.

There was a knock on the door. Vos felt wary. Was it another unwanted visitor? He pulled the front living room curtain slightly to one side.

It was only Marc.

Did he want a drink?

Twelve

With business of his own to attend to in the city, Rainer had agreed to provide a taxi service to Brussels at a bargain rate.

Vos still had some misgivings about the plan to talk to Webers. Whilst appreciating Rodenbach's intentions, Katerine had made it clear she was worried about his involvement and the risk of *unintended consequences*.

Rainer was a fine driving companion who seemed to know instinctively when to talk and when to shut up. Vos had told him about the purpose of his trip and had received a positive response. *Make the man aware that you've got muscle at your disposal but play it low key with no direct threats.*

Zipping along in the outside lane, Rainer asked him to slot in a Jefferson Airplane tape and crank up the volume.

"I thought a young man like you would have been into downloads?"

"I'm not that young and besides, having taken the time to make a load of tapes over the years, I'm not suddenly going to stop using them. You hear about Kirchner being taken?"

"Yes – Neumann told me. How did you get to know about it?" Vos asked.

"A local farmer, friend of mine, saw it happen. Didn't realise what was going on until it was too late. Do you want a chat with him?"

Vos wondered if there was anybody locally who Rainer didn't know.

"Thanks, that would be really helpful."

"OK, we can call in there on the return journey. Tricky business you're involved in, Harry. Of your two possible candidates, one has just been kidnapped and the other might not even exist."

"Tell me about it," Vos said.

+ + +

Rainer parked near the Atomium.

The building looked as if it was playing a part in a late 1950's sci-fi film. Vos could remember being completely blown away by the new structure on a school trip. This time he was dazzled by the gleaming new stainless steel panels, which had replaced the old aluminium ones.

They found a café outside the Stade Roi Baudouin and sat in the sunshine drinking coffee. When his phone rang, he expected it to be Rodenbach. But it was his nephew. Did he want a six year old Berlingo, in good condition at a very reasonable price? It was an easy question to answer.

"Do you know where Webers lives?" Rainer asked.

"Yes, Leo told me and I checked the location of the apartment online. It's in that block over there," he said, pointing to a multi-storey building a couple of hundred metres away.

Just after Rainer bought a second round of coffees, Rodenbach arrived. Vos did the introductions and explained that his taxi driver, a bit of a trader, had business to carry out in the city.

"Ah! A man after my own heart," Rodenbach said. "And if you're a friend of this feller, that's a good enough recommendation for me. Here's my card. You never know, our interests might overlap. Now, as I mentioned on the phone, Harry, I've had somebody keeping watch on Webers and he's definitely in. You ready to go?" Vos nodded.

As Rainer drove off towards the city, they walked across to the apartment block. The lift took them up to the tenth floor where the view from the landing towards the city was impressive. They knocked and waited.

+ + +

Since he'd have struggled to get by on fare income alone, Rainer had managed to develop a number of interesting sidelines over the years. The taxi provided cover for him to be in strange places at odd times and some of his customers provided useful, potentially lucrative information.

He liked Harry Vos, but couldn't work out what made him tick. On the one hand he seemed to be very domesticated, a big family man and yet from what Marc had mentioned, he'd got himself tangled up in some risky cases in the past without making any money from them. And then there was his current Brussels trip which was all about firing some warning shots over the head of a recently released villain who might – or might not – be on the warpath.

Vos was a difficult man to fathom.

His own business was to be conducted on a side street just off the Canal du Charleroi. Despite the traffic being worse than usual, he managed to arrive more or less on time. As the warehouse doors closed automatically behind him, he saw the man with the big beard slowly descending the steel staircase from the second storey portacabin above. Three boxes were loaded into the boot of the taxi and Rainer handed over the cash. The doors slid open and he was away. The whole thing had taken only minutes and barely a word had been spoken.

Rainer made his way slowly back to the Atomium, wondering whether Vos' appointment had gone as smoothly.

+ + +

It hadn't started well, but Vos thought that, in the end, it had been worthwhile. Webers had been completely thrown by the sight of him on the doorstep. After a tense stand-off and some initial raised voices, they'd managed to come to an understanding of sorts.

Rodenbach had certainly been worth his fee. Vos had expected him to be firm, but hadn't anticipated his underlying calmness, a quality that had seemed to be completely lacking when they'd first come across each other.

Back in Rainer's taxi, Vos was about to doze off in the slow-moving city traffic when he remembered about Kurt's laptop and his inability to access any useful information that might be stored there. He asked his driver whether there was an IT expert in his list of contacts. There was – and Vos was looking at him! Just before Liege they stopped to refuel themselves and the car.

Over a beer and a sandwich Rainer talked passwords.

"Of course, it could be a completely random set of characters, in which case we've got no chance. However, people often choose something which is obvious and easily memorable for them, but which they assume nobody else will be able to guess. Very much a longshot though, trying to narrow down a password in this way. A more productive way of going about it would be to search for any written reminders. Given that modern life seems to require a bloody password or number for almost everything we do – even coming in and out of the house – a lot of people keep a list of them."

Vos succumbed to sleep as soon as they left the service area and didn't wake until they were bumping along a farm track a few miles north of St Vith, marshy ground and a meandering stream to their left. Rainer pointed out Kirchner's rented house on slightly raised ground to their right. They drove to the end of the rutted track, parked outside the farmhouse and walked towards the sound of a tractor chugging in the entrance to an adjacent barn. Once he'd spotted Rainer, the farmer turned off the engine, jumped down from the cab, greeted his friend and lit a cigarette. Vos was unable to follow the initial exchange of banter.

"This is the man I was telling you about," Rainer said, "the one who's been checking whether Kirchner has the right qualifications to inherit old Kurt's estate." Vos thought Rainer's tone was a bit heartless, given that the man had just been abducted, but the farmer just grinned.

"Pleased to meet you. I was telling Luka yesterday about what happened. Kirchner's not been in that house long. I've spoken to him a couple of times, but he's not really one for a chat. No visitors, to my knowledge anyway, until yesterday morning, about nine. Arrived in a Toyota, an old estate, and knocked on his door for a while. Kirchner eventually opened up. They started talking. Nothing out of the ordinary at first. Then Kirchner made to go back in and close the door, but one of them must have stuck his foot in the gap. The pair of them hauled him back out, closed the front door, frogmarched him across to the car and shoved him into the back seat. One of the men joined him there – to keep him out of mischief no doubt. All happened pretty fast. By the time I'd twigged what was going on, they'd scarpered. No way I could I have stopped them."

The farmer reached into the back pocket of his overalls and pulled out a piece of paper.

"Soon as I could, I wrote down a description of the pair of them and the car – as much as I could pick out from a distance anyway. I've already spoken to the coppers, so you're welcome to it."

Vos read the descriptions of the two abductors, but unfortunately they lacked detail."

"Thanks very much for this," he said. "Anything else you can remember about them?"

"Not really…except maybe their voices. A couple of times the wind picked up and I caught a snippet of what they said. Spoke in

German, but with quite strong accents. Hope that's a help. Now if you'll excuse me, I've got some beasts to sort out."

Rainer drove them on to Kurt's house. Vos removed the laptop from its hiding place and set it up in the study.

Having looked in a few obvious places for evidence of a password and found nothing, Rainer turned his attention to the bookshelves, examining each volume and flicking through it before placing it back on the shelf.

"Can I help?" Vos asked.

"You can. We're looking for a codebook, maybe something hidden inside an innocuous-looking cover. I know people use them, especially older people."

Before he could join the search, Vos' phone rang. It was Josina. She'd spent a fair bit of time searching online for a prospective Sebastien Baumer – without success. But she'd keep trying.

Vos knew there was something else he needed to ask her. Something to do with Kirchner. Ah! That was it. His idea of trying to find someone else to talk to who'd known both Elias Kirchner and his mother. He asked Josina about it.

"That could be difficult as we've not much to go on," she replied.

Vos had a bit of inspiration – a long shot perhaps, but worth a try.

"I know Ursula's wedding was a long time ago – 1963 I seem to remember – but could you try locating one or other of the witnesses named on the certificate. That's assuming that they maintained links with Ursula long enough to get to know Elias – and of course that they're still with us."

"Hm. Not sure of the chances of success with that, but I'll give it a go."

"Thanks, Josina."

While Vos had been on the phone, Rainer had come the end of the final shelf without discovering a code-breaking guide.

Vos remembered there were more books upstairs and their search resumed. Halfway along the second shelf in Kurt's bedroom they struck gold – a thin notebook, within a hardback.

Rainer selected his top three likely code candidates to access the laptop. With the third one he let out a whoop.

They were in!

Thirteen

He'd never got around to retiring. This was mainly down to a perpetual shortage of money to maintain a lifestyle he'd become addicted to. The house in Cape Town was not cheap to run and the garden far too large. Security costs were extortionate but it didn't do to skimp on them. And he and his wife still liked to travel.

It was also partly that he didn't want to stop work. Work less – certainly. But the idea of stopping altogether? Well, why would you? He was a dealer, of whatever he could get his hands on, a bit of import and a bit of export, some on the right side of the line and some crossing over.

Ever since the 'elopement' as they still referred to it, he and his wife were persona non grata when it came to the family. The only exception was his elderly aunt. He liked to turn up unannounced at her house in Kinshasa. As she seldom went away, that made it easy. But he could never persuade his wife to accompany him.

Not unusually, the flight to Kinshasa was delayed. In the bar, a card game was in progress. He was good company, had an easy way with words, a seemingly endless supply of tall tales and an ability to deliver jokes non-stop. It turned out the card players were all waiting for the same delayed flight. After an hour, a small stack of ten rand notes sat next to his whisky glass. He was well up, pleasantly drunk and had made a couple of new business contacts.

Eventually their flight was called and they trooped off to their seats. Five hours later, after problems with turbulence, they landed.

He didn't like the local taxis, preferring to ride with a friend of a friend who was also far cheaper. When they pulled up outside the gates to his aunt's house, something felt different. It took ten minutes for someone to arrive and let him through, someone he didn't know.

As he entered the house he was taken aback. There were no animals inside. But the ground floor was still impregnated with the smell of them. Why had they been banished from the house? He recognised the tall elegant woman – his aunt's PA. She had bad news.

It took a moment for him to take in that his aunt had passed away.

"We tried to contact you, left messages on your telephone about the funeral." He'd received nothing. When he asked to check the number they'd used, it was clear they'd transposed two of the digits.

He wondered whether it might have been deliberate, a ploy to keep him away from the funeral in order to avoid the difficulty and embarrassment of a confrontation with his brother.

The PA said there'd been mention in his aunt's will of a box to be given to him, containing 'keepsakes with memories' as they'd been described. Damn! Was that all? Over the past few years, he'd frequently thought about what she might leave him when she finally went. But then, given past events, he couldn't really be surprised that there was nothing. And his wife had always poo-pooed the idea that, when the time came, he'd inherit anything. 'You'll be behind a long queue of animals,' she'd told him.

The 'keepsakes' included some photos his aunt must have taken when he'd visited decades ago and the memories came flooding back.

He'd been just twenty-one, newly graduated, brimming with confidence and about to start a job in Kenya. In those days he'd got on well enough with his brother, despite the age gap and had been invited to stay with him for a few days en route to Nairobi.

Congolese independence was approaching and his brother would be moving on, so it was a last chance to catch him in Kinshasa.

Although he'd heard a lot about her, he'd not previously met Miriam, his brother's fiancée. She'd taken his breath away. From the first day he'd been captivated. What amazed him was the look in her eyes, the way she gazed straight at him. He felt awkward around his brother, but not at all around her. Ridiculous thoughts bubbled up. On the third day of the visit, his brother fell ill, with one of his recurrent bouts of malaria. He and Miriam were thrown together sampling the attractions of daytime Kinshasa as well as its nightlife. When she confessed to him that she'd made a mistake in agreeing to the engagement he saw his chance. Although they agreed to be open about the decision they'd reached, in the end neither of them could face a direct confrontation with his brother and their plans remained secret right up to their day of departure.

They'd never been forgiven.

And since then, there'd been no contact between the brothers.

Fourteen

Kela had arranged to meet Jules Fontaine in an Antwerp bar just off the Jordaenskaai. Not yet ten in the morning and they were the only customers.

"How did it go?" Fontaine asked nervously, hoping the delivery had been completed successfully. With Baumer still off the radar, she was becoming more anxious.

"Relax, Jules. You always worry too much. It all went to plan. By my reckoning, over half the pieces in Eyckman's gallery would be worth going for. Here, have a look."

Fontaine didn't know anyone else who had Kela's ability to appear both laidback yet fully focused. She scanned the notes about the exhibits on Kela's phone and wondered whether it would be wise to move onto stage two straight away or delay for a while.

"I'll tell you what's really worrying me. Kurt hasn't been in contact!"

"That's most unlike him."

"Exactly – he's usually so reliable," Fontaine said. "And I haven't been able to reach him at all."

"Doesn't he live in some remote place near the German border?" Fontaine nodded. "Why don't I go down there and check the scene? I've never been to that part of the country before and could do with a break."

Fontaine was relieved by Kela's offer. She didn't really have the time to make the journey herself and as a city girl through and through, she disliked spending time in the countryside.

"That would be good. We can make a decision about Eyckman's gallery when you return – hopefully with Kurt by your side."

+ + +

Magnus Neumann was feeling lucky.

Item One on his lucky list related to the Baumer diamonds. Much to his surprise, he'd managed to get hold of the specialist *Ice Squad*, as they were nicknamed. An analysis of the gems had been carried out and a 'signature' established. They'd originated in the DRC, but it was not yet known how they had ended up in Kurt Baumer's possession. Neumann had his own idea about how this might have happened. Vos had said something about possible dodgy art dealing. So, in return for supplying valuable under-the-counter Congolese artefacts, Baumer could have been paid off in gems.

Item Two was the unexpected receipt of information concerning the abduction of Elias Kirchner. A farmer had witnessed what had happened out on the moss. Although his description of the two abductors was fairly basic, it was consistent with that given by old Ella of the of the pair who'd visited Baumer's place on the night he died. So, it was likely the same men were involved on both occasions. Different car though.

And the third – and best – item on his lucky list was dinner with the doctor.

He was all fingers and thumbs with the tiny buttons that secured the ends of each collar. Had he overdone both deodorant and aftershave? Too late now, as there was no way he could remove either. Should he take a present or would that be seen as too much, too early? He was completely out of dating practice. What was it – ten, eleven years? And so much had changed in that time, like social media and dating websites. He'd got as far as looking at some of them, but hadn't had the nerve to go any further.

The last thing he agonised over was tie or no tie. He'd always been a tie man, both at work and socially. But he'd heard that views had changed and that neckwear could be seen as stuffy and old-fashioned these days. Damn it! He just didn't feel comfortable without one. Single colour won out over stripes and blue beat red. He was ready.

It was a fifteen minute walk from his house to the new tapas restaurant. Would she drive there? He hoped not, as it would mean he'd have to limit his alcohol intake so that it didn't exceed hers by too much.

He sat in the pre-meal drinks area, wondering whether she made a habit of being fashionably late or whether a medical emergency had reared its head. Checking his phone for the third time he found nothing.

He pretended to read the menu as he sipped his Stella, then switched to a quick bit of revision of the two small file cards which listed possible topics of conversation. But not wanting to be caught with them in his hand when she arrived, he pushed them hastily back into his jacket pocket.

He was too hot. Would it be acceptable to take his jacket off before she arrived? He'd have to take the chance or he'd overheat and start sweating.

Suddenly she was there in front of him looking just as cool and attractive as he'd hoped she would. But what was she doing out on a date with him? Perversely, he wondered whether her judgement might be a little in question if she saw him as suitable dating material.

She kissed him on the cheek, a waft of perfume and a move away just before he got his brain engaged fully. She caught the waiter's attention and ordered a white wine. They clinked glasses, took a few sips and studied the menu.

"Do you know I'm starving, nothing to eat all day. Tell my patients off for that sort of behaviour. What are you going to have, Magnus?"

They each ordered three dishes. When she suggested putting them all in the middle of the table, he had to force back a thought about not really wanting to share his choices. But then found he actually enjoyed her dishes more than his.

A second drink was followed by a third. Assuming she hadn't come by car, he began to relax. But it wasn't easy. At social events, he felt constantly on call even when technically he wasn't. Maybe it was the same for her.

After the food was finished and coffee served, her autopsy stories started. Unlike him she was a natural raconteur, funny but not longwinded. When she disappeared to the ladies, he took the opportunity to check his phone which, most unusually, he'd left on silent. Six messages, but thankfully none of them important.

"I've settled the bill," she told him on her return. "You can pay next time!" That completely disarmed him. No point in making gallant comments about *paying for the lady*. Clearly, that wasn't the way it worked any longer. But his lucky streak was continuing. There'd be a next time!

As they rose from the table, he felt the panic rising. Just a few minutes to get it right … or wrong. Her place, his place, or no place? Outside, he spotted her car parked next to a large white van. So, she had driven, but surely with the amount she'd had to drink …

"Do you fancy an evening amble?" she asked, linking her arm through his. Why hadn't he thought of that?

They strolled along in the twilight, bats swooping between trees either side of the lane.

"Not far from your house, are we?" she said, smiling. How did she know where he lived? Or had he mentioned it? He couldn't remember. It didn't matter.

He returned her smile and that was enough.

Fifteen

The woman said she was calling from Belgium and assisting her father who had the job of trying to trace any living relatives of a Kurt Baumer who'd lived in St Vith, a small town near the German border.

Christ! Past tense. First his aunt and now his brother. A heart attack the woman said. Sebastien's brain was in such a whirl that he found it difficult to take in what she was telling him. He'd even failed to make a note of her name.

Was he Kurt's brother? Of course he was. She mentioned the possibility of inheritance. Would he be able to forward evidence to confirm his identity and his status as Kurt's brother? Yes, he would do that.

When the woman asked whether he was aware of a nephew of Kurt's, he over-reacted, telling her in no uncertain terms that there were no nephews in the family.

As the conversation continued, the full impact of the news of his brother's death began to hit him. Why hadn't he made the effort to contact Kurt over all those years? Yet it had been the same with his sister Ursula who'd died a few years back. Both estrangements had been triggered, decades ago, by acrimonious family bust-ups and he'd never seen either sibling again. Talk about a dysfunctional family!

Feeling suddenly very emotional, it was all he could do to stop himself breaking down over the phone. The woman caller's sympathetic and patient manner gradually calmed him down and he apologized for his earlier abruptness.

He told her the relevant documents would be forwarded and she gave him her father's contact details and thanked him for his help.

He was completely unable to think about anything practical for the rest of the day. A dreadful feeling of guilt, about how he and Miriam had treated Kurt, swept over him. His wife was unable to understand the depths of his anguish, reminding him that it had been their deliberate choice not to re-establish contact with Kurt and re-open old wounds.

It wasn't until the following day that he felt able to summon the energy to start making plans. He recalled the phrase the caller from St Vith had used...*the possibility of inheritance*. Having got nothing from Aunt Ada would there be a chance of a boost to his finances from his brother's estate? He'd need to be on the spot to pursue his claim. A trip to Belgium was required. And being there would also give him the opportunity knock the idea of a nephew on the head. It really rankled. There was no nephew. The man had to be a chancer, a fraudster and it was his duty to unmask him.

It took all his persuasive skills to convince Miriam to accompany him on the journey. He knew why she was so reluctant. Like himself, she'd never addressed their failure all those years ago to tell Kurt face to face about their momentous decision.

Sebastien found it hard to believe that Kurt had ended up in St Vith. He'd always imagined that a potential high-flyer like his brother would have spread his wings much further.

Having left the town when only a boy, his own memories of the place were hazy and he'd never been back.

That was about to change.

+ + +

The flight was long, tedious and tiring.

They picked up a hire car at Brussels airport and the satnav delivered them to the door of Kurt's house. Sebastien felt suddenly very nervous and Miriam confessed she was similarly affected.

The house looked a little run down. He hoped it wasn't an indication that Kurt had been short of money. Sebastien had expected the man who'd been searching for heirs to be at the house, but the only response to his repeated knocking was the opening of the front door of the adjacent house. A man with a glass in his hand and a smile on his face spoke to them. Could he help?

When his visitor introduced himself as Sebastien Baumer, Marc felt it was like one of those dreams when everything seems normal apart from one small but incredibly important detail. It wasn't that he thought old Ella had made up the story about a Baumer brother. Just that he'd never expected the sibling to make a flesh and blood appearance. Not that he looked well. Maybe it was just the after-effects of long-distance travel.

Marc led them inside his house. Did the couple already know about Kurt's death? Marc had never been much good at personal stuff. Was he now going to have to break the awful news? The longer he left it the worse it would be. Harry was expected, but hadn't given him a time. It was no good. He'd have to do it by himself.

But before he'd had chance to open his mouth, Sebastien spoke.

"We only just found out about my brother. It's been such a tremendous shock. Do you by any chance know about the man who has been looking for relatives of Kurt? We kind of hoped he'd be here."

Marc told them that the man was called Harry Vos, happened to be a friend of his and would be arriving shortly. He sat his visitors down and offered them a drink.

Far from calming them, the brandy seemed to stir some deeper emotions. Sebastien was the first to lose control. The woman tried her best to hold things together, but after a few moments she succumbed to floods of tears. Gradually their story came out.

He hovered over them, offering tissues and more brandy. Eventually the couple regained some composure. Thinking the worst might be over, he risked asking what seemed like an innocuous question. How long was it since they'd seen Kurt?

It was a big mistake. The couple stared into each other's eyes and within seconds the tears restarted. Unable to cope with such an uncontrolled display of emotion, Marc asked to be excused and without waiting for a response, sidled out. In the sanctuary of the kitchen, he made plenty of noise, moving kettle, coffee pot, cups and saucers. A visit to the toilet followed. By the time he returned to the living room, the crying had stopped. He didn't dare repeat his question.

A knock on the door, easily recognisable as Vos' heavy rat-tat-tat. Relief at last. A hurried briefing in the hallway ending with a shout from the new arrival. *You're joking!*

Vos introduced himself and confirmed that it was his daughter Josina who'd managed to locate Sebastien, thanks to her online genealogical skills. They told him they'd come to pay their respects to Kurt and hand over in person the identification that Josina had requested.

"I'd thought you'd probably provide the documents electronically but it's very good that they've been hand-delivered and that we can meet both of you," Vos said. No doubt they'd also wanted to be here in person the better to pursue Sebastien's claim to Kurt's estate he thought, rather uncharitably.

"Would you like to see Kurt's house?"

"No thank you. I think we'd both find that too difficult. We've booked a room at a hotel in St Vith. What we'd like to do is go there and rest. It's been a long and extremely emotional journey. Perhaps we could meet you tomorrow, Mr Vos, to show you the paperwork and talk about ... you know ... my brother's estate."

They agreed a time to meet in the morning. Vos waved them off.

"That's you sorted then, Harry. Thanks to Josina's good work the heir's virtually fallen into your lap!" Marc said, as he poured them both a Brugse Zot Dubbel. "A brother will trump a nephew any day so that's the end of Kirchner's claim!"

Marc was quite right, Vos thought. There'd be some formalities for sure but it was almost case closed.

"I'm surprised they've just turned up, unannounced and not a word to either me or Josina beforehand. Still, now they're here, hopefully it'll only be a question of dotting i's and crossing t's. She did a grand job, my daughter."

With no need to continue looking for evidence in Kurt's boxes and wanting some fresh air, he decided to walk back to St Vith. Marc pointed out the track on the map. It was a pleasant slow-paced stroll.

There was this niggling thought. Why did he always seem to have these? Sebastien and Kurt didn't look much like each other. Admittedly, it was difficult to make an effective judgement as he'd never actually met Kurt Baumer alive, but he'd seen plenty of photos of him during the searches through the boxes. And he'd also persuaded the good doctor to let him see the body. He knew other brothers who didn't look much alike, but there was usually some aspect of their appearance or something more intangible that hinted at a link. Granted, intangibles were harder to pick out in a dead man, or a photograph but even then ...

Back at the B&B, he called Josina to let her know about the surprise arrival of Sebastien Baumer.

"I agree it's a bit odd, him turning up without letting us know. What's he like?"

"That's what's bugging me. He doesn't look at all like Kurt."

"But that applies to lots of siblings," Josina said. "If he's got the right ID details, that's all that matters – isn't it?"

"I suppose you're right. I'll find out in the morning. They're in no fit state to talk about anything just now."

"They?"

"Oh, yes – sorry. Sebastien and his wife Miriam."

"I see. So, if he's who he says he is, EK's claim will fall by the wayside."

"EK?"

"Sorry, I mean Elias, the nephew."

"Of course. Yes, you're right."

+ + +

After another of Helga's fulsome breakfasts, Vos felt ready to face the newly-arrived Baumers. Their hotel was a fifteen minute walk away.

Part way there, the weather suddenly changed for the worse. His umbrella blew inside out as he turned a corner and the rain hit him full in the face. It had been a mistake not to wear a waterproof. It was hard to credit just how wet he could get in such a short time. Standing dripping in the foyer of the hotel, he wondered whether it would be better to turn around, go back to the B&B, change into dry clothing and return wearing a waterproof – rather than inflict his wet self on the couple. He was about to walk back out when he was hailed by the man himself.

"You look like you could do with a towel and a warm drink! Come on up to our room." Sebastien seemed to have recovered his composure.

Vos felt he couldn't refuse such a kind offer from someone who was virtually a stranger. Miriam was out which made it decidedly less embarrassing to stand in the bedroom, half undressed, and dry off. They chatted about the unpredictable weather and St Vith. The coffee went down well. Only when he'd finished the drink, could Vos bring himself to talk business.

"Look, thank you for helping me out. Is it OK it we have a talk about ID?"

"Of course – as we agreed yesterday. We're in a better frame of mind today. I think it was a combination of delayed grief over my brother's death and the effects of a long flight. Now – about my passport. The thing is my wife keeps both our passports. I'm a terrible one for losing things whereas she's a stickler for security. But she won't be back until tonight. Gone shopping in Liege. She needed some retail therapy after yesterday's events. Perhaps you could pop round again tomorrow to do the necessary – if that's OK with you."

"That'll be fine. I'll also need a copy of your birth certificate – you know just so I can check your parents are the same as Kurt's."

"Ah! I'm really sorry about this. I left it out to pack and it's still sitting there on the dining room table. Stupid of me. But never mind, I can arrange to get it scanned and a copy emailed to you."

"That would be very helpful. I'll check with Kurt's lawyer whether he'll also need to have sight of the original, or perhaps a certified copy."

"Well, that would obviously take a bit longer to arrange. Let me know if it's required."

As they shook hands on departure, it struck Vos that Sebastien didn't look well.

On the walk back to the B&B he thought about the conversation. It seemed a little strange that the pair of them hadn't placed their passports in the hotel safe. After all, wandering around shops with the documents stuck in a handbag didn't seem like the best of security arrangements. And the whole point of him calling in to see Sebastien had been to get sight of the passport. A tiny bit of planning ahead could have avoided the problem. As for the birth certificate! Well, perhaps Sebastien just wasn't very organised.

Back in his room, he removed Kurt's laptop from its bag and entered the newly-discovered access password, the B&B wi-fi code and the email username and password that Rainer had successfully picked out from Kurt's codebook. There was something almost decadent about snooping around somebody else's online life and Vos had to try and discipline himself to stay on the straight and narrow and concentrate only on information that might be relevant to his enquiries.

Although a few informative emails had emerged, he'd actually been rather disappointed by the lack of any hard evidence of Kurt's involvement in art dealing. Opening a recent document, he clicked on an attached photograph of a small bronze statuette. Which set him thinking. He wondered whether other artefact photos might be stored on the computer. A few clicks revealed an absolute treasure trove, a comprehensive photographic record of African artefacts, all carefully annotated. The earliest pictures dated from the 1950's and were mainly black and white. The most recent were from the previous month. With instant access to such a record, it was no wonder that collectors had beaten a path to Kurt's doorstep.

A significant amount of information had now been unearthed – the carbon copy schedules, incoming letters from dealers, emails sent and received and hundreds of photos. Vos really needed some specialist help to make sense of it all. He thought about Katerine, but she wouldn't be available for such an exercise for a while yet.

Then he thought about the dealer who advised him from time to time on the sale of paintings he'd inherited from his father.

One of his father's old schoolfriends had been a struggling artist. Vos senior had bailed him out on several occasions and had even provided him with lodgings when things were really tough.

The friend had paid him back in paintings which at the time were worth no more than a few francs each. On his father's death, Harry had inherited these. A few years later the artist had been 'discovered' and the value of his primitive works had risen considerably. Vos had used the art works as an alternative savings account and had used the dealer occasionally to cash in a painting in order to fund something that would have otherwise been out of his reach.

Maybe he could provide some specialist advice.

Vos tried to recall his name. It was written down in a notebook, but that was in the desk drawer back in Heist-op-den-Berg. His mother would have remembered the name but regrettably he couldn't ask her.

As he tried to clear space in his mind to recall the name, his phone rang. It was Neumann. He'd heard about Sebastien's arrival and wanted a briefing. Might he know something about the origin of the diamonds? Aware of the total lack of contact between the two brothers over much of their lifetimes Vos doubted it. But he agreed to pop across to the police station and tell Neumann what he knew about Sebastien.

+ + +

Kela had never set foot in the Ost Kantonen before. Fontaine had told her a little about it and how most people there spoke German. But she'd been reassured they'd speak French as well, her German being non-existent.

She knew from past experience that some in rural communities could be less than welcoming to people of colour. Despite Belgium's exploitation of the Congo during the colonial era, and the multiple problems faced by the DRC in the present day, there were those who resented the presence of Congolese migrants in the 'mother' country. So, she was prepared for a potentially difficult reception.

Having reached Baumer's house, she was surprised by the very modest nature of the property. Knowing something of Kurt's past life in the diplomatic service in different parts of the world, including her own country, she'd expected him to be a man of some wealth, living in a large detached house standing in its own grounds. And yet here was a small building, attached to others. Perhaps he'd been only a minor diplomat, she thought – or alternatively, just very bad with money.

It was a pleasure to be able to stretch her legs after their long confinement in the small car. She knocked on the front door, waited and then repeated the process. Nobody in. She tried the house next door.

"Sorry to bother you but I've travelled here from Brussels to see Herr Baumer." Fontaine had advised her to use the German title.

"In that case, you'd better come in. I'm Marc by the way." She had no hesitation in following. He didn't feel at all threatening.

Kela followed him into a cluttered living room. The walls were covered in photographs of mountains. A number featured a much younger version of Marc standing on one peak or another, looking ecstatically happy.

"Hard to believe but yes, that's me, back in the day. You're not a climber by any chance, are you?"

"Well, as it happens, I am."

The two of them exchanged brief references to various European and African peaks and their respective ascents of Kilimanjaro.

"Sorry," Marc said after a short while. "Much as I'd love to carry on talking about mountains, I really need to give you some bad news before we go any further."

Kela found it hard to take in. She'd been well aware of Kurt Baumer's advanced age and knew that his health hadn't been brilliant of late. But to hear that he'd died ... Well, it really took her aback. Apart from her feelings for the man himself, Baumer held information which, if it now got into the wrong hands, wouldn't do any of them much good. And she'd no idea how securely he might have stored it. Marc didn't seem to know much about his late neighbour, or if he did, wasn't giving anything away. Kela asked about cause of death and was told it was heart-related. She explained how Baumer had been a colleague, that they'd shared an interest in Congolese artworks. The comment seemed to stir Marc's interest. Kela was careful to keep her answers short and avoided going into detail. She'd need to phone Fontaine and tell her about Baumer's death as soon as possible. They'd have to consider all the possible implications.

She heard a noise through the party wall, a door closing.

"Not ghosts I hope!"

"No, it'll be Harry arriving, a friend of mine. He's a bit too substantial to be a ghost. You might want a word with him though. He's got the job of tracing any living relatives of Kurt's. Didn't leave a will, you see. In fact, Harry would probably like a word with you. Come with me."

+ + +

Vos was somewhat surprised to find Marc standing next to a black woman on the doorstep. So far during his stay in St Vith he'd come across few people who weren't white. But then, judging by the presence of a car with Brussels plates parked at the roadside, the woman wasn't local.

Having made introductions, Marc excused himself, muttering something about urgent business. Vos took Kela indoors, made coffee and listened as she explained how she knew Kurt.

He was immediately interested in finding out more. Maybe this woman could help to fill in some of the many Kurt-shaped gaps in his knowledge.

But she wasn't slow in asking her own questions. Vos gradually realised that the two of them were both trying to find out as much as possible from the other, whilst at the same time revealing the minimum.

He had a feeling that Kela's visit had something to do with the diamonds, but that she'd probably be wary about asking directly about them. And Vos certainly wasn't going to bring up the subject himself. He'd need to make more of a connection with her, build up a degree of confidence about where she was coming from, before saying anything.

"How about going into St Vith for something to eat?" Vos said. "Don't know about you but I'm starving." She agreed.

As Kela drove them into the town, she mentioned Marc's mountaineering conversation and asked Vos if he'd been a climber.

"I was for a while, but not like Marc, nowhere near as keen. And my accident put paid to my mountaineering career," he said, patting his knee and lifting his stick. Just as he steered his mind away from memories of the accident, he found the name Ruud Okker coming to the surface – the dealer who'd handled the sale of some of the paintings he'd inherited. He'd check online for a phone number.

Sixteen

The day of Kurt Baumer's funeral was far too hot. Although the inside of the church was relatively cool, the churchyard lacked shade and following the service, mourners stood in small groups, tugging at their collars, over-dressed for the weather. It was a relief for all to be able to escape to the air-conditioned Hotel Renard. Vos counted the mourners – sadly only twenty – perhaps a reflection both of Baumer's solitary nature and the likelihood that a number of his former work colleagues and friends were already dead. Two things surprised him. Firstly, he could name all but two of the mourners and secondly, Kela was present. He'd assumed she'd have already returned to Brussels. The evening meal they'd shared had been full of lively conversation but he hadn't learnt much that was new about Kurt Baumer. Here was an opportunity to try again.

Before that, despite the fact that it wasn't really an appropriate occasion, he needed to have another word with Sebastien about his passport. Despite his promise to ring, he hadn't been in touch.

He was apologetic, said that the document was no longer in his wife's handbag but was securely lodged in the hotel's safe and promised it would be available for viewing without fail the following morning. Vos began to wonder whether Sebastien was stringing him along, perhaps because he had something to hide.

Vos spotted Kela standing by the double doors that opened out onto the hotel garden. She was friendly enough, but when he tried again to find out more about Kurt's art-related activity and his links to dealing, it was clear she didn't really want to go down that conversational route. After a short while, she excused herself and walked across to the bar where Marc was standing, drink in hand.

Although disappointed not to have got further with her, Vos took the opportunity to have a word with the two guests he'd been unable to name. The first was a very old woman, long grey hair just touching her shoulders, who told him she'd only got to know Baumer within the last few years. The two of them had shared an interest in African works of art but whereas he'd been a real expert, she was just a dabbler. It quickly became apparent to Vos that she'd be unable to add anything to what he already knew.

His second unknown mourner, a much younger woman, was standing in the hotel garden, talking to a man of similar age and tucking into an over-laden paper plate of food with a plastic fork. Vos' reluctance to return to the outdoor heat was outweighed by his desire to find out what she knew about Baumer. Moving outside to stand a few paces away from the pair, he tried to gauge an appropriate moment to break into their conversation. She looked to be in her late thirties and wore large-framed spectacles, baggy linen trousers and Jesus sandals as Vos called them. Once aware of his presence she turned to face him. Somewhat embarrassed, he apologised for eavesdropping, introduced himself and said he'd like to talk about Kurt. The young man drifted off.

She was Sophie, a lecturer at Liege University, a specialist in African art. Out of the corner of his eye, he noticed Kela walking towards them. Sophie, seeming suddenly nervous, told Vos that it would be good to have the opportunity to talk more about Kurt and his work – only not there and then. Handing him a business card, she asked Vos to ring to arrange a time to meet.

Kela joined them.

"So, has Sophie been filling you in on Kurt's art world?"

"Yes, she was just saying how knowledgeable he was and how his expertise will be missed. Now if you'll forgive me, I really must get inside again. This heat is a bit too much."

He left the two women in the garden. Had Kela been keeping tabs on him? And what was it that Sophie wanted to talk about that couldn't have been said there and then?

+ + +

In the end it was something of an anti-climax having Sebastien's passport in his hands. Because of the delays in getting sight of it, Vos had imagined it would present a problem. A different name perhaps, or a date of birth that didn't fit with the facts he already had. But there were the details in black and white. Date of birth: 7/4/1939; place of birth: Bonn; name: Sebastien Baumer.

Now all that was needed for him to be able to confirm his place in the Baumer family, was sight of a birth certificate. Vos asked about it.

"I've spoken to our friend back home who's authorised to access our house in an emergency, which this is in a way. Without that authority, the security people wouldn't let him in. He's agreed to go there, pick up the certificate and scan and email it. Has Ahrendt said whether he also needs to see the original?"

"A certified copy will be fine. Can you ask your lawyer to arrange that?"

"Certainly."

"Thank you, Sebastien, that'll be helpful. I hope you don't mind me saying, but you don't look well. Do you need to see a doctor?"

"I've not felt right since arriving here. May have been something I picked up on the journey. As it happens, I saw a doctor yesterday. She gave me antibiotics, did some tests and I'm waiting for the results. It's a real shame because it would have been nice to have had more of a look around the old place. But I don't really feel up to it."

Despite Sebastien being unwell, Vos felt he needed to raise the subject of Elias Kirchner. But Sebastien beat him to it.

"When she called me in Cape Town, your daughter mentioned something about a nephew. I can tell you here and now that there are no nephews. So, if there's someone claiming to be one, he must be a fraud!"

Vos felt very awkward breaking the news to Sebastien that his sister had a child.

"But that's just not possible," he said. "I'd have known about it."

"Have you been in contact with Ursula over the years?" Vos asked. Sebastien's mouth opened but no words came out of it. His face reddened. Eventually he spoke.

"No. We seem to specialise in non-communication within my family. It just seems so unlikely that my sister became a mother and that I was completely unaware of it."

"Well," Vos said, keen to take the heat out of the issue, "once I've had sight of your birth certificate, that should make Kirchner's claim academic. As far as I'm aware, your claim would take precedence over his."

"That's reassuring. But in any event, I think he must be a fraud. Has he provided any evidence of this family connection?" Sebastien seemed to be only just managing to control his anger.

"Yes, he has the right documentation. Unfortunately, he's just gone missing, abducted in broad daylight by two men."

"What? Well, perhaps this isn't the only fraud he's perpetrated and a previous victim has caught up with him. It all sounds very strange. I might need to speak to Ahrendt about exposing Kirchner."

"Let's hope he turns up," Vos said. "In the meantime, you'd need to put any thoughts of legal action on hold."

"Yes, I appreciate that. Anyway, thank you for what you and your daughter have done so far."

After leaving the hotel, Vos phoned Ahrendt. He'd be free in an hour, which gave ample time for a café visit. Strolling along a pleasant tree-lined street, he thought about the call from Jalloh the previous evening. Because of his wife's illness, he'd had to postpone his next business trip to Kinshasa, which meant the chance of digging around for information at Aunt Ada's animal sanctuary also had to be put on hold. Vos reflected that when he'd originally floated the idea, part of the reason for such a visit was to try and find evidence of Sebastien's existence. Since then, he'd turned into a flesh and bones reality. But a Jalloh visit could still turn out to be very helpful if it threw any light on the origin of the diamonds.

Somebody had left a copy of the local Grenz-Echo on a table on the terrace outside the café. Vos decided to test his German and see how much of the news he could understand while he sipped his coffee. As that meant real concentration, he didn't notice Dr Vermeulen's arrival.

"Do you mind if I sit here?" she asked, taking a seat without waiting for a reply. "So, you're keen to find out what's going on around here, are you?" she continued, gesturing at the newspaper.

"Keen but struggling with my German, which means it's a good time to take a break and find out what local news you might have."

"Well as a doctor, there's an awful lot I know but unfortunately most of it is not for sharing. But tell me, what's the latest on Sebastien? Has he passed your identity test – or is that also confidential information?"

Vos was impressed with the speed of the local grapevine.

It suddenly struck him that she might have been the one who'd examined Sebastien. After all he'd said *she,* when talking about the doctor. He wondered whether there might be a need to confirm

Sebastien's status as Kurt's brother by means of a DNA test. Given that Kurt's body was now underground, the ability to carry out a comparative test would be dependent on Dr Vermeulen having retained some small part of him from the autopsy. He might need to ask her about that at some point.

Still – he was jumping the gun. Sebastien's passport had turned out to be fine and there was no reason to suspect that there'd be a problem with his birth certificate.

"I think we're on the way there," he replied in answer to her question about Sebastien's identity. Such a statement didn't feel like he was breaking any confidences. "In fact, I'm off to see Ahrendt shortly to update him."

The doctor ordered a fruit juice and a waffle, before fixing him with an inquisitive look.

"What?" he asked.

"Nothing," she replied. "It's just that … don't you find sometimes things aren't quite what they appear to be?"

Was this her way of telling him something whilst appearing to tell him nothing? Perhaps he should err on the side of caution. After all, now there were two claimants to the Kurt Baumer estate, he'd need to be scrupulously fair.

"I do agree," he said. "Take my friend Marc for example …" Having picked up on her hint, he wanted to move the conversation away from Sebastien.

The doctor really was very easy to talk to. A glance at his phone reminded him the appointment with the lawyer was due. He left just as her waffle arrived, covered in berries and cream, the kind of temptation he'd have found hard to resist.

Ahrendt was preoccupied, fiddling with the knot of his tie, before rising mid-sentence to water the plants on the windowsill, using a small green can with a long snout, oblivious to the drops he spilt as he went. But once he'd retaken his seat, his mind re-focused immediately on what Vos had been saying.

"I appreciate Sebastien is being a little slow in getting hold of his birth certificate," the lawyer said. "But we could also try other avenues. There'll be nothing in the local registry because, according to his passport details, he wasn't born here. But I could ask a contact of mine in Bonn to carry out a search there. I'm afraid I don't have the expertise to do that kind of online work myself."

"That would be very helpful," Vos said, "although I've no idea whether records from the late thirties in Bonn would have survived the war. Would you know?" Ahrendt shook his head.

"No news on the nephew, I take it?"

"Nothing," Vos said. "I'm hoping to speak to someone who can independently confirm details about him."

"Yes, that's sensible. You've probably already realised that Kirchner will only get a look in if Sebastien turns out not to be who he claims to be."

"Indeed. I'll be in touch again once I have further useful information about either of them."

As soon as he left the lawyer's office, he texted Josina, gave her Sebastien's DOB and asked if she could try and get hold of a copy of his birth certificate. She was on the phone to him within minutes.

"I'll certainly have a look for the certificate. But that's not why I'm phoning. I've managed to find one of the witnesses at Ursula Kirchner's wedding!"

"Really – that's amazing!"

"Yes, it certainly surprised me. Frau Emmerling. I gave her a ring and she'd be happy to talk to you. I'll text her number. Lives in Hamburg."

Kurt

As soon as his plane touched down in Kinshasa, he felt at home again – even though it hadn't been his home for over fifty years.

He'd never wanted to leave but there'd been no choice at the time. And going back later? Well, the right opportunity had never arisen.

He'd met up with Aunt Ada several times over the years. They'd always got on – unlike him and his father. Most people called her eccentric, but he'd always considered this to be an understatement.

A phone call had informed him of his aunt's death at the ripe old age of 95 and given details of the funeral arrangements. As he now found international travel such an effort it had been difficult to summon up the necessary energy. But there were three reasons which drove him to book his flights. The chance of one last visit to the Congo – sentimental really but, given his own age, it was probably now or never. An opportunity to say goodbye to his aunt. They'd shared a lot of memories and she'd been such a support after Miriam had deserted him. And the third reason? Well, Aunt Ada had been looking after something of his and he wanted it back.

The airport taxi dropped him off in the Matonge area of Kinshasa. It had changed a lot since his day of course, but the buzz and energy were just as pronounced and the smells just as strong – the street food, the market livestock, the drains. For a while, he wandered around in a daze, as if hooked on some drug that was both freely available and highly addictive.

His friend and colleague Kela Mpenda rented an apartment in the city and they'd arranged to meet up in a new nganda restaurant that had recently opened. As they ate fish in a hot pepper sauce and drank dark Turbo King, Kurt said he was keen to catch up on the latest developments in the city. She told him about attending *the official opening of a new gallery of indigenous art in the city, small in scale, quite unlike the huge new national museum that was being developed in partnership with the South Koreans. They talked about trade and plans for the next shipment.*

Kela told him she'd been saddened to hear of the death of his aunt and was pleased to be able to accompany him to the funeral. Kurt said that, for his part, he was pleased not to be staying in a hotel and thanked her for making available the spare bedroom in her apartment.

They talked long into the evening and wrapped up the meal up with glasses of white elephant.

+ + +

The rain on the church's tin roof drowned out most of the funeral service, which was fine by him. He'd just wanted to be there and spent the time thinking about his aunt's unconventional ways and the risks she'd taken traveling on her own, in earlier days, to so many out-of-the-way places, in search of the two A's – art and animals. An accomplished artist herself, she also been a collector of local artefacts. Then there was her obsession with animals, particularly those that had suffered. The extensive grounds surrounding her house had become a cross between a small safari park and an outdoor veterinary centre. Orphaned monkeys shared space with injured zebras and a three-legged wildebeest. Several of the smaller animals frequently roamed the ground floor of the house, his aunt being oblivious to the dirt and the smells.

The rain stopped just as the service did and the mourners were able to move out from the stifling heat of the church to the relative coolness of the tree-shaded graveyard.

Kurt didn't recognise the man who sidled up to him and introduced himself as Mr Seymour. An Englishman. He was small and wore an incongruous-looking baseball cap and completely opaque sunglasses, so that Kurt was unable to get any real idea of what he looked like.

"You'll know about your aunt's will of course," the man said in poor German. It was a statement rather than a question. But Kurt knew nothing about the will. "Everything has been left to her animal sanctuary. She set up a trust to keep it going once she'd passed on. Without her at the helm, I'm not sure how things will develop. We shall have to wait and see."

Kurt's hopes were dashed. For years he'd held onto the idea that his aunt would treat him favourably in her will. It was nothing she'd said specifically, but rather a bond he felt, one that was mutual or so he'd thought. Having been all too familiar with her animal obsession, Seymour's news shouldn't have been a surprise. But it was still a huge disappointment.

He tried to resist feeling resentful. Because of a permanent inability to handle money and a series of badly-advised investments, not to mention a very poorly performing pension annuity, he'd never been able to fund the kind of lifestyle he'd really wanted. Which is how he'd ended up in his poky little house outside St Vith. And now his aunt's property and worldly goods were to be committed to the continuation of the menagerie. For her, in death as in life, humans came a poor second to her precious animals.

But there was still the matter of **his** property which had been left in Aunt Ada's safe hands, until such time as he could get it out of the country. Strictly speaking it was her's, but she'd gifted it to him. Would the lawyer have been instructed about this item? Before he'd had time to ask the question, Seymour answered it.

"You may not have been mentioned in your aunt's will, Herr Baumer, but I do have something for you." Had the Englishman been able to read his mind?

A small white envelope was handed over. Inside was a key. There was hope after all.

"Your aunt told me you liked mysteries and was confident you'd solve this one. But to do that, you'll need to visit the house. I'm afraid she told me nothing else, so I'm unable to help you further."

Kurt tucked the key into his inside jacket pocket. How typical of Aunt Ada. Nothing was ever straightforward. But then that was one of the things he'd always liked about her. There'd only been a few years between the two of them. They'd been more like a pair of cousins than aunt and nephew.

The mourners moved into the church hall, where sandwiches, tea and stronger drink were available, a surprisingly modest spread, Kurt reflected.

Apart from Kela, he knew hardly anyone in the room and found it hard work making small talk with strangers. People were polite enough but most of them appeared to have very little to say – which was no doubt how they also assessed him.

He didn't like gatherings – of any kind – and always wanted to leave them as soon as was decent. And the key was an additional factor pushing him away from the wake and pulling him towards his aunt's house.

He took it from his pocket. It was old, the type that might open a drawer or a door to a piece of furniture. Something rang a bell, a connection with his past.

He tried to think himself back into the house, where he'd stayed when first arriving in the country as a young man and on subsequent visits over the years. It was difficult attempting to picture the furniture. One hazy memory melded into another. A huge double wardrobe – but did it have a lock? A Chinese cabinet decorated with intricate sketches of rural life, the two poorly hinged doors difficult to close, but ... lockless as far as he could recall. A mahogany dresser was a more likely candidate, but he couldn't recall any detail apart from its great weight. Dragging the thing just a centimetre or two in an attempt to retrieve an important sheet of paper that had dropped behind it, had required enormous effort.

These half-memories were no use. As the lawyer had told him, he needed to be there, in the house. How would the experience affect him though? What unwanted memories might a visit drag to the surface?

Having phoned for a taxi, he told Kela it was time for him to go as it was all getting a bit much. She understood. The taxi moved slowly through the busy streets. It was stimulating being back in the city, but every now and then, it felt like one of those dreams that start with a familiar location before turning into something unknown – where one minute you think you know your way around and the next, you're almost completely lost.

Traveling down a broad avenue he thought of his old office, in the colonial administration building. Surely it should have been on that corner he thought, craning his neck to look back. But the space was filled with shops.

The animal sanctuary was on the edge of the city, the house itself set well back from the road. The taxi dropped him off at the gatehouse.

+ + +

The staff on duty were new to him. Nobody he even half-recognised. At first, much to his frustration, they were reluctant to allow him access to the house. However, he gradually won them round. His passport showed that he shared a surname with his aunt. But it was the few black and white photos he'd brought with him, snaps of the two of them at the house in the late 1950s that convinced them. Despite the passage of time, they recognised the youngish woman and the even younger man in the pictures. He watched as they studied each of the photographs carefully and listened to their comments about how the house and the garden had changed.

With the ice broken, he was given the go ahead to explore the house for as long as he wanted.

The first thing that hit him was the absence of animals – and their droppings! There'd always been an intense smell about the place. It hadn't entirely disappeared, but someone must have worked very hard cleaning the place from top to bottom.

In his younger days he'd been willing to put up with animals in the house, but in later years, he'd been unable to cope with them and had stayed instead in hotels or, more recently, in Kela's apartment which had provided a welcome refuge.

He lit a cigarette and started his search on the ground floor. Although each room held different memories, none held a piece of furniture that matched his key. At first, he found he could cope alright with moving around his aunt's home, picturing Ada in her favourite chair or at the piano. But when he entered the formal dining room, which hadn't been used for years, all he could see was his brother, seated next to Miriam at the large oak table. It was too much to handle. Upstairs, the unwanted images gradually faded. It was lighter and airier. But there was still no sign of a lock awaiting his key.

Even though he hadn't been up the narrow winding staircase that led to the attic for decades, it seemed very familiar. His knees complained about the steepness of the flight. There were three doors off the attic landing. Behind the first two, the rooms were empty, dark, dingy and dusty. But when the door opened to the third room, he was taken aback.

It appeared to be almost unchanged from the days when he'd slept there. An iron bedstead, chamber pot beneath, a washstand with jug and basin, a cane-bottomed chair eaten away in parts by insects and a small wardrobe. The bedside cabinet was familiar. His hands shook as he tried the key. At first the lock wouldn't budge. After two more unsuccessful attempts, he tried turning the key and simultaneously, lifting the small door slightly on its hinges.

It worked!

The cabinet was full of papers – bills, accounts, receipts – dating years back.

A strange sensation crept over him, a vision of Aunt Ada stooping in front of the cabinet telling him something important.

Of course – that's why it had seemed familiar. The cabinet had originally been in the family home in Belgium. His father had given it to Ada and she'd brought it out to the Congo. He remembered what his aunt had told him, what she'd shown him. A hidden catch at the back of the cabinet, above the top shelf, a catch that opened a secret compartment. His excitement rising, he removed the papers from the shelf to create the space for his fingers to explore the rear of the upper part of the cabinet in search of the catch.

A voice shouted up from below. Was he OK? Had he got lost? He went to the top of the attic stairs and called back down that he was fine and was just spending a little time reminiscing in a room he'd slept in many years ago. Footsteps receded along the first-floor corridor.

A second search for the catch was successful. When released, a tiny panel sprang open, revealing a small compartment. Inside was a business card issued by a Kinshasan bank.

On the back of the card was a number.

Seventeen

Skip had worked for Eyckmans for over ten years. Nobody else had lasted anywhere near as long. The boss was difficult, a natural bully with a short fuse. Skip had stood up to him in the early days which had earned respect. More importantly, he'd shown real skill in extending the supply chain and running a tight ship. As the years went by, he'd been increasingly left to run things his way. As long as he continued to produce the goods, Eyckmans kept his interventions to a minimum.

But Skip was worried. Although Mpenda had been vouched for by sources he trusted and had made several successful deliveries, there were things about her that made him uncomfortable. For a start she was a sculptor. None of the other team members, past or present, practised any of the arts themselves. He was instinctively wary of artists and felt they were unreliable and prone to drift off-message. Then there was her … he wasn't sure how to put it…detachment, perhaps. As if she was never really part of the team. Perhaps, most basically, she was suspect because she was a woman. People told him he was outdated, old-school, that the world was changing, that he should keep up. But that wouldn't happen. He felt his suspicions were well-founded.

The problem was he had no hard evidence against her – just gut reaction. But then he'd never been wrong before. Eyckmans wasn't a man to confide in. If there was a problem, he'd just want it sorted.

The woman wasn't due back in the DRC for a while, taking a break, she'd told him. He'd act once she was back.

+ + +

Vos felt good being back home in Heist, even if it was only a flying visit. There'd been practical reasons to come back, like taking delivery of the Berlingo Ryck had found for him, stocking up on clothes, checking his mail and forgetting about heirs for a couple of days. But he also missed the place and wanted to feel its familiarity again.

Best of all, Katerine had travelled home from Luxemburg for the weekend. Although both confessed to being a little wary about the risk of Webers suddenly turning up, they hoped that Rodenbach's warning visit had provided a sufficient deterrent against any ideas of revenge.

Barto was on a weekend home visit as well. Having grown used to having the dog around, Ryck had rather reluctantly dropped him off, with the Berlingo, before being driven back home by Magda.

Not only had Vos missed the regular walks, he knew his waistline had too. It was time to weigh himself again. He could have bought a pair of scales for the bathroom, but didn't want to be distracted into checking his weight every five minutes. Instead, once a month, he slotted a fifty cent coin into the machine in the Heist pharmacy and made a note of how far the pointer swung around the dial. His stroke check-up was approaching and he wanted to be able to report that his weight was under control and avoid the need to have to cut back any further on his favourite diet rule-benders.

They took advantage of the good weather and walked down to the flea market, Barto continually distracted by familiar and unfamiliar smells. As they wandered from stall to stall, Katerine asked her husband about progress in the search for a Baumer heir.

"Still waiting for Sebastien's birth certificate," Vos said. "He hasn't got hold of a copy yet, Ahrendt's official channel of enquiry in Bonn has produced nothing so far and poor Josina, my unofficial channel, is unfortunately out of action, laid low by a bug and confined to bed. So, we're treading water at the moment."

"And what about the nephew – Elias is it?"

"Yes, that's right. Unfortunately, there's been no news of him since the abduction. For reasons I can't really explain I don't like the man but it's an awful thing to have happened."

"Any ideas as to why he's been taken?"

For a while, Vos had felt uncomfortable about his failure to tell his wife about Baumer's diamonds. It was time to put that right.

"I'll tell you in a minute. Fancy a coffee?" She nodded.

A small coffee bar that served a particularly good brew, was a frequent market stop of theirs. Once they'd settled onto a pair of red, fold-up garden chairs under an awning, Vos told her about what had been found in Kurt Baumer's stomach.

"And what's this got to do with Elias?" she asked.

"Possibly nothing. But there's a similarity between the descriptions of the two men who took him away and the two men who arrived at Baumer's house on the night of his death and returned that evening we were playing cards. My instinct and Neumann's as well, is that they were after Kurt's diamonds. If they knew about Elias being – or claiming to be – Kurt's nephew, then he'd be a good target to work on to find out where they were."

"I assume the police are pursuing this," Katerine said, "and that you're not getting involved. After all it's got nothing to do with finding Baumer's heirs, has it?"

He knew she was right. Not wanting to dwell on the subject, he told her about Sophie, the art lecturer he'd met at the funeral who had information about Kurt.

"She wasn't comfortable talking about him at the time and we were going to meet sometime afterwards, so she could spill the beans. But that's proved impractical, because of her busy schedule, so in the end I settled for a phone call."

"So, what did she have to say?" Katerine asked.

"Well, from the sound of it, Kurt was no angel. What she told me was all a bit cloak and dagger. He was part of a network called Circle 10. They're involved in unauthorised movement of African art and artefacts, paintings, sculptures, masks, you name it. Baumer was their expert adviser – or one of them. I found this stash of photos on his laptop. Neumann is sniffing around because he thinks Kurt's connections with the art world might have had something to do with both his death and the presence of the diamonds. Because it's art, it sounds nice and fluffy, *no danger here* sort of thing, but from what I've picked up so far, the reality is much different, because there's big money involved. Sorry – you'll already be aware of this kind of thing through your job."

"Very much so! But again, you'll need to leave this for the police to follow up, won't you?" Vos nodded half-heartedly. "Why's it called Circle 10?"

"Apparently because that particular shape is easier to protect – you know, circle the wagons sort of thing – and there are ten of them in it. Simple as that! Except of course there's only nine of them now."

"There's no need to get involved any further though, is there? You just need to get a legitimate heir sorted. Whether or not Kurt was up to his ears in something shady or illegal is not really relevant to that task. Take it from me, a lot of the art-dealing world is dodgy or a rip off or both and the people who are buying often have more money than sense. Better to steer clear."

Although her advice was right, it didn't extinguish his continuing interest in the likely link between Kurt's death, his dealing and the diamonds.

Leaving the coffee stall, they wandered on through the market, coming to a halt at a junction between two stalls. Vos was trying to move to the left, but Barto was having none of it. A regular visitor to the market, he had a set route which involved a number of key locations. After a few seconds of lead-pulling, Vos gave in to Barto's determination and they went right.

Twenty metres further on, they stopped so that Barto could receive a treat, a pat on the head and a bit of TLC from Maggi, one of the stallholders.

"Told you before, Harry. I could do with a dog like that. Let me know if he ever gets too much for you."

"You wish!" he replied and walked on.

"I had a call from Eddie," he said to Katerine, eyes half-closed as he soaked up the sun.

"Oh yes – how's your son doing? We haven't heard much from him recently."

"You're right, although I haven't been in touch much either. He's had a lot to do sorting out things after that fire in the place next door to his bar. Got a bit more time now, I think. How about going out for a meal with him and Sibilla?"

"Yes, that would be good. Tomorrow evening?"

"Great, I'll give him a ring," Vos said, thinking it would be another challenge for his waistline. But what the hell.

Back home, he was just about to settle into his armchair to have a snooze under cover of pretending to read the newspaper, when he remembered about Frau Emmerling, the witness at Ursula Kirchner's wedding Josina had unearthed.

She answered his call promptly and immediately started talking about Ursula, how she'd been a good friend over many years, how awful it had been when Berthold had left her and disappeared to Bangkok, how delightful Elias had been – at least up until his early twenties. No, she'd seen very little of him since then, but Ursula had provided regular updates on his activities. Had she known Kurt? Only by name and reputation. Did Elias have any contact with him? Not as far as she was aware.

Did she have an up to date photo of Elias? No, but she had one from way back – a group shot. Could she forward a copy? Yes, but it might take her a while as she didn't want to send the original and wasn't sure if the photography shop still did copies. Scanning and emailing wasn't an option. She'd never managed to get her head around that kind of thing.

+ + +

Josina felt a little better. She wasn't sure whether it was something she'd eaten or a bug but it had laid her low for 48 hours. At least she now had the energy to do a little light online research on the births section of the Bonn registry site. But she could find no reference to a Sebastien Baumer born on the 7th April 1939. Maybe, because of all the wartime upheavals that followed so soon afterwards, records for births in Bonn in 1939 were incomplete. Or maybe the date of birth was wrongly recorded. She searched using dates a few days either side of the 7th. Still no luck. What about the surname? Could that possibly be wrong?

She checked all the births on the 7th. Finding a Sebastien was totally unexpected – but there it was. *Sebastien Ziegler born 7/4/1939. Mother Elsa Ziegler. Father Hans Ziegler (deceased).* Poor thing: a new mother and a widow. She ran off a copy.

Could this possibly be *her* Sebastien? She gave free rein to her imagination. Perhaps he'd started off as a Ziegler ... maybe his mother had subsequently died ... and he'd been adopted by the Baumers because ... well maybe she'd been a close friend of the family.

It was a theory worth testing out.

Josina switched her search from births to deaths and from Sebastien to Elsa Ziegler. Much to her frustration the site crashed. Despite repeated attempts to get back in she was unable to make any progress. Tiredness crept over her and she was unsure whether to continue. After a break for a decaf tea and a stomach-settling plain biscuit she made one last try and managed to get back online.

Her new search started from 7/4/39, aware she might have to trawl through months or years of records before coming across a possible Elsa death. The much more likely outcome was that there'd be nothing. But she actually found it very quickly. Elsa died only a month after Sebastien's birth. Maybe there'd been post-natal complications. Josina found it heart-breaking, thinking about what had happened to the young widow.

Aware that it would be useful to have some form of corroboration, she made one further search. Death notices published in the Bonn newspaper. The search engine led her to digitised 1939 editions of the city's daily paper, the General-Anzeiger.

But before she could make a start, there was a call from the salon. The Vercammen woman was kicking up a fuss, insisting that only Josina could get her colouring right. She calmed the woman down and mentioned about possibly still being infectious. The woman was suddenly very understanding and happy to accept a re-arranged appointment in a few days' time.

Back to the search. Within minutes the newspaper revealed what she'd been looking for.

Elsa Ziegler (12/5/17 to 8/5/39), widow, passed away after a short illness, leaving a son, Sebastien...

There was the confirmation she wanted – *leaving a son Sebastien*. No father, no mother. That could have been when the Baumers stepped in.

It was hard to believe it had been possible to piece together such a story, decades after the events had happened. But any feeling of satisfaction was tempered firstly by the realisation of how awful things must have been for both Elsa and her son and secondly by the thought that all this might turn out to be pure conjecture. And just supposing she was on the right track, the chances of being able to find an adoption record were slim. After all, she had no idea where or when an adoption might have taken place. Rather than wasting a lot of time on what might be a fruitless task, it was time to ask Harry whether he'd be willing to have a conversation with Sebastien about his past.

Eighteen

Rainer's trip to Liege had a two-fold purpose. Drop something off and pick someone up.

It was time to shift the last of the three boxes he'd collected when he'd taken Harry Vos to Brussels. The contents of the other two had already been sold on. After loading the box and a chill-bag into the boot of the Passat, he made coffee, filled a travel cup and grabbed a couple of chocolate biscuits. Traffic on the A27 to Verviers was surprisingly light and the full-volume Deus tape helped swallow up the kilometres.

He'd got into the burner-phone business by accident. A conversation with one of his fares a couple of years back had set the wheels in motion. Prepaid, unlocked, no requirement to register at the point of sale and no tracking of personal data. What was not to like? OK, they were used by bad boys to stay under the radar but there were far worse things that they got up to. He had a burner himself – for those occasions when he wanted to avoid using a smartphone.

The A3 took him into Liege, where he headed for the city centre, crossed the Pont des Arches and parked on a side street in Outremeuse. Removing the box and the chill-bag from the car boot, he walked to number 3A. The door was solid timber. He pulled on the wrought-iron rod that hung down to the side and listened as the bell clanged somewhere deep in the house. The door was opened by a middle-aged man with a huge moustache.

"Georges! How are you?"

"Good thanks and all the better for seeing that box of goodies. Big demand for them. Still got the taxi I see. Thought you'd be too well off for that now?"

"Of course I am, but it's a very useful sideline and as for picking up gossip, well I couldn't do without it. How's the Free Republic of Outremeuse? Still going strong?"

"Come back on the 15th August and find out!"

"Might just do that. Can I come in?"

"Yes, yes, of course. Where are my manners?"

Rainer dumped the box on the old wooden kitchen table and pocketed the cash his friend handed over. The two men had served in the army together and kept in touch since discharge. In addition to their trading contact, they had occasional nights out in Liege, meeting up with other ex-army buddies.

"Let me know when you need more phones. Any coffee left in that pot?"

Georges nodded and filled two St Vith mugs.

"Do you miss the place?" Rainer asked.

"You must be joking! Far too small for a man like me. I can get lost and be anonymous in Liege – well up to a point anyway."

"Did you hear about Kurt Baumer?"

"I did. Strange old gent. Never got much out of him but he did buy one of my phones. A friend of his put him in touch," Georges said.

"Really! Now that *is* interesting. This guy Harry Vos has been hired to find any heirs Kurt might have had. I'll have to let him know. The only phone he found in the house was the landline."

"Kurt told me he needed it for business, by which I assumed he meant something related to artworks, given that he was always banging on about them. Maybe the dealing was a bit questionable and that's why he needed a burner." Georges said. "Now, what do you fancy this time? No steak unfortunately, but I've got pork or lamb chops – both very tasty – or calf liver."

Rainer was partial to lamb chops and said he'd take a couple of packs. The chill-bag was put to good use.

"Well, thanks for the drink, the chat, the meat – and of course the cash. Sorry I can't stay any longer, but a customer will be waiting for me in the city centre and, naturally, it doesn't do to keep a punter waiting."

Every man and his dog seemed to be trying to reach the same destination at the same time. Eventually he managed to pull up outside the Musee des Beaux Arts, and ignoring the sound of multiple car horns, used his own to grab the attention of Sebastien Baumer who was sheltering from a downpour under a large 'Visit Cape Town' umbrella. He moved slowly across to the car and got in.

Traffic was just as heavy on the way out of the city.

"How did it go then?" Rainer asked.

"Waste of time. They didn't know a thing about Kurt in the gallery. But at least there were some excellent pictures of industrial Wallonia in there. No, I think he must have operated elsewhere, Brussels maybe. Have to say, when you told me about the art dealing it really threw me. A side of him I knew nothing about; one of many, no doubt, given our complete lack of contact."

+ + +

Vos had arranged to get a lift back to St Vith with Josina. After making his own way to Leuven, she picked him up at the station.

They discussed the delicate issue of Sebastien's parentage and his possible adoption. Vos was wary about raising it directly with him. Although very frustrated that Sebastien has still not produced his birth certificate, Vos felt it might be a step too far asking him if he'd been born a Ziegler. There was also the awful thought that he might be unaware of some of the details of his very early life. How might any such revelations affect him, particularly given that he was already suffering physical ill health. Maybe it would be wiser to wait for Sebastien to produce his certificate. Surely it wouldn't take much longer!

"So, you're OK to spend today working on Kurt's boxes," Vos said. "Given that we now have two potential claimants to Kurt's estate, both with a degree of uncertainty to their claims, I feel we should have another search, just in case there's some crucial piece of evidence that we've missed."

"Yes, I can manage today Harry, but having already missed three days at the salon with that bug I won't be able to stay any longer – more's the pity. I enjoy the work. By the way, did you manage to get anywhere with Frau Emmerling?"

"She was very helpful," Vos said "and gave me the confirmation I was after. A photo of Elias is on its way so I can double check that it matches *our* Elias."

"That's good. And have the police managed to find him?"

"Not yet. I've been wondering about why he was abducted. Has he been involved in something questionable and would that put a question mark over his claim to Kurt's estate?"

"Possibly, but he's more likely to be just a victim. Let's hope they find him soon."

"You're probably right. By the way did I tell you about a Congolese woman called Kela Mpenda?"

"Briefly. A colleague of Kurt's?"

"That's right. I can't really work her out. I found out from somebody I spoke to at the funeral that she and Kurt were part of a group called Circle 10 who apparently trade in African artefacts. There's something dodgy about what they do, but as yet, I don't know what. I was wondering whether you could have a word with Kela today. She might open up more to you. I'm sure her presence in St Vith has something to do with the diamonds although I have to say she does seem genuinely upset about Kurt's death."

"I'll speak to her if there's time but I don't want to set off home too late."

"Thanks, that's good. We should be OK for time. I'll give her a ring."

"Oh, I meant to ask. You haven't left Katerine on her own in Heist, have you? Not with that nasty man on the prowl!"

"No, don't worry. She's on her way back to Luxembourg, more work still to do there." Vos knew Josina had been right to raise it as an issue though. Perhaps he was too inclined to take risks which might have consequences, not just for himself but also for others. "Before I forget," he continued, "Rainer gave me an interesting piece of news. A pal of his apparently sold a mobile phone to Kurt some time back. One of those basic unsmart ones. I'm going to have another search round the house and see if I can locate it. Why Kurt would have wanted to hide away such a basic phone is beyond me. Still – that man has been full of surprises."

"How was your Heist weekend by the way?" Josina asked.

"Very pleasant. Even managed a meal out with Eddie and Sibilla. They've been really busy recently and it was good to have a catch up. Hang on, I'd better just take this call."

It was Sebastien with news that a copy of his birth certificate had arrived. Could Harry come to the hotel?

"Well, that's a relief," Vos said, once the call had ended. "I was beginning to think it was never going to arrive."

Josina was puzzled. If the certificate was genuine – how come she'd missed it?

+ + +

By the time they arrived at the hotel, Sebastien was in a bit of a state. Doctor Vermeulen had confirmed the results of his medical tests. He had a rare infection. She'd put him on a course of powerful medication and told him not to think about going home until he was considerably stronger.

Miriam removed her arm from around her husband's shoulders, walked across to the desk beneath the window, picked up a piece of paper. And handed it to Vos.

After reading the document, he showed it to Josina. Having scanned through it, she glanced at Harry and turned towards Sebastien, about to ask him a question.

But he cut her off.

"I must apologise for not explaining my origins before now," he said, looking drained. "It's very difficult for me to talk about and hardly anyone else knows about this. In a nutshell, as you will have seen from the certificate, although my father was Heinrich Baumer, my mother, Elsa Ziegler, was not his wife. He had an affair with her. She died, tragically, not long after giving birth to me. Heinrich took me into his own family and very laudably, my step-mother brought me up as her own son."

Vos couldn't help noticing Miriam's fleeting reaction to her husband's story. Was it a look of incredulity?

"Well thank you for being so frank," Vos said. "I can quite understand how difficult it must be for you talking about this. Once you feel up to it, we can meet with Ahrendt and go through whatever formalities he requires."

Vos caught Josina's eye briefly. A shared implicit assumption that any discussion about the disparity between the birth certificate she'd found and the one produced by Sebastien would have to wait.

"I think my husband needs a rest now," Miriam said. "If you can arrange the meeting with the legal man and let us know, that would be most helpful."

Vos and Josina said their goodbyes and went to sit in her car.

"That was awful," she said. "The certificate he produced must have been doctored to show that Heinrich is his father, not Hans Ziegler, so that he can inherit."

"And if you hadn't found the original certificate, we'd have been none the wiser. I'll need to speak to Ahrendt and check how he wants to proceed. What a mess! And did you notice Miriam's reaction?"

"I did!" Josina said. "It was as if she'd never been told about Elsa Ziegler. Look, assuming my research is accurate, the question of adoption might still arise? It'll be difficult, but I could have a look and check whether anything's out there?"

"That'll be good, if you've got the time. But as you said, I think it'll be a long shot. No wonder Sebastien was so concerned to hear about Elias Kirchner. A rival for Kurt's inheritance who might turn out to have a better claim. Now, as a bit of light relief let's try and finish those boxes off. You never know, we might strike lucky and find something that helps our search for a legitimate heir! After that, as long as you're still OK for time, it would be really helpful if you could have a quick word with Kela. To be honest, I'm surprised she's still here in St Vith."

+ + +

Josina had found the day very demanding, not helped by the fact that she was still not feeling one hundred percent. But despite that, sleep wouldn't come.

The discussion with Kela had gone well enough. According to her, Circle10 was an informal club of people with an interest in Congolese art and artefacts. Some dealing was involved but it wasn't the primary purpose of the group. She'd been very concerned about the two men who'd been in Kurt's house, convinced that they must have precipitated his death in some way and disappointed that police had made no real progress in identifying them. Josina was sure that her grief at Kurt's death was genuine.

When, at her father's request, Josina had told Kela about the diamonds, she'd been really thrown, unable to understand why

Kurt would have had such things in his possession. Another very honest response, Josina had reported back to Vos. It looked very much as if the diamonds had nothing to do with Circle10.

Josina gave up on the struggle to sleep and got up to make a drink. Sitting in her favourite armchair, a moving-in gift from her mother, a mug of herbal tea to hand and a Café del Mar mix on her headphones, she had another look at Sebastien's online profile which had links to a number of other sites.

Her search picked up something she missed previously. Sebastien and Miriam had a daughter, Suzanne, a successful dancer and choreographer back in Cape Town. No doubt she was also in the dark regarding Sebastien's origins.

Nineteen

The duty officer took a call from Luc Torfs, a diamond dealer in Antwerp. It was transferred to Chief Inspector Neumann. Hearing the reference to diamonds, he decided to record the call.

"I'm phoning about the late Kurt Baumer." He was all ears. "Do you know about him? Good, that helps. The thing is, he came to see me, wanted to get some diamonds valued." Neumann smiled. At last, some progress.

"Just a minute. Given the nature of the information you're providing, I need to double-check your name and ask for your dealer registration number." Neumann made a note of the details. "Thank you. I'm going to put you on hold while I confirm these at our end. Is that OK?" Neumann was being over-polite, not wanting Torfs to ring off.

Neumann waited while his deputy checked an encrypted online register. He got the thumbs up.

"Hello. Yes, that's fine. Please continue."

"I gave him a provisional valuation and asked if he wanted to leave the diamonds with me – for safe-keeping, you understand. In addition to our own extensive security precautions, you'll be aware that we also have armed guards operating in the district. A lot of my clients take advantage of this service. But he decided not to. I'm sure he'll have wanted to get a second opinion on the valuation. The thing is, I've only just found out about his death. What concerns me is that this happened the day after he came to see me. I'm worried his death might have had something to do with the diamonds. He could have let something slip about them. So, I wanted to check that you knew about the diamonds and that they are in a safe place and – god forbid – haven't disappeared."

Neumann was unsure what to make of the enquiry. Was Torfs just doing his public duty or was there perhaps more to it than that? Whatever, it would do no harm if he confirmed that he knew about the gems and that they were indeed in a safe place.

Having passed the information on he asked the question he'd been wanting to ask from the off.

"We have had some concerns about the diamonds. So far, we've been unable to trace their origin. I wonder, are you able to throw any light on this, sir?" Hesitation at the other end of the line.

"Well, given that Baumer is most unfortunately no longer with us, I'm at liberty to tell you that he didn't bring any evidence of provenance with him. I did emphasise that my valuation was provisional and would only be confirmed once I'd seen the relevant documentation."

Neumann had a feeling that the longer the conversation went on, the less assured the dealer seemed to be. But maybe that was down to a degree of nervousness…talking to the police about a man with possibly questionable diamonds.

He thanked Torfs for his help and rang off.

Ever since his date with Dina Vermeulen, his head had been in a spin. They'd spent the night together, something he'd never really expected would happen. And since then, nothing had gone wrong. It was hard to believe his luck was continuing.

He tried to concentrate on work, but all he could see was her face, framed by dark, slightly greying curls, the unexpected red lipstick and that smile.

Eventually he managed to force himself away from this vision and made a note of the key points arising from the call. His fingers made slow progress over the keys. He'd never properly adapted to the computerised keyboard world. Earlier in his career, he'd made his own handwritten and typed records. Later, as he'd risen through the ranks, there'd been the luxury of dictation, albeit to a machine rather than a real live secretary. But more recently, following the closures and mergers within the new division, admin back-up had been hacked away, along with most other things and he didn't cope well with the new world.

He played the recording of Torfs' call. Something bothered him about the conversation but he couldn't put his finger on it. Should he have said anything at all about the diamonds? Had he been suckered unwittingly into revealing something? He didn't think so.

The internal phone rang. A black woman was at reception wanting to speak to him about Kurt Baumer. Why was everything about Baumer all of a sudden? Although not really wanting a further interruption to his already overloaded schedule, he was intrigued about what she might have to say about the dead man, and asked for her to be brought through to his office.

She was striking, tall, very short hair and had an immediate air of self-confidence.

Someone connected to Harry Vos had suggested she come to speak to him. Of course – he should have guessed. When the private investigator had first appeared on the scene, Neumann had assumed that he wouldn't be around long. But the man was still in town and, what's more, seemed to act like a magnet for trouble, break-ins, abductions, con artists, diamonds. You name it. So, what did this woman want?

She claimed to have been an art world colleague of Baumer's, though to his mind, they'd have made a strange pair. However, as far as he could judge, her regret, perhaps even sorrow, regarding his death seemed genuine enough. Her particular concern was about the underlying cause of death – not the heart attack as such but what might have caused it. She was aware that two unknown men had been at Baumer's house on the night of his death and wanted to know what, if any, progress the police had made in tracing them?

He reiterated that a heart attack had been confirmed as the cause of death and there was no investigation about that as such. However, the presence of the men was of concern and an investigation was in progress. They had not yet been traced.

Having decided, at the start of the interview, not to say anything about the diamonds, he was very surprised when she mentioned them herself. Was there anybody who didn't know about the damn things?

How had she found out about them? Vos' daughter had told her. So, he was roping in family members to help now! No, he couldn't comment on their origin or on why Baumer had them in his possession. Did he think they might have been linked to his death? He was unable to comment.

Then it was his turn. Did *she* know why Baumer had the diamonds? Given his involvement in the art dealing world, had he obtained them as a form of payment?

She found that hard to believe, but it was a source of worry to her. He thought the comment sounded heartfelt. Did she know anything about Baumer's nephew, Elias Kirchner? Kurt had never mentioned any relatives. It sounded like she was telling the truth.

The more they talked, the more Neumann suspected that she was aware of reasons why Baumer had attracted the attention of the two men, but he was unable to prise anything further from her. He briefly contemplated holding her for further questioning, but knew he had no grounds for doing so.

Watching through the window as she walked to her car, he wondered what the real purpose of her visit had been. It must have been something to do with the diamonds, but he couldn't work out what her angle was. Oh, for a bit of time to digest the implications of both the earlier phone call and her visit. But it was straight on to the next pressing task.

Sometimes he wondered why he continued in the job. It had been different in earlier days, before the cynicism, the cuts and the extra bureaucracy had set in. Now it felt like he could do what he defined as the proper job for a maximum of about ten percent of his day. The rest of his activity was what the machine made him do.

Still, it wouldn't be long before he'd be on his boat. For a fortnight, he'd be a completely different person. Was Dina a sailor? He didn't imagine so, but it would be worth asking. It wasn't as if he'd be venturing out onto the high seas, just a coastal run up to Harlingen and then on to the Frisian Islands. Would she want to join him?

+ + +

Although Miriam Baumer had known her husband since her early twenties, she'd never been told much about his life before they'd met. Sebastien had always been vague about his early years, so the revelation that the woman he'd called mother was actually his step-mother had come as a complete shock.

After Vos and his daughter had departed, Sebastien had tried to brush it off, saying that as he'd never known his real mother it was all a bit of an irrelevancy.

She'd been pinning her hopes on him inheriting his brother's estate. Judging by Kurt's reduced circumstances – as indicated by his very modest house – it was unlikely to involve a huge amount of money. But anything that would help boost their bank balance would be welcome. It was the only reason she'd consented to accompany her husband on his trip to Belgium. She wanted to keep an eye on progress towards the inheritance prize. Not that she'd admitted it to Sebastien.

She was worried about his health. The doctor had clearly been concerned and the medication was strong stuff. How long would it take him to recover sufficiently for them to be able to return to South Africa?

Resting on the sofa, Sebastien asleep in bed, she reflected on how life had turned out. Although she still loved her husband, he could be infuriating. What would it have been like had she married Kurt? Because their paths hadn't crossed for so long, there was no way of knowing, but from what she'd picked up since arriving in St Vith, he seemed to have turned into a dry old stick, very different from the man she'd become engaged to. How much had that been down to staying single, she wondered. Would he have turned out very differently had they stayed together? She knew such speculation was pointless … but it didn't stop her.

She felt suddenly tired, not falling asleep tired, but a deep-seated weariness. Life in South Africa demanded so much of her energy and there wasn't much of that left. Unfortunately, she had no real connection to any other country and Sebastien would never entertain the idea of living anywhere else.

+ + +

"Harry?"

"Yes, Josina."

"Listen, I haven't got much time. Work is a bit mental at the moment. It's about Berthold Kirchner. I think he might not be dead!"

"But Elias told us he was."

"That's right. But there's no documentation to back that up. He and Ursula only knew about the death because a family friend told them. It wasn't like they went to the funeral. Anyway, out of curiosity I tried searching for a death certificate for Berthold. You told me Frau Emmerling had mentioned about him being in Bangkok, so I looked there, but couldn't find anything. When I searched various other Bangkok sites, I stumbled across a very-much-alive Berthold Kirchner. According to his website he has an extremely pleasant house there, a wife who looks to be at least forty years younger than him and a property company specialising in holiday lets. No mention of a son, so he might be a completely different BK and not Elias' father, but I thought you might want to give him a ring and find out!"

Twenty

Fontaine had been really unsettled by Kela's news of Kurt Baumer's death. Although the officially-stated cause of death was a heart attack, the revelation that there'd been two callers at Kurt's house the night he died was very troubling. As was the news that he'd been in possession of some diamonds.

She'd contemplated delaying the next step in the Eyckmans plan until they knew more about what had happened on the night of Kurt's death. But she was reluctant to tread water. And they were primed to go. She decided they shouldn't hold back.

A recent break in at the gallery had been covered by the local press. Nothing had been stolen, but walls had been sprayed with graffiti. The raid had been put down to petty vandalism.

Leon, one of the vandals, who also happened to be an alarms expert, occupied the left rear seat of the 4x4. Kela sat in the right-hand rear seat. Fontaine was with the driver up front. All were dressed in black, face masks at the ready.

They'd checked the forecast, heavy cloud, but no rain. Traffic was light on the N26. An Aphex Twin download kept them chilled. The driver took the Haacht turn off and shortly afterwards turned onto a side road and cut the engine, lights and music. Two of the upstairs rooms of the large house were lit. The rest of the building was in darkness.

Leon slipped out of the vehicle and disappeared through a gap in the fence – one he'd prepared on his previous visit – and crossed the field up to the house. The other three waited. After ten minutes a single word text appeared on Fontaine's phone. *Deactivated.*

The two women took the same route across the field, leaving the driver to guard the vehicle. The grass was still wet from late evening rain and they were glad of their boots, lightweight and waterproof.

Leon was waiting in the doorway. They followed him inside and took off their backpacks. The blinds were closed in the gallery rooms. Their head torches provided the necessary focused illumination. They'd memorised the exhibit details Kela had collected on her previous visit and moved swiftly to pick out the targeted artefacts, wrap them in protective packaging and place them in the backpacks.

At the sound of movement from the floor above, they froze. A minute went by. The sound of a toilet flush. A silent minute followed. The packing re-started. They moved as quickly as possible through the other three gallery rooms.

Masks created by the Yaka, Ndop statuettes, Kuba textiles, Nkisi figurines of the Kongo people. The bags were full.

Another noise from upstairs. They stood stock still and waited. A creak on the stairs. A brief trickling sound, the clink of glass against metal, footsteps ascending the stairs. The bliss of silence.

They left the house, re-crossed the field, loaded the backpacks into the rear of the 4x4 and sank into their seats. The driver set off slowly, initially without lights, back to the Haacht road, a right turn, a couple of kilometres and into a small layby screened by birch trees.

Much to their relief, the white van was already there. The 4x4 reversed towards the open back doors of the van and the backpacks were transferred. Kela and Leon were swept away in the van, leaving Fontaine and the 4x4 driver to fix new plates, dump the old ones and travel on to Antwerp.

Just outside Leuven, the 4x4 was stopped by a police road block. Although it seemed absurdly quick for this to have any connection to their raid, it didn't stop Fontaine worrying. However, nothing remained in the 4x4 that might compromise them. Everything, including the head torches, the dark outer clothing and the face masks had been switched to the van.

The driver lit up two cigarettes and passed one across to Fontaine. When they reached the line of uniformed officers, they were told to extinguish the cigarettes and step out of the vehicle. A thorough search followed. They were given the all clear. Much to Fontaine's annoyance, the driver asked what they were looking for. She wanted to keep as low a profile as possible. Cocaine, they were told. There'd been a tip-off.

+ + +

Vos thought he'd probably have only one chance to get anywhere. If he didn't pitch his enquiry right, Berthold Kirchner would no doubt just put the phone down.

Best to be upfront from the start. He was calling from Belgium on behalf of a local lawyer in connection with the estate of a Kurt Baumer. This was the critical moment. From what he'd picked up about the family, the two men had probably never actually met. Nevertheless, there'd have been no love lost between them.

To his relief, Kirchner didn't terminate the call there and then.

"I've never had anything to do with Baumer and had no idea he was dead."

So, he was the right Berthold Kirchner.

"I'm sorry to have to break the news. The reason I'm calling is that a man claiming to be your son Elias, has recently arrived in St Vith, where Kurt lived and has staked a claim to his estate." The news was greeted with initial silence.

"I've only ever had sporadic contact with Elias, so it's not surprising he's not bothered to let me know about his uncle's death. But I'm very surprised to hear that he's after Baumer's worldly goods. As far as I'm aware the two never met or had anything to do with each other. Still, if he can get his hands on the old miser's money, good luck to him."

Vos tried to rein in his expectations. Things were going too well.

"The thing is," he said, "I need to be able to verify that the Elias Kirchner who's here in St Vith is the real thing."

"What exactly do you want from me, Vos?"

"A reasonably up-to-date photograph of your son if you have such a thing. You see there's always a risk of someone making a false claim. The fact that the Elias I've met has the right kind of identification and relevant family information regarding yourself and his late mother isn't quite sufficient. I need someone who knows him to authenticate a photo of him."

"Ah, his late mother!" Damn – from the changed tone of voice, Vos suspected he'd made a big error by mentioning her. "She blamed me for everything but rebuffed all my offers of help. I was completely ostracised by her and she made sure my son viewed me in the worst possible light. It's taken me decades to establish what is still only a minimal level of contact with Elias. Several weeks since I last spoke to him. Be that as it may, there'd be a certain degree of poetic justice if he inherited Kurt's money, so I'll do as you've requested and send a photo of him. It's not bang up to date, probably a couple of years old, but it should do the job. Now, if you can give me your email address, I'll forward it to you."

Given all the potential pitfalls, Vos couldn't believe how well the conversation had gone. He just hoped the old man wouldn't take too long to do the necessary.

+ + +

change of plan
why's that
it's too risky to try smuggling it all back to the DRC
thought you'd checked that out
yes, but given K's death
fair point, what's the new plan
we film all the pieces and put it online with a commentary
that'll put us right in the firing line
no, we can do it anonymously and use a vocoder
I like it – how soon
tomorrow

+ + +

Vos stared at the man in the photograph, took account of the way photos can distort features, made allowances for the fact it had been taken a few years ago and thought…it could well be *his* Elias Kirchner. But, very frustratingly, he couldn't be certain. And to add to his frustration, he still hadn't received Frau Emmerling's photo of EK. He was on the phone straight away. She was very apologetic. There'd been problems trying to get a copy, but now she'd managed it. The photo was in the post.

At least that was progress but it meant yet another wait, until he could be certain about the nephew's identity. His mood was not helped by the failure to unearth Kurt's burner phone, despite another search. There was a third area of non-progress, niggling away at him, but for the life of him he couldn't bring it to mind. And thinking about it directly probably wouldn't help to shift it from the back of his mind to the front. Some distraction was necessary, to allow the information to trickle through in its own time. Involvement in a few routine tasks might help the process, so he concentrated on making coffee in the B&B kitchen, taking a tray through to the guest sitting room, flicking idly through a bird magazine and trying to ignore the twinges of pain in his knee.

He felt almost affronted when a middle-aged couple suddenly joined him in the room. Given the total lack of other guests to date – with the exception of his family – he'd come to regard the room as his own private space. What was worse, they seemed keen to talk. As quickly and politely as possible he made his excuses and retreated to the sanctuary of his bedroom.

As soon as he sat on the bed the thought popped into his head. The task that had been nagging away at him. Contact his art dealer to get a professional view of Kurt's art-related activity and documentation.

A quick search online and there was Ruud Okker's website – *specialist in nineteenth century landscapes, originally from Utrecht, now settled in Antwerp, valuations and sales arranged.* Minutes later he was speaking to the man himself.

Was there any chance he'd be able to come down to the Ost Kantonen to assist with a professional opinion on an art-dealer called Kurt Baumer, who'd recently died?

A positive response. It might be in a day or two, but he'd definitely help out.

+ + +

Although all the surrounding industrial buildings had been abandoned years ago, the specialist metal fabrication company had continued operations mainly to provide cover for lucrative dealing in a range of products from drugs and under-the-counter cigarettes to small arms. Beyond this cluster of buildings, the new commercial Charleroi had sprung up, a very different world of biotech, telecommunications and aerospace companies.

Elias Kirchner was bewildered. His life had been turned upside down by the visit of the two men in the Toyota. He'd assumed they were debt collectors, easy enough for him to handle.

But they'd turned out to be in a different league. Kurt Baumer had been holding something of theirs. Although they were very sorry to hear he'd passed away, they needed their property back. *Could he assist?*

Property – what property?

Their initial politeness evaporated once it became clear that he wasn't going to help them. His claims that he didn't know about any such property were ignored. He'd been bundled into the Toyota and blindfolded.

After a seemingly endless journey, he was frogmarched into a building and left in a storeroom. His attempts to shout his way out had led only to a headbutt, with a promise of more to come should he try again.

Hours later they'd come to question him, bringing a sandwich and a bottle of water. When he was asked where his uncle had hidden the diamonds, his worst fears were confirmed. So, he wasn't the only one who knew about them. Nobody could have been more amazed than him when Kurt had first dropped them into the conversation. And now he was going to have to pretend he knew nothing about them. He was used to being evasive, creative even, in responding to questions about debt. But questions about diamonds? Well, that would require a whole new level of creativity.

And how on earth had they found out about his connection to Kurt?

Twenty One

When his resident caretaker had phoned in the early hours to tell him about the break in and the thefts, Eyckmans had been apoplectic. Although he lived at the gallery, his business frequently took him away. His wife had left him several years previously and his adult children had flown the nest. It had been a catastrophic twin failure – the security system and the caretaker – each of which cost him thousands.

The 4x4 had been parked too far away to be picked up clearly on his own CCTV footage and there was no public system on the lane that led to his house. The three masked figures were on camera, but had no identifying features. And the thieves had left no prints. Keen to avoid the risk of awkward questions being asked about the provenance of the artefacts, Eyckmans had initially decided against involving the police, preferring to mount his own investigation. Which would have had the additional advantage of being free of the constraints the police had to work within.

But once the online film show made its public appearance, he was obliged to change his approach. The police could no longer be kept away from the investigation process.

The 4x4 had not been found. No one had witnessed the intruders – but then there were no near neighbours. The caretaker had been completely unaware that he'd had company. And the police techies had got nowhere trying to establish who had posted the video online.

Eyckmans was asked to provide a valid paper trail – from the respective African states of origin to his gallery – for each of the exhibits which had starred in the online video. Most of these pieces had been acquired years ago. In the early days of building up the gallery he'd been cocky and far too lax. Back then, it had been easy enough to bribe officials either to overlook the lack of a document or ignore a forgery that didn't pass muster. His paperwork for these items resembled not so much an auditable trail as a mystery tour, which meant he was faced with the prospect of having to pay out an awful lot of money in order to fill the gaps with high class forgeries. All within a tight timescale.

It was no longer possible to get away with tricks of the past. Over the years the authorities had tightened up on the traffic in stolen items. An electronic database listing hundreds of missing works had been developed. If one of these items surfaced, the team responsible for monitoring the illegal trade in cultural objects would spring into action. This hadn't put an end to illegal trading but had made it much more difficult.

Eyckmans had previously turned a deaf ear to rumours of a group of art thieves doing the rounds of private galleries. Now, he was paying for it. He had to assume that the black woman who'd made the recent delivery to the gallery must have infiltrated his network. She'd staked out the place and he kicked himself for allowing her to wander around, even with a chaperone.

Having started off on the back foot, he moved quickly to seize the initiative.

His first step was straightforward. He spoke to Skip, his man in Kinshasa and instructed him to get on the next plane to Brussels, find the woman and deal with her.

The second step involved more risk. Through one of his many contacts, he arranged to do a TV interview – fronted by a man who just happened to be a friend of his. Although aware of the danger of putting himself in the spotlight, it was clear nobody else was going to come to his defence. On the contrary, he'd made a number of enemies during the course of his dealings and they would be hoping to witness his comeuppance. His plan was to play victim on camera.

It wasn't a role that came easily to him, but he felt his story sounded convincing. He placed a strong emphasis on the money and effort that had gone into developing the gallery, so that important African artefacts could be viewed by discerning members of the public – people who would appreciate the skills that had gone into every piece. And now access to such opportunities had been threatened by thieves out for a quick buck! He concluded by stressing how the gallery had kept high professional standards and made a significant contribution, over many years, to the artistic life of the country.

At the end of the interview, the host, who'd given Eyckmans a very soft ride, turned to face the camera and said that art lovers should rest assured that it wouldn't be long before the net closed in on the criminals involved.

+ + +

Despite trying several times, Vos had been unable to get through to Berthold Kirchner again. And the arrival of Frau Emmerling's photo of Elias Kirchner was still awaited.

His next immediate task was a pre-meeting with Ahrendt, to discuss the problem of Sebastien's birth certificate, prior to the arrival of the man himself.

When he heard what Vos had to say, the lawyer pulled a face. He'd wanted a simple solution to the quest for a Bauman heir and yet Vos seemed to be continually bringing him problems. However, he was a realist. There was no alternative but to put all their Sebastien cards on the table.

Vos, who'd been feeling very uncomfortable about the whole situation, was impressed by the way the lawyer took ownership, once Sebastien arrived.

"I'm sorry to have to raise these issues," Ahrendt said, "but perhaps you can help me to understand the position. I have these two birth certificates. I'm assuming that the one you gave me is correct, but I'm puzzled that the one I obtained online does not contain identical information. You'll appreciate that it's my duty to make sure that a document so crucial to the inheritance process is properly verified, hence the need to be thorough. Perhaps you could have a look through both these certificates and help me to understand?"

Ahrendt sat back in his seat and watched Sebastien as he read through the online document, then suddenly slumped forward onto the table. Vos wondered, belatedly, about the wisdom of going ahead with the discussion. Given Sebastien's poor health, the meeting was obviously proving too much for him. But Ahrendt remained calm, fetched a glass of water and whispered a few consoling words to Sebastien. There was a gradual recovery.

"I have to apologise," Sebastien said. "It was a foolish thing to do. The truth is that although Heinrich was a father to me from my birth onwards, he was not actually my father. The prospect of being able to inherit Kurt's estate clouded my judgement and I decided to try and make it look as if Heinrich was my biological father. It was a huge mistake on my part not to realise that you would be thorough in your duties and that trying to fabricate a story in this way would be doomed to failure. I hope you can forgive me."

Vos felt Sebastien's regret was more to do with the failure of his plan than the morality of it.

"You realise it's a criminal offence to pose as a claimant to an inheritance! By rights, I should report this to the police," Ahrendt said, his voice almost harsh. He left the threat hanging in the air.

Sebastien was unable to look the lawyer in the eye. "However, I'm prepared to overlook what you did." Ahrendt continued after a very lengthy silence. "What we need to do now is work out where this leaves you." Vos was surprised by, but not opposed to the lawyer's leniency. A focus on the practical seemed sensible. "So, you're not a blood relative of Kurt's. But can I ask whether you were adopted by Heinrich and if so, is there any paperwork to substantiate that?"

His comments seemed to breathe new life into Sebastien.

"Forgive me. I should have been upfront with you from the start, but I was unsure of the implications of me being Heinrich's adopted son, rather than a blood relative. I will arrange for a copy of the adoption certificate to be forwarded from Cape Town."

So, he hadn't brought it with him as a contingency, Vos thought. There'd now be another delay. He wondered whether Josina would be able to find the document online.

+ + +

He was on another Brussels-bound train. The continual travelling was beginning to tire Vos. Were all these journeys really necessary? Why wasn't he better organised? The private investigation work had always involved plusses and minuses, but he was starting to feel that the minuses were taking over.

The search for someone who might inherit Baumer's worldly goods was becoming tedious. A few steps forward followed by almost as many backwards. Overall progress limited. It was the other factors surrounding Kurt that enabled him to keep his enthusiasm. And he'd just made a big discovery.

It was one of Kurt's hats that had triggered the find. A row of hooks in the hallway of his house held coats and an array of hats. Being something of a hat wearer in the past, Vos hadn't been able to resist the temptation of trying on each of them in turn, standing in front of the full-length hall mirror. One had a small zipped pocket, similar to a hat of his own. He just had to check the pocket. Inside was a business card.

Luc Torfs, Diamond Specialist was printed on one side of the card, together with relevant contact details. On the other side was the figure €100,000 in Kurt's handwriting.

A diamond connection! One that had to be followed up immediately, he'd decided.

His seat in the almost empty carriage was so restful, that, half-asleep, it took him a while to realise his phone really was ringing.

It was his cousin Bernard Antoine who he hadn't spoken to for several months. Their paths had crossed frequently during the Redline case, but since then contact had been intermittent.

"How are you, Harry?" Despite this introductory pleasantry, he could tell the chief inspector was phoning on official business.

"Very well as long as I continue to rest in this very comfortable train seat, Bernard. What's up?"

"We've just rescued a friend of yours. Told us he'd been abducted and held captive in this place we've just raided. Does the name Kirchner mean anything to you?"

"That's amazing! Not quite a friend, but, yes, I certainly know him, though I can't work him out. Claims to be the nephew of a man called Kurt Baumer who died recently. I've got this job down in St Vith, trying to trace any living relatives, which is proving to be a bit more difficult than I'd imagined. But how come Kirchner's turned up on your patch? Do you know who abducted him?"

"It's a long story, but here's the shortened version. We've been keeping an eye on this old metal workshop in Charleroi for a while. All sorts of naughty stuff going on in there and we've been waiting for the right moment to clean up. We took a big broom to it early this morning and Kirchner was one of the people we swept out. Obvious that he wasn't there because he wanted to be. Seems to know very little about the men who'd abducted him and nothing at all about anyone else in the building. When we interviewed him, the story about his uncle and your role came out. Quite a surprise I can tell you. Apparently, the men who were holding him wanted to retrieve some property of theirs, claimed that it had been taken by Baumer and were convinced Kirchner knew where it was. So, they held onto to him for several days trying to sweat the information out of him. Bashed him around a fair bit, but he claims they got it all wrong."

"Did he say what the property was?" Vos asked.

"Diamonds supposedly!"

Vos told Antoine what he knew about the gems.

"So, if diamonds were the ultimate prize, that would explain why they held onto him for so long. We haven't been able to get that much out of Kirchner as he's still in a state of shock from the whole experience."

"Are the abductors in custody?"

"Unfortunately not! We got the rest of the pack, but those two got away. Kirchner gave us a good description of them though. I'll send a copy of it to my oppo in St Vith. What's he called?" Vos gave him Neumann's details. "The two men are brothers, from Moldova, it seems. Have to admit – I'm not exactly sure where that is!"

"Me neither – somewhere near Ukraine, I think. Just our bad luck that they got away. Apart from anything else it would have been good to find out how they knew about the diamonds. Are you still holding Kirchner? I'd like a word with him if that's possible."

"Stay on the line and I'll transfer you to the interview room. Before I go, how's the lovely Katerine? The four of us must get together. It's been far too long."

"She's very well thanks and still putting up with me, thank goodness. You're right, it's been ages. I'll arrange something once I've finished in St Vith."

Kirchner sounded as if all the stuffing had been knocked out of him. He'd be coming back to St Vith as soon as possible, but wouldn't be returning to his rented holiday house, as he no longer felt safe there. Vos decided to leave his questions – and the issue of a DNA test – until they were both back in the town.

At least, having checked with Dr Vermeulen, he knew such a test would be possible. She'd retained some of Kurt's tissue samples from the autopsy. Ahrendt had in fact made a request for this to be done – as a contingency.

Call finished, he noticed an incoming text from Jalloh. He hoped to be free to travel to Kinshasa shortly. Could Harry send him a brief and the necessary documents authorising him to make enquiries regarding the two Baumer brothers. He'd also see what he could find out about the diamonds!

+ + +

Having arrived at Heist station, Vos walked to his house and had a short break before setting off in the Berlingo to Antwerp. He was lucky to find a parking space almost directly outside his son's bar.

It was busy, with staff rushed off their feet. Eddie told his dad that after a worrying dip of a few months, his new chef had managed to lift the quality of the food back to their previous high standards.

After enjoying a late lunch, Vos took his coffee onto the first-floor balcony over-looking the docks with the marina beyond. Once the rush was over, Eddie joined him and asked how things were going on the job. His father complained about slow progress and commented that he seemed to be relying more on others, particularly Josina, to do a lot of the investigative work.

"But that's what you're good at, Dad," Eddie told him. "Getting other people with the time and the right skills to carry out specific tasks and then pulling it all together."

Vos hoped there was something in his son's assessment.

"Thanks, Eddie."

"You mentioned something about a diamond dealer when you were on the phone. Is that's why you're here in Antwerp?"

"Yes, one of the few areas where I've made some progress." Vos mentioned the business card and his plan to go and talk to the dealer Torfs about Kurt Baumer's diamonds. "Of course it's not strictly related to my search for a Baumer heir, but I sort of feel responsible for trying to find out what I can about something that may have been a factor in his death."

"Are you going on your own?" Eddie asked. Vos nodded.

"Well, given what you've told me so far, I'm not sure you should be pursuing this at all. But if you're insistent on going ahead, then you certainly shouldn't be venturing there on your own. I'm pretty well finished here now, so how about I ride shotgun?"

Vos' instinctive reaction was to say no. But he paused to give it some thought. Maybe his son was right. Katerine would have said he was definitely right.

"OK – you're on, Eddie. Thanks."

Not wanting to be stuck the wrong side of a pair of armed guards, Vos had phoned ahead that morning to make an appointment with Torfs. As it was a very pleasant day, they decided to walk into the city and on down towards the Stadspark. The office was just off Appelmansstraat. The guards asked for their appointment details before letting them through.

+ + +

When the buzzer announced a customer arrival in reception, Luc Torfs rose from his seat at the oval mahogany table in the room he called his softening-up space. Standing in front of the mirror, he checked his appearance, twisting a large gold ring on the middle finger of his left hand, this way and that. Figure still trim, although there was perhaps a hint of a double-chin lurking, hair longer than might have been expected in his business, but well-groomed, a well-cut suit, expensive but not too expensive and a sober but not too sober tie. The gold cufflinks which protruded just below the sleeves of his jacket caught the light from the chandelier above.

Although he'd come a long way from the boy selling cheese on the stall in the Borgerhout area of Antwerp and was now able to savour the good things of life, he was still a market trader at heart.

Satisfied with what he saw in the mirror, he flicked a switch on the intercom and asked his receptionist to show the customers in.

Two men took their seats at the table, one older, one younger. They introduced themselves. Father and son as he'd guessed.

"I understand from your phone call, Mr Vos, that you'd like some advice on the valuation process. Do you have the merchandise with you?"

"No, I don't. It's some initial advice I'm after. You see my uncle passed away recently. Very generously, and very unexpectedly, he left me a small number of diamonds. I understand he came here to ask for valuation advice, name of Kurt Baumer from St Vith."

"I don't recall anyone of that name, I'm afraid. But let me just check to make doubly sure." He opened a small drawer in the table and looked momentarily puzzled. "Ah – just a moment – the diary's next door." The intercom was put to use again to summon the diary and an assistant brought in a leather-bound book. "Right, when was it you think he came here?"

"It was the 2nd of last month."

Torfs flicked back through the pages.

"Can't find a reference to that name. Maybe you were mistaken about the date."

"I don't think so. You seemed to go through those pages quite quickly. Could you just check again for me?"

Torfs felt irritated by this request, but looked through the pages again in a slower, more exaggerated fashion.

"Ah, apologies, I must have turned over two pages at once. Yes, Kurt Baumer. I remember him now, reminded me of one of my father's friends. I'm sorry to hear of his death. Let me see now," Torfs said, pausing for a moment. "He brought the diamonds with him and I gave him a provisional valuation there and then. Understandably, he wanted to consider this before making a decision about a sale. I advised him to let me keep them here, securely, in the meantime. Most homes are very insecure. But he chose not to take up my offer. Now, before I could give you details of my initial valuation, I would need ID and proof of your link to Herr Baumer. Alternatively, you could bring the diamonds here and I could re-confirm their provisional value and give you further advice regarding a sale."

"That would be very helpful," Vos said. "But before we get to that stage, there's one thing I'm concerned about. You see, his death occurred the day after his visit here. That evening he had two unexpected visitors who we have reason to believe knew about the diamonds. And my uncle died of a heart attack. Now these events might have been entirely coincidental. But I need to ask the question. Could there have been a breach of confidentiality here? Could someone have overheard your conversation with him and decided there might be easy pickings in St Vith?"

Torfs felt suddenly very uncomfortable. His breathing became laboured and he could feel his cheeks reddening.

"I resent such an implication, Vos. This is a highly professional service. As I've already emphasised, I'm sorry to hear of your uncle's death, but I can assure you that it had absolutely nothing to do with any unauthorised disclosure of information from my office. Given your attitude, I can tell you now that I'm no longer willing to advise you regarding the sale of your diamonds. I'll see you both out."

A very revealing interview, they agreed on the walk back to Eddie's bar. After a light meal, Vos set off on the long drive back to St Vith in the new Berlingo.

Twenty Two

The force's diamond specialists had given Neumann a valuation of around €150k for Baumer's gems and about two thirds of that figure if evidence of provenance was missing. Either way, it was the sort of sum that might well have stirred up the wrong kind of interest. The officer he'd spoken to had given him a mini-lecture on how such valuations were carried out. It was all down to the four 'c's'; weight in carats, how well the diamond had been cut, how close the colour was to being white or colourless and the clarity, in other words, how free it was from inclusions.

When Neumann mentioned Baumer's connections with the DRC, the officer had mentioned the possibility of there being a fifth 'c'. Conflict – or blood – diamonds, mined under the control of rebel groups who used the proceeds from sales to fund their operations. He stressed that there were controls in place to try and prevent conflict diamonds getting into the legitimate market but that some still found their way there.

The specialist officer asked what information there was about how Baumer had acquired the diamonds? Right from the start, it had puzzled Neumann how a quiet-rural-backwater of a man like Baumer had come to be in possession of anything so ritzy as a set of diamonds. It had also worried him, because their presence in the dead man's stomach cast some doubt on the idea that death was solely down to natural causes.

Neumann responded to the question by passing on Vos' information about the deceased's involvement in African artefact dealing. The specialist confirmed he would make enquiries with colleagues in the art division regarding this dealing and the possibility that payment for one or more of these deals could have been made in the form of diamonds. Neumann thanked the officer and made a note to contact Luc Torfs to find out whether he might know more than he'd let on about Baumer and his diamonds.

Neumann recalled that a fellow chief inspector had once described his approach to policing as being akin to painting by numbers. For every crime situation, there was a standard response to be used which could be selected from a list of officially approved remedies. Neither instinct nor gut feeling had ever got much of a look in with Neumann and he had a natural aversion to even bending, let alone breaking the rules.

But it occurred to him that he might be changing and that in part this might be down to his relationship with Dina. And it was now definitely a relationship. The night they'd spent together had been everything he'd hoped for. Earlier in the evening, prior to the pillow talk, there'd been some shop talk and she'd encouraged him to be more flexible and to use his intuition once in a while. Maybe more of that would be needed in relation to Baumer and his diamonds.

Having been concerned that Elias Kirchner's disappearance would be followed sooner or later by the discovery of his body, Neumann was very relieved to hear from Vos that he'd resurfaced. It meant that he could stop the search which had been frustratingly fruitless. However, his boss' attention had now switched from finding the man who'd been abducted to finding the men who'd carried out the abduction and he'd given the investigation high priority. *Can't have villains from the big city coming down here and kidnapping folk. We need to find out who took him, Chief Inspector!*

Naturally this order had come without any additional officer time to assist in pushing the case forward. So the unexpected assistance offered by Harry Vos had been welcome. The man was something of a will o' the wisp and prone to doing his own thing maybe, but Neumann was also aware that he could be useful.

Vos had put him in touch with his cousin Antoine, who happened to be a chief inspector in Charleroi. Neumann had never had anything much to do with the industrial town, either personally or professionally. Liege was about as far from St Vith as he ventured, with the occasional trip to the capital for specialist events.

According to Antoine, the Metal Gang, as they'd been tagged by the press, had been involved in all sorts of illegal activity. As luck would have it, although most of them had been rounded up, the two men that Neumann was now after had escaped the net. Still at least Antoine's team had been able to extract names and descriptions of the two abductors from one of the captured gang members. Azov and Zig Donici originally from Moldova. In addition, Neumann would soon be able to speak to the abducted man himself.

But before that, he wanted another meeting with Vos.

+ + +

They sat opposite each other, arms on the interview room table, notebooks at the ready. Neumann decided against playing the cop / interviewee game. He figured he'd get more out of Vos by being sort of equals – at least for the time the meeting took.

"Feels like progress at last!" Vos said. "It's highly likely that the two Moldovans who kidnapped Kirchner were the same two men who visited Kurt and precipitated his death."

"And no doubt, the same pair broke into Baumer's house, only to be disturbed by you and your wife."

"I think we've already worked out between us how things went that night," Vos said. "The brothers somehow found out that Kurt was in possession of some nice shiny gems. They paid him a visit and asked him to hand them over. He must have pretended to go and fetch the diamonds but then instead of doing a handover, swallowed them instead. A very secure hiding place – if only for a strictly temporary period. When he refused to hand them over or say where they were, that would have really pissed them off. Threats would have followed, maybe bringing on the heart attack. Faced with a dead man, the pair of them panicked and scarpered."

"What I've been wondering," Neumann said, "is whether on their second visit to Baumer's house they could have come across something which tied Kirchner to Baumer."

"I haven't considered that before. But yes, it's possible I could have left papers out on the kitchen table relating to Kirchner's claim to be Kurt's nephew. I had been working on them."

"Well, that's another useful link in the chain," Neumann said. "It surprises me that Kirchner held out against the brothers for as long as he did. I'll be interviewing him right after we've finished here. You mentioned on the phone that Kirchner knew about the diamonds. Are you aware how he found out?"

"Well, from his captors I assume. But it's just occurred to me that he might already have known about them prior to his abduction. I found out that he actually met Kurt, not long before his death as things turned out. It's possible Kurt mentioned them."

"That seems unlikely, unless their relationship became very close very quickly!"

"You're right," Vos said. "You'll need to ask him. Where are the diamonds now, if you don't mind me asking?"

Neumann hesitated for a moment, wondering whether it would be OK to tell the PI.

"In our safe. I tried to persuade the Ice Squad, as they're known, to hold onto them once their own work was completed, but they've learnt from bitter experience not to keep too many of the things in the same place."

Neumann thought about the phone call he'd had from the dealer Torfs and decided it would be a step too far to reveal such information to a civilian. Instead, he asked whether Vos was any closer to finding out how Baumer had acquired the diamonds in the first place.

"No, I'm still none the wiser. However, I do have a contact who'll shortly be making some enquiries for me over in the DRC. I'll let you know how he gets on." Neumann wondered just how extensive Vos' network was.

"But I do know roughly how much they're worth," Vos continued. Neumann couldn't hide his surprise.

"I beg your pardon!"

"I found some information in Baumer's house which triggered a visit to the Antwerp diamond quarter, where I spoke to a dealer Kurt used to get an initial valuation."

"Was his name Luc Torfs, by any chance?" Neumann asked. It was Vos' turn to look surprised.

"How could you possibly know that?"

"I'll tell you in a moment. Please finish your story."

"Right … OK. Well Torfs confirmed he'd provided Kurt with a valuation – a provisional one. But there was something about him that I didn't like. A shiftiness maybe. Anyway, he was surprised to learn about Baumer's death."

"Are you sure?" the policeman interrupted. Vos stared at him.

"Yes, of course I'm sure. Why do you ask?"

"Sorry, I shouldn't have interrupted again. Please continue."

"I told him that Kurt had died the day after he'd been given the valuation and asked him whether there might have been a leak of information about the diamonds from his office. I'm afraid he rather lost it, which just reinforced the idea that his company was guilty of leaking. Unfortunately, I can't prove that's what happened. What we could do with is evidence of a link between Torfs and the Moldovan brothers, but that seems unlikely."

"Thank you for being so open with me. I need to tell you my Torfs story now."

Neumann ran through the details of the phone call he'd had from Torfs, emphasising that the dealer certainly had known about Baumer's death.

"Doesn't add up, does it?" Vos said.

"No, I'll need to speak to him again."

"Just a thought, why don't we share valuations, the one Kurt got from Torfs and the one your specialists provided?"

Neumann hesitated. But when Vos gave him a figure, the chief inspector reciprocated.

"Well, that was a very helpful discussion," Neumann said, "but I'm short of time and need to speak to Kirchner now."

When Vos asked if he could sit in on the interview, Neumann's initial thought was to turn him down. It would be stretching the rules. But then, reflecting on Dina's comments about flexibility, he reconsidered. After all, in relation to the abduction, it wasn't as if Kirchner was a suspect. He was a victim.

Elias Kirchner had bags under his eyes, a large bruise on his forehead and a shocking lack of colour. The hand which held a mug of coffee was unsteady. He managed to rouse himself sufficiently to give them detailed descriptions of the brothers and what they'd done, but then went on to complain that he'd already given the police in Charleroi exactly the same information.

"They didn't give much away, just kept going on and on about the diamonds. But sometimes they spoke Russian in front of me, unaware that having worked for a few years in Moscow, I'm fluent in the language. Despite their Moldovan accents, I was still able to follow most of what they said. They moaned on and on about not being able to find the diamonds in Uncle Kurt's house even after going back there for a further search."

"And it was after that they paid you a visit," Neumann said. "Do you know how they discovered the link between you and Kurt?"

"I'm afraid I've no idea."

"So how did you find out about the diamonds in the first place?" Vos asked, hoping he wasn't treading on Neumann's toes. Kirchner hesitated before replying.

"Kurt told me about them." Vos exchanged glances with Neumann. "I was amazed when he said he'd share the proceeds with me once he sold them."

Vos found it difficult to believe what he'd just heard. Why would Kurt have made such a promise? Might it have been through guilt at having cut Elias and Ursula out of his life? But then again, maybe Kirchner was just making this story up as he went long.

"Does the name Luc Torfs mean anything to you?" Neumann asked

"No! Look how much longer is this going to take? I'm exhausted and just want to get back to my hotel and sleep."

Neumann said he appreciated Kirchner had been through an awful ordeal, thanked him for his help and told him the interview was over.

Vos followed him out of the police station.

"Look, Elias. I'm sorry but I have just one more question. Is this a photo of you?" He held up the photograph that Berthold had sent him.

Kirchner stared at it but didn't say anything. Sweat began to bead on his forehead. Perhaps after his lengthy incarceration, it was all getting too much for him. Finally, he managed a response.

"Yes. It was taken some time ago but I've never seen it before. That's why I was a bit hesitant. Where did you get it?" His voice had suddenly taken on a much sharper tone.

"From your father!"

Elias put his hand to his forehead and staggered to a bench. Vos gave him time to recover.

"So, he's not dead. Why would someone have told me and mother that he was? What kind of twisted and perverted action is that?" Vos felt the response was genuine. Why indeed would anyone have done such a thing? "Where is he? How did you find him?"

Vos explained.

"Look, you'll appreciate I'm at the end of my tether and this news – well it's just so much to take in. I really need to get back to my hotel to rest. After that, if we can finally have our meeting with the lawyer, that would be a great relief."

Vos decided not to make things even worse for Kirchner by raising the issue of a DNA test. Depending on what the much-delayed photo from Mrs Emmerling showed, such a step might not be necessary.

Back at the B&B, Vos tucked into coffee and a slice of Helga's homemade chocolate cake and thought about the photo. Why hadn't it arrived yet?

His phone rang. It was Ruud Okker who'd just arrived in St Vith, was parked by the museum and available to run a professional eye over the dead man's art-dealing correspondence. Vos walked to the museum and Ruud drove them out to Baumer's house.

He got to work straight away, sifting through the carbon copy schedules, the pile of handwritten letters from dealers, some relevant documents on Kurt's laptop and his extensive cache of photographs. An hour later he shuffled the paperwork together, closed the laptop and turned to Vos.

"I have to emphasise that there's a lot of ambiguity in what I've seen and read. But I'd say that your man Kurt was very likely to have been involved in the illegal trading of artefacts. He's clearly very knowledgeable. It's not my field at all but he seems to play the role of an expert fixer, although it's not clear how he makes any money out of it. What I've seen so far has given me a partial picture of what went on. It's a pity there aren't a few more documents to assess to help provide a more rounded view."

"Thanks, Ruud. That's very helpful and more or less confirms what I've been thinking. He was involved in this group called Circle 10. But there's no mention of them in what you've just read. That level of secrecy is another indication that he was involved in some questionable activity."

"You're probably right, Harry."

"Come on then. Enough of this. I'll just phone my police contact to update him and then we can go next door to meet my friend Marc. We'll no doubt be offered a drink or two and then we can go back to town for something to eat."

+ + +

Another late evening in the office trying to clear a mountain of paperwork. The performance returns were the worst. It was always tempting to put them off but Neumann's boss was a stickler for prompt submission.

Still, another date with Dina was a strong motivation to get finished. Given how frequently emergencies and unpaid overtime cropped up for both of them, they'd got into the habit of booking late slots for their get togethers.

Just before leaving, Neumann tried Torfs again, but had to settle for leaving yet another message. Convinced he wasn't going to get anywhere, he phoned a friend in the Antwerp force and asked him to arrange for a local officer to pay the dealer a visit.

Twenty Three

Eyckmans hadn't spent years developing his trading network, without picking up some very influential contacts. Officially, importing art works from the DRC was frowned upon. There were state agencies that could come around asking awkward questions about dodgy imports and unpaid duties.

But in practice it was still possible, with the right degree of influence and creativity, to do business. He'd cultivated a senior police officer over a number of years who'd been particularly helpful and had become a friend. 20:20 vision was not helpful in this world. A more nuanced approach to what was seen and what was overlooked was encouraged. Regulation was light touch. The key players benefited from this creativity – not least the senior officer.

Which was very helpful for Eyckmans, who still had unfilled gaps in his artefact paperwork. With assistance from influential friends, those gaps went unseen.

And Kela Mpenda? Well, his man Skip was now in the country and had assured him that it was only a matter of time before that particular difficulty was removed.

+ + +

Someone must have talked. Jules Fontaine had been brought in by the police for questioning about the raid on the Eyckmans' gallery. She planned to deny everything and wait for them to reveal how much they knew. They'd seen the online video but had no way of linking it to her. Not yet anyway.

After they showed her the CCTV footage of the raid, she answered their questions. She'd been in Leuven that evening. Yes, her boyfriend would confirm that. (The wry thought crossed her mind that she had actually been out once with the 4x4 driver). Could anyone else vouch for her? Yes – their police colleagues who'd been operating a road block near Leuven, looking for drugs. They'd even searched the vehicle. No, she'd never been involved in the theft of art works. And the figures in black picked up by the CCTV? Well, they could have been anyone, couldn't they?

That was when the threats started. The accusations of breaking and entering and theft hadn't surprised her, but she was brought up short by their allegations of money-laundering.

When she asked to see their evidence, they told her it would be presented in due course. In the meantime, she'd be held for further questioning, but was allowed to make a phone call.

Her lawyer, fully briefed prior to the raid, made clear to the police that their right to continue holding a suspect was dependent on the existence of some evidence – and they didn't have any! Fontaine was bailed.

She was torn. Part of her wanted a trial to happen, in order to use it as a platform to expose Eyckmans in public. But she worried about evidence being fabricated, about the activities of some of Kela's associates and above all, about the fate that had befallen Kurt Baumer. If he'd been taken out, might she be next?

+ + +

After the lengthy postponement of his trip, Jalloh had finally made it to Kinshasa. His first priority was business arising from the twinning arrangements between the Matonge areas in the respective capitals of the DRC and Belgium. Having completed this, he drove out, in a friend's car, to the house and animal sanctuary that had been owned by the late Ada Baumer. Harry Vos had asked him to see what he could find out from the staff there about Ada's nephews – the two brothers Kurt and Sebastien Baumer. Harry had told him about evidence he'd found confirming they'd both visited the house a number of times over the years. In addition, Jalloh would attempt to make some discreet enquiries about Kurt's diamonds.

When he pulled up outside the gates to the house and sanctuary, it brought back childhood memories. He'd spent the first twenty-five years of his life in Kinshasa and this was by no means his first visit to the sanctuary. As a boy he'd been mad about animals. There'd been no money to pay for trips to the big reserves but visits to the menagerie, as it had been known back then, had been just about affordable for his father. He'd even got himself an unpaid job there, filling feed bins for the smaller, animals.

Jalloh introduced himself to one of the guides and explained that he'd like a tour followed by a conversation about the previous owner and her family. The paperwork provided by Harry was his way in.

Initially it looked as if things hadn't changed much since the old days. But after an hour spent with his very knowledgeable guide, he was worried. Worried for the future of the whole enterprise. It was often the case, he thought, that projects were held together by the drive of one person with a vision and a lot of energy. And when that individual was taken out of the picture, there was really no guarantee that the show would continue. But he didn't want to wallow in nostalgia and maybe the place had had its day.

It turned out that Jalloh's guide hadn't come across either of the brothers. He was one of a number of new staff. There were still workers who'd known the old lady and might have come across the brothers, but as it happened, none of them were on duty. Perhaps he could come back the following day.

Jalloh said that, unfortunately, he was pushed for time. Was there anybody else he could talk to?

The guide paused, took off his hat and waved it fan-like in front of his face. There was the aunt's lawyer, Mr Seymour, an Englishman, who still had an involvement in the charity that ran the sanctuary. Jalloh put the number he was given into his phone, made the call and waited. It went to voicemail. As his English wasn't good, he decided to respond in French and hope for the best.

There was no point hanging around the sanctuary any longer. The place was beginning to depress him. He could envisage it closing down all too soon.

+ + +

Back at the hotel, his phone rang.

"Mr Jalloh, it's Edgar Seymour returning your call." The voice sounded to him just like one of those posh men from an old black and white British film.

"Everybody calls me J," Jalloh said. "Thank you very much for calling me back. Would it be OK to talk in French? My English is not good." Seymour switched instantly to almost impeccable French, and asked how he could help.

Jalloh broke the news of Kurt's death. Seymour said how sorry he was. Jalloh went on to explain about the lawyer Ahrendt, Harry Vos and his own role.

"What I'm wondering is whether you'd had any recent contact with either Kurt or his brother?"

"Well, I only ever met Kurt once and that was at his aunt's funeral. He seemed pre-occupied about something and anxious to leave. Not an easy man to get to know I'd have said."

"And what about, Sebastien? Just to put you in the picture, he and his wife are currently visiting St Vith, the town in Belgium where Kurt lived. I understand he'll be involved in discussions about a possible inheritance – you know, in relation to Kurt's estate. Do you know Sebastien by any chance?"

"I met him a couple of times at the aunt's house. Sorry – do you know about Ada?" Jalloh said he did. "I'm surprised to hear he's travelled to Kurt's old stomping ground, but then, as you mentioned, it'll be the inheritance he's interested in. From what Ada told me, the two brothers fell out decades ago and had no contact with each other since. Sebastien was definitely persona non grata within the family, except with his aunt who made a habit of welcoming all and sundry."

"My friend Harry told me about Sebastien's mother dying not long after he was born and how he was brought up his step-mother – and Heinrich of course. Is that something you're aware of?"

"I am. Ada Baumer could be quite mischievous and at times would tell me things I had no right to know, like Sebastien having been adopted by Kurt's parents."

"So, it was an adoption, "Jalloh said. "Harry was led to believe that Heinrich was Sebastien's father…"

"Ah! Of course, this all has a bearing on the inheritance," Seymour said, the lawyer in him coming to the fore. "I feel a little uncomfortable talking about these matters without checking one or two details beforehand. Once I've done that, perhaps we could meet face to face to continue our conversation."

"That would be very helpful. But there is one other issue I wanted to raise – which is also sensitive. It concerns some diamonds that were in Kurt's possession?"

"You're right! It is a sensitive area." Jalloh wasn't sure whether that meant the lawyer would or wouldn't open up on the subject. "Before I can talk to you any further on either of these matters,

I need to make some phone calls. The first of these will be to Kurt's lawyer. Could you give me his contact details? Hopefully I'll be done in an hour or so and we can meet up. Can you suggest anywhere convenient?"

Jalloh told him about his involvement in the Matonge twinning and they agreed to meet in the organisation's small office.

+ + +

As it happened, it took Seymour more than two hours to carry out his enquiries. He turned out to be nothing like Jalloh had imagined. A considerably younger man than the voice on the phone had suggested and instead of a trademark crisp white linen suit and a traditional sunhat, he was dressed in jeans, t-shirt and a baseball cap.

They drank mint tea. Seymour asked to see Jalloh's ID and his authorisations from Baumer's lawyer and Harry Vos.

"I managed to speak to Ahrendt and am fully satisfied you are bona fide. So, let's talk first of all about Sebastien's family background. According to Ada, his father, a Mr Ziegler, died a short while before the birth and his mother not long after the birth. Tragic circumstances and all this happened just prior to the start of Second World War hostilities. The Baumer's, who were friends of the Zieglers, stepped in and adopted little Sebastien. But the adoption was kept secret from all but Ada and one or two other close relatives. They wanted to treat Sebastien as if he were their own son."

"Do you happen to know whether the adoption was formalized?" Jalloh asked.

"Unfortunately, I don't. I'm not sure whether even Ada would have known about that."

"Thank you for being so open about all this," Jalloh said. "It really is very helpful."

"Well, in the matter of the inheritance, it's important that these facts are known. Now, you wanted to know about Kurt's diamonds! In the normal course of events, I wouldn't be able to tell you anything about them. But given that unfortunately both Ada and Kurt have passed on, I don't see what harm it can do. It's very interesting to hear that the diamonds survived their journey to Belgium."

"How did Kurt acquire them?" Jalloh asked, uncertain whether he'd receive an answer.

"We have to start the story with Ada. She was given them by a friend for 'safe keeping' as it was described. No papers, no provenance! The friend subsequently disappeared. Nobody turned up to ask for them back so she held on to them. I wasn't entirely convinced by her story but there we are. The next part of the tale I know to be fact, because of my involvement. A few days before her death, well aware she didn't have long to go, Ada asked me to make sure Kurt received the diamonds. She must have been confident he'd attend her funeral. The handover here wasn't to be straightforward, but then she always liked her little games. When I asked her what she expected Kurt to do with them she said … well to use her exact words … *he knows a lot about smuggling, he'll know how to get them home.* And clearly, given that you told me they are now in Belgium, she was right in her assumption."

"Presumably without any paperwork, they'd be more difficult to sell."

"Indeed. But from the little I know about the trade, even with the circumstances I've outlined, it will always be possible to find a buyer. You'd get less for them and you'd probably end up dealing with someone who wasn't entirely reputable. Do you know if he did try to sell them?"

"From what Harry told me, he'd obtained a valuation but hadn't actually arranged a sale."

"Well, that might have been enough to alert the wrong sort of people."

Jalloh had suspected as much himself.

He'd taken a liking to Edgar Seymour. More tea was ordered.

"Could you tell me a little more about Ada?" Jalloh said. "I'm intrigued by what you've said so far."

Seymour told him a few of Ada's tales. He turned out to be a natural raconteur.

"So that's Ada for you, a very unusual woman, involved in all sorts of activities, some of which, I think, were a little questionable. Hugely energetic, not easily put off and about as liberated as you can get."

"Sounds like a real character. One thing Harry has been puzzled about, is why the two brothers had nothing to do with each other. Was that because of something specific that happened?"

"Very much so. Ada told me about it, how Sebastien came here to visit his brother, back in 1960, the year of independence. Kurt was engaged to Miriam, but by the end of the visit she'd switched her allegiance to Sebastien and the two of them ran off together. Ada maintained that Kurt never really recovered from being jilted. It's a sad story, but please ask Harry to keep it to himself. Now, J, if we've completed all the formal business, do you have a little time to tell me about this twinning organisation of yours? I have a number of clients in Matonge. Maybe I could help spread the word."

+ + +

On her return from the Ost Kantonen, Kela, updated her boss on what she'd found out. Fontaine, who'd also been close to Baumer, found it hard to come to terms with what had happened and was particularly concerned about the existence of the diamonds.

"There's another thing I need to mention," Kela said. "I met this guy called Harry Vos who's been hired by Kurt's lawyer to trace any possible heirs. From the sound of it, he's not making much progress but he's poking around too much in other areas for my liking. Wanted to know about Kurt's art 'dealing' as he put it and, his daughter, who's helping him out, asked if I'd known about the diamonds and why Kurt would have had them."

"What exactly did you tell Vos and his daughter?" Fontaine asked, knowing that Kela wasn't a blabbermouth, but worried that she might have inadvertently let something slip that might be harmful to the Circle.

"I made it clear that the news about the diamonds was a complete surprise. I can't imagine what Kurt was doing with them," Kela said. "I was very careful talking about his involvement in the art world and referred to him as a helpful expert advisor. At the funeral, Vos spoke to a couple of other people about Kurt – I was keeping tabs on him. One of them was harmless, knew nothing about us, but the other one was Sophie."

"Shit!"

"Exactly! She was well aware what I was up to and as a result didn't say anything much. But she gave Vos her card and suggested they met up. I'm sure she'll have spoken to him by now. Given her views about us, I'm wondering whether we should get Vos on board and tell him enough so that he doesn't cause us any problems."

"That would be sensible. Do you think he'd come here?" Fontaine asked.

"I'm sure he would. He's only in St Vith temporarily, actually lives in Heist-op-den-Berg which is just down the road from here. And we can always tempt him with some information about Kurt."

"Good. Give me his number, I'll arrange it. And maybe he could do something for us. Just an idea that's beginning to take shape. I've been informed that the trial's going ahead and we could really do with some dirt on Eyckmans. Perhaps we could get Vos to help us out."

"It's certainly worth a try."

"And maybe we can find out more from him about those fucking diamonds. It really worries me that Kurt had them. I mean, was he doing something on the side?"

"I agree, it doesn't look good, especially if the opposition found out about them."

+ + +

Sebastien Baumer had given a copy of his adoption certificate to Harry Vos, who'd forwarded it to his daughter.

As it had been particularly busy at the salon, Josina had been unable to find time to check it out. Her boyfriend had been round for the evening and having just said goodbye, she now had an hour or two to spare. In bed, with a cup of drinking chocolate on the bedside table and her tablet propped up against her knees, she started her research.

The certificate had been issued in Bonn, two months after the death of Sebastien's mother. But Josina could find no trace of it in the official records. Which meant that either they were incomplete – which wouldn't be surprising, given that they were being kept in mid-1939 Germany – or that the certificate was not genuine.

Having doctored his birth certificate, had Sebastien been so desperate to inherit that he'd forged an adoption document?

She examined it in closer detail and then compared it to some of the certificates from the same period on the official site. There were some clear differences. The wording of the questions appeared to be identical, but the layout differed. Not only that, but several of the answers included insufficient detail, a couple of the questions had not been answered at all and the signature was illegible. Surely anyone checking the form at the time would have refused to accept it without more detail.

Her conclusion was that either someone – Heinrich most likely – had cobbled something together back in 1939, sufficient to meet their immediate needs, but had never actually registered the adoption, or that Sebastien himself had arranged for a false document to be prepared, in order to assist his inheritance claim. Either way it was a minefield.

Before attempting to find a way through it, she needed a second opinion. The Active Archivists Association had access to all kinds of expertise and she'd been a member for some time. It took a while but eventually she found a fellow member whose specialisms included German adoption paperwork. Copies of the certificate Sebastien had provided and 1939 examples from the Bonn site were forwarded.

She was reluctant to phone Harry because she knew just how disappointed he'd be to hear that her research might end up pulling the rug out from underneath the more promising of the two possible heirs.

How common was it for estates to be left with no successor, she wondered? There was something very sad about the end of a line. What happened to inheritances in such cases? Did the money go to the state?

And what about Kurt's diamonds – who would get those?

+ + +

The letter had slipped behind a pair of wellington boots left by the front door, just underneath the letterbox. It had probably been there for a day or two.

From the postmark, Vos knew what it was immediately and was all fingers and thumbs trying to open it.

The envelope contained a letter and a photograph of a group of friends who looked to be in their early twenties, on a beach. Not a warm summery beach but a cold windswept one, judging by the big coats and the breakers behind the group. Vos picked out Elias straight away – despite the picture being from way back. Not just his face but something about his stance and the superiority of his gaze.

Vos turned the photo over and read the details written with a fountain pen on the back. *The gang by the Baltic, November 1990.*

The letter, in Frau Emmerling's neat italic script, gave apologies for the delay and went on to list the names of the group of four – which she'd taken from the details on the back of the original photo.

From left to right. Elias, Hans, Lothar and Richard.

Surely that wasn't correct. Elias was second from the right. The man on the far left certainly looked similar, but …

Was it too late to phone her? Would she be asleep? Vos decided he couldn't wait. He had to know.

She sounded pleased to hear from him.

"I'm so glad it arrived, Harry. You say you have a question for me."

He explained.

"No, no. The young man on the far left is definitely Elias. You're correct in thinking he looks a lot like the other young man. That's his close friend Lothar Kramer. We used to joke about the pair of them, similar looks, same school, same college. And, if I'm honest, both with high opinions of themselves."

"So, what does Elias do for a living? He hasn't really said much about himself."

"Oh, he made his money in banking, enough to be able to take a very early retirement. I don't really have any contact with him these days but from what I've heard he spends a lot of his time at those – what do you call them, the isolated places that Buddhists go to?"

"Retreats?"

"Yes. Those. Usually in India or Nepal, cut off from contact with the rest of the world."

Vos couldn't wait to have a conversation with Lothar Kramer.

He tried Berthold Kirchner again and this time managed to get through. It took a while to relate the full story. Vos asked if he'd be able to contact his son to let him know about Kramer's identity theft – and the small matter of Uncle Kurt's estate.

Berthold said it might be difficult. The retreats he spent time at were off grid – all phones and computers surrendered at the gate. But he'd try.

Kurt

It wasn't the first time he'd resorted to smuggling.

The business card hidden in the attic bedroom at Ada's house had led him to the bank. The number on the card, together with his passport ID had given him access to a safety deposit box. The plain white envelope inside the box had contained four sparkling diamonds. They were mesmerising.

Although he implicitly trusted Aunt Ada to look after them, there'd always been a fear that something could go wrong, that somebody might find out about them and they'd disappear.

The big problem had been the complete absence of paperwork. That's why they'd been left in his aunt's care, until a solution emerged for moving them safely back home from the DRC. In the end he'd decided there was only one way to achieve this. He'd have to smuggle them out.

Desperate measures were required. Hidden in the toilet shortly before boarding at Kinshasa airport, he ate the little beauties. An online search had established that, as diamond was not a metallic mineral, the presence of them in his stomach, along with his half-digested breakfast, ought not to set off the airport scanning machine. But there'd been no way of being certain about this. "Do you think I could get a few diamonds, hidden in my stomach, through an airport scanning machine undetected?" wasn't the sort of question he could safely ask anyone. An illicit cigarette in the confines of the toilet calmed his nerves.

Waiting in line, he worried that the sweat drenching his cotton shirt would give him away, until he noticed that almost everyone had been similarly affected by a sudden breakdown of the air-conditioning system in the terminal. Nevertheless, he felt mightily relieved when the scanner didn't react at all to his unusual meal.

During the long flight, his biggest problem was finding enough distractions to stop him thinking about how to retain the contents of his stomach for the duration. The last thing he'd wanted was to end up flushing the diamonds into the void within the restricted area of an aircraft toilet.

The scanner at Brussels airport also stayed mercifully silent. Once through passport and customs controls, he virtually ran to the nearest toilet, where, after some difficult juggling with a plastic bag, he managed to retrieve his valuable internal cargo without mishap.

Only when he stepped out into the cool, early morning air, did he realise quite how much of a toll the act of smuggling had taken on his body and how tense he'd been during the whole of the lengthy journey. It was such a relief to be able to sink into the rear seat of a taxi for the drive to the city centre, completely ignoring occasional questions from his driver.

He was dropped off outside Kempen, his favourite Brussels bar, the first priority being to eat. Coffee, sausages, frites and a small cognac – not his usual breakfast but it did the job nicely. After a short walk, he retrieved his car, which, prior to his flight to Kinshasa, he'd left in a friend's office car park. That way he'd been able to avoid the extortionate airport parking fees.

The Rekord started first time. Within a short while he'd be back home.

+ + +

The longer he left it, the more it felt like the diamonds were burning a hole in his pocket. Weeks had passed since his return from Kinshasa and he'd done nothing about getting them valued and sold.

And then his nephew turned up on the doorstep!

His first instinct was to deny any family link, but curiosity got the better of him. Ursula had died and he'd known nothing about *it. Much to his surprise, the news hit him very hard – and yet he'd been the one who'd cut off all contact. He found himself in tears, apologising to his nephew, a feeling of guilt overwhelming him. Over coffee he began to recover and they exchanged stories about their pasts. He found Elias very congenial company. Having re-established contact, he wanted to do whatever he could to maintain it.*

Money wouldn't wash away his guilt, but it might at least be a form of penance. If he sold the diamonds, he could split the proceeds.

On his nephew's second visit, he took a big risk and told him about the diamonds. Although Elias said he wouldn't be able to accept such a generous gift, Kurt felt that in the end, his nephew would come round.

It was time to get it done.

After a call to one of his art dealer contacts, he had a name, Luc Torfs, a man who would give him a valuation, no questions asked. Torfs proved difficult to get hold of, but eventually an appointment was arranged.

Although it would be a long drive to Antwerp, the thought of going by train had made him nervous. All those people around him. Would they be able to sense he was carrying something very valuable? A Brahms violin concerto on the car radio and a couple of cigarettes helped to keep him calm through the last part of the journey.

As he headed towards the city centre, second thoughts about his plan began to surface. Without paperwork to vouch for the provenance of the diamonds, he'd be dependent on Torfs' discretion, which would, no doubt, come at a price.

But then the diamonds were proving to be an unwanted distraction, their security a source of worry, whereas the cash a sale would generate would be instantly useful – to both himself and his nephew.

His second thoughts drifted away.

It took a while to find somewhere to park close to the office and further delays were involved in getting past the armed guards outside the building and the rather unsavoury-looking man on reception inside.

Torfs was reassuringly well-dressed in a good quality suit, polite, professional and very slightly deferential. Once it had been established that there was no supporting paperwork, the matter wasn't pursued and he seemed more than happy to deal with an unknown customer on the basis of a known mutual contact.

After examining the diamonds carefully, Torfs said he could give a preliminary valuation. Baumer was pleasantly surprised as he'd assumed it would take a few days before such information would be available. But the figure he was given was an unpleasant surprise – much lower than he'd hoped. Torfs emphasised the provisional nature of his valuation, subject to a later, more detailed analysis. Baumer worried that the final figure might be even lower.

When Torfs suggested he might want to take advantage of secure storage for the diamonds, until a sale could be arranged, Baumer was tempted. But with his concerns about the valuation, he felt it would be unwise to hand them over there and then, particularly as he knew very little about the dealer. Despite his worries about security, he needed a little more time to make a decision. And maybe he'd get a second opinion.

Walking back to his car he felt strange. The diamonds fascinated and worried him in equal measure. Knowing what they were worth, even though it was less than expected, he felt more vulnerable and worried irrationally again that something about his facial expression or his body language might give away the fact that he was carrying something very valuable.

Had it been foolish of him to turn down the offer of safe storage?

No, his caution had been understandable. He hadn't wanted to rush into anything. And, yes, he'd definitely get a second valuation.

After all, the more he could get for them, the more he and his nephew would benefit.

And on cooler reflection, on the drive home, he decided there was really no logical reason for him to feel vulnerable.

Twenty Four

Luka Rainer had not expected the call from Leo Rodenbach. But his business proposal made a lot of sense. At the end of their discussion, Rodenbach said he had another proposal – which was to do with Harry Vos. He reckoned the PI needed some protection from the ex-con who still bore a grudge. The verbal warning given to Webers in the apartment near the Atomium had been fine as far as it went. But Rodenbach's assessment was that there was a need for more. How about they teamed up to provide a surveillance service? Rainer had grown to like Vos and needed no convincing to say yes. And Rodenbach would pay him a retainer to keep watch – so it was all good.

Rainer arranged for a tracker to be fitted to Webers' Citroen. It wasn't the first time he'd used the technology, which enabled him to follow a vehicle's movements via alerts from an app on his phone. At times when he was too busy with other things, or asleep, he delegated the monitoring task to a couple of pals who owed him favours. To date, it appeared that Webers hadn't ventured outside Brussels. This concerned Rainer who worried that the man might have a second vehicle which he used for unofficial trips. But as he would have no reason to suppose the Citroen was being tracked in the first place – why would he be so cautious? His two pals had been asked to carry out the odd site visit to Webers' apartment to check for other vehicles but nothing was spotted.

Rainer had just made a delivery in Hasselt, when his phone beeped. An alert from the tracker app. The map showed a flashing icon moving from Brussels, towards Mechelen. It might be an innocent journey on Webers' part. Time would tell.

Realising he was only around 60 kilometres from Heist, Rainer thought it would be worthwhile heading in that direction, just as a precaution. If Webers was going to be breaching his parole licence conditions by visiting Vos' house, then Rainer wanted to be able to get there in time to capture the event on camera.

As far as he knew, Harry and his wife were both away. To be on the safe side he gave Vos a ring to check his whereabouts, only to learn that the PI was in fact heading home and would be in Heist within about an hour. Rainer felt he had to come clean and explain about the monitoring arrangements, the Citroen tracker and Webers' movements. Vos sounded concerned.

Held up for a while by roadworks near Aarschot, Rainer watched the icon getting closer to Heist. So, his hunch looked to be right. From Aarschot, he made good time, reached Vos' house and parked up within about 10 metres of the Citroen. Webers had to be in the house. Rainer would wait for him to emerge and film the moment on his phone. As Webers had never met him or his car, there was no danger of being clocked.

He liked the feeling of knowing quite a lot about the man he was tracking, whilst Webers knew absolutely nothing about him.

Once he had the man on film, there'd be an anonymous call to the probation service in Brussels, to let them know one of their clients had breached his licence conditions. A memory stick containing the video would be sent to them, anonymously, by express mail.

+ + +

Given his status as a parolee, Webers had to be careful not to get caught in the wrong place at the wrong time.

He should really have left well alone. But despite all the warning lights and alarm bells, he couldn't resist the urge to exact some form of revenge against the PI.

For a man with his skills, breaking into Vos' house without leaving a trace was easy. A friend had checked in advance and confirmed that the property was empty. Once inside, he wandered from room to room, taking care not to disturb the contents. The paintings in the living room surprised him, more modern than he'd have expected. And there were lots of family photographs, scattered across tables and the tops of bookcases throughout the house. The dog hairs were another surprise and for a moment or two he wondered whether their owner might be somewhere loose on the premises. But a quick search proved otherwise.

Mounting the stairs, he reached the top, only to feel dizzy and be forced to sit down on the landing. It wasn't the first time he'd been affected in this way. After a few minutes his head cleared sufficiently for him to be able to get up and move into the bathroom. He removed the cistern lid, inserted a shrink-wrapped package inside and replaced the lid.

Satisfied with his handiwork, a warm glow came over him and, despite the earlier dizziness, he decided to indulge. The armchair in the front bedroom looked very comfortable. He sat down carefully, pulled a hipflask from his jacket pocket, unscrewed the top and took a sip. The single malt tasted good. He held it in his mouth for a while to savour the taste, before swallowing and feeling the liquid coursing through his body. Two more sips and the cap was replaced. Rising from the chair, he checked to make sure he'd left no lasting impression on the seat.

It was time to leave. Once he'd made his getaway, there'd be the pleasure of phoning the police, posing as a concerned citizen, with a suggestion that they should pay a visit to the house.

+ + +

Vos had been reluctant to drive all the way from St Vith to Antwerp, particularly as his knee would probably play up, but there were problems with the trains and the lure of hard information about Kurt Baumer and his art dealing had proved too strong to resist.

The call from Rainer had come out of the blue.

On learning that the taxi driver and Rodenbach had teamed up to keep tabs on Webers' movements, he'd felt such gratitude. Perhaps it had been foolish to think that a single warning visit would be sufficient to deter a man like Webers. Thank goodness Katerine was still working away from home.

The news really worried Vos. Perhaps he'd just been lucky that this sort of thing hadn't happened before. After all he'd made a number of enemies during the course of his investigations and had tangled with some nasty pieces of work – like Webers! It really wasn't sensible to put himself – and more to the point Katerine – at risk in this way.

Vos kept his speed within the limit. There was no sense in risking being stopped by the police and missing out on the chance to catch Webers red-handed.

There was so much to think about.

Like the chain of events following Josina's discovery that Sebastien's adoption certificate was likely to be invalid. Ahrendt had made further enquiries which had confirmed this view. The news had dashed Vos' own hopes that Sebastien could be confirmed as the inheritor of his brother's estate. But his own disappointment was as nothing compared with Sebastien's reaction. There'd been absolutely no doubting the genuineness of his response. He hadn't forged the certificate. It must have been drawn up at the time of his adoption but never submitted for approval. Sebastien had been completely distraught.

Miriam had accused Vos of waging a vendetta against her husband. She claimed that as he seemed to be going to any lengths to deprive Sebastien of what was rightfully his, he must be secretly working for the nephew.

Vos felt awful and began to wish he'd never taken on the heir-hunter job. It didn't feel anything like either of his two previous big investigations. There'd been a structure to those – maybe not from the start, but certainly once he'd got his head round what was going on.

But Vos felt he'd got precisely nowhere with this one. It had been like wading through treacle. Every time it looked like there might be a breakthrough, something happened to thwart him. Between them, he and Josina had demolished the claims made by both Sebastien and the man who'd claimed to be Elias Kirchner.

Still, that's what he'd been paid to do. Look for relatives and check they were who they claimed to be.

A meeting had been arranged with the unsuspecting Lothar Kramer aka Elias Kirchner, with two items on the agenda…the abduction…and the question of his true identity. Chief Inspector Neumann had been briefed.

Rainer was on the phone again.

"I'm parked near your house. Webers' car is just up the street. He must be still inside. How near are you?"

"I've almost reached Heist. Hopefully I'll be there before Webers does a runner."

+ + +

Having parked up, Vos slid out of his own vehicle and into the taxi.

"Still there, I take it?"

"Yes – odd really. Can't imagine what he's doing, unless he's fallen asleep in front of your telly!"

"That could be the case. The stuff that's on this time of day is enough to send most people to sleep. I'll go and have a look."

"Not on your own, you won't! I'm coming with you."

"I don't want to drag you any further into this mess."

"No arguments. We're both going in."

"Well, if you're sure. Have to say I'm really impressed with the service you and Leo have provided for me. But isn't it going to cost me a packet?"

"It's free, Harry, courtesy of the two of us."

It felt very strange trying to creep as quietly as possible into his own house. They stood in the hallway listening. Not a sound.

"Are you absolutely sure he came in here, Luka?" Vos whispered.

"No! But given his car's parked right outside I thought it was a fair assumption."

Vos walked down the hallway and noticed the lower part of a pair of legs sticking out across the kitchen doorway.

"What the fuck…!"

A loud groan.

Webers was sprawled on the kitchen floor, his face twisted in pain.

"Get me an ambulance…please."

"What on earth's happened to you?" Vos asked.

"Had a dizzy spell and fell down your fucking stairs, didn't I. Must have busted my hip. Dragged myself this far to try and get to my phone on the table there, to call for help. Do us a favour, will you, and call them for me?"

Vos was very, very tempted to make the man suffer for a bit longer. All the time he'd spent worrying what his enemy might do. And now he'd broken into his house and … and what? He'd no idea what Webers had been up to – apart from falling downstairs.

But Rainer was already on his phone, making the call.

"Shouldn't be long," he said. "Harry – get him a pillow, will you, and a blanket. Don't want him catching cold."

Vos couldn't understand what Rainer was up to. His own instinct was to ignore the man, let him stew. Pocketing Webers' phone – didn't want the man making any sneaky calls for back-up – he went upstairs to find the necessary. Rainer followed.

"Harry, you're getting this all wrong!"

"*I'm* getting it wrong?"

"Yes – you! Think about it. What's been your aim all along? To get him off your back. Only what you've done so far hasn't got you very far. So, we need a different approach."

"And what might that be?" Vos asked, wondering where this particular conversation might be going.

"Right now, he's in your hands and needs something from you – your help. If you deny him that, it'll just feed his resentment and the desire for revenge. Provide it and he'll be in your debt. I reckon even a man like him will cut you some slack as a result and back off."

Vos hadn't thought about it this way, maybe because his judgement had been clouded by a wish to make Webers suffer.

"You could be right. Here, take this pillow while I find a spare blanket."

Webers seemed grateful for the attention.

"What were you doing here? Why did you break in to my house?"

"I was just going to cause some damage … when it came to the crunch though …Jesus this hurts … it all seemed a bit pointless."

"You mean once you'd finished damaging yourself on the stairs, you were in no fit state to damage anything else." Webers didn't reply.

Vos left the kitchen, phone in hand. Rainer followed him – again.

"What are you up to now, Harry?"

"Calling the police of course. I don't want the bastard getting to hospital and slipping through the net."

"You haven't been listening, have you? Think about it! If you don't report this to the police, he'll be even more in your debt, plus you'll have something over him, with me as a witness. It's not worth pursuing. They'd get him on breaking and entering but nothing else. He'd be back inside for a while for breaching the terms of his release, but he'd be out before you know it – seething!"

For the second time, Vos realised his taxi driver was making a lot of sense.

Rainer had a conversation with Webers and explained the plan. They wouldn't bring the police in. Everyone would draw a line under what had happened and there'd be no reprisals.

Webers nodded in agreement, his face screwed up in pain.

Twenty Five

The timing was lucky. A minute earlier, Kela had been glued to her phone and wouldn't have seen him until it was too late. But she caught a glimpse of Skip, half-hidden, near the entrance to her hotel, staring at *his* phone and was able to melt back into the crowd unnoticed.

There was only one reason for his presence. He'd put two and two together and worked out that she wasn't really one of them.

Now he'd be out to get rid of her.

As it wouldn't be safe to return to the hotel, she'd have to make do with what was already in her backpack.

With her cover blown, everything else would have to be put on hold.

But she'd need to warn Fontaine.

+ + +

Vos, his mind drifting, watched the fields flashing by on the short train journey from Heist to Antwerp.

Josina had told him about Suzanne, the daughter of Sebastien and Miriam. Out of curiosity, he checked her website. She was a choreographer and before that, an accomplished dancer. The site was full of references to career highlights, with performances in different parts of the world. One of the press articles on the site referred to her age, which set Vos' mind whirring. Something

Jalloh had told him about the two Baumer brothers. He rang the contact number on the site and left a short message.

Two incoming calls in quick succession.

Katerine telling him how glad she was to get his message that the Webers' threat had been resolved – fingers crossed – and how lucky he was to have help from someone as sensible as Rainer. And the other good news was that the work in Luxembourg was nearly finished and she'd be back home within a few days.

Vos' second call was from Neumann. Given that he been unable to make contact with Luc Torfs by phone, he'd arranged for an Antwerp-based chief inspector to pay the dealer a visit. Torfs had been adamant. He'd never made a phone call to Neumann to ask about Baumer and his diamonds and had no idea how anyone else would have been able to access his dealer registration number. Neumann said Antwerp would be investigating further.

Vos felt Torfs was trying to muddy the waters and the news served only to reinforce his mistrust of the dealer.

Jules Fontaine met him at Antwerp station and they walked to Café Philosophie nearby. She told him that, unfortunately, Kela wouldn't be able to join them. When he asked why, she hesitated. But then the full story came out of how Kela had managed to infiltrate a Kinshasa-based, art-dealing gang, with the aim of uncovering their supply routes and locating stolen artefacts. Unfortunately, the gang leader must have finally worked out what she was up to and was in Antwerp on her trail. She was about to make herself scarce.

Vos was intrigued. This story put a very different slant on the activities of Circle 10.

"I'm sorry to hear about Kela," Vos said. "Is there anything I can do to help?"

"That's a nice offer, but given the potential risks, it wouldn't be wise to get involved. But there is another way you may be able to help us which is why I invited you here. Let's talk about it in the café."

What did she have in mind, Vos wondered, and would he really want to take on anything else?

Seated at a café table, he suddenly felt very hungry. Only a coffee for breakfast and with all the Webers drama, he'd barely eaten a thing the previous day. Luckily there were plenty of dishes on the menu that tempted him and he went for the charcuterie platter and a glass of house red. Fontaine who was on first name terms with the staff and seemed very much at home, opted for a salad and a mineral water.

"Let me tell you about Circle 10 first of all and then I'll explain how you might be able to help," Fontaine said. "No doubt Sophie told you something about us. If that was the case can I ask you to forget what she said. Sophie is not aware of what we really do. What brought us together, several years ago, was concern about the illegal trade in African artworks and artefacts." This was news to Vos, the complete opposite of what he'd suspected. "There's an agency which monitors illegal trade in cultural objects. Their funding has been repeatedly cut, which has led to a shortage of people on the ground. We've developed this unofficial arrangement with them. We fill some of the gaps and provide expertise – using people like Kela and Kurt. Our main objective is to stop artefacts leaving the DRC in the first place. But if our attempts at interception are unsuccessful, then, where possible, we try to track the objects, locate them in their new Belgian homes and switch our attention to getting them repatriated, one way or another. We also lobby to get DRC artefacts here in our museums, returned home."

Vos was struggling to take it all in. There'd been a number of factors which had helped form his view that Circle 10 were the baddies of the story, rather than the goodies of Fontaine's portrayal. Firstly, the contents of Kurt's documents which pointed in the direction of underhand activity. Secondly, Kela's attempts to keep him away from any discussion about Circle 10's activities, like the way she'd tried to prevent him speaking to Sophie. Then there was Sophie herself, who had indicated that Kurt had been involved in suspect trading. And finally, there was the detail Jalloh had unearthed about Kurt and his smuggled diamonds which smacked of money-laundering connections.

Yet Fontaine was now painting a completely different picture. When he told her about his suspicions that Circle 10 was involved in illegal movement of artefacts, her almost permanent look of concern disappeared momentarily and she smiled. On the contrary, she told him, their job was all about making life difficult for the real smugglers.

"So, what you do must be pretty high risk!" he said.

"You're right. And we do push it to the limit…and beyond. Some of what we do is illegal. I'll tell you about an example of that in a moment. But we think it's justifiable. We don't say anything to the agency about these activities because if they were aware, they'd refuse to continue working with us. One or two of them might have guessed, but kept it to themselves – luckily for us. Our interventions can put us in danger. Because the illegal trade in artefacts is highly profitable, the smugglers are well defended and have a long reach. That's why I'm worried for Kela. And Kurt may have paid a very high price for his involvement. You see he had an almost unrivalled knowledge of Congolese artefacts and their origins. And, he was able to track down a lot of the pieces taken from the DRC to their new homes in this country. So, he could have become a target for one or other of the smuggler networks."

"I presume Kela's told you about the two men who visited his house on the night of his death?" Vos said. Fontaine nodded. "And about the diamonds?" Another nod. "Well, we now know they were definitely after the diamonds. Maybe they were linked to one of the smuggler networks, found out about them and thought there'd be easy pickings."

Fontaine ordered coffee.

"Those diamonds really worry me," she said, shifting her chair away from the table so that she could stretch her long legs. "It's so unlike Kurt to be involved in anything like that. Do you know how he got them? Was it as payment for something? If so, that could open up a real can of worms."

"Well, it's still something of a mystery. A colleague of mine managed to find out that Kurt inherited them from a recently-deceased aunt who lived in the DRC. At the funeral, he was informed by her lawyer that the diamonds were being held for him in a local bank. Given that his aunt had no paperwork for them, Kurt must have smuggled them back here. Then there's the question of exactly how his aunt got hold of them in the first place."

"That's a murky story but not quite as bad as I'd feared," Fontaine said. "Although, given that they originated in the DRC there's a risk of them being blood diamonds which would be a real worry. But at least it looks like Kurt didn't acquire them as a form of payment."

Vos said it was a surprise she'd revealed so much information about Circle 10 when she knew so little about him.

Fonataine's face relaxed a little.

"Ah! That's down to Kela. I've learnt over time that she's an excellent judge of character. You got the thumbs up from her."

"That's good to know."

"Now, as I mentioned earlier, there's something else I want to talk about," Fontaine said in mock hushed tones. "I've got a job for you. Let me tell you about a man called Claus Eyckmans."

+ + +

Vos stopped for a good hour at a service station on the drive back to St Vith. Time for a snooze in the car and then something to eat. His reluctance to take on another job had evaporated once Fontaine told him what it was. He'd be doing it for the good guys and in a small way, continuing Kurt's work.

When a call came through, he didn't immediately recognize the name Suzanne. But the South African accent helped him to make the mental link. He hadn't really expected her to call back.

"This better not be some sort of scam!" she said. "Talk about cryptic. I've really no idea what you're after Mr Vos."

"Please, call me Harry. I didn't want to tell the answering machine too much. Let me explain."

He told her who he was and about Kurt and his search for relatives. When he started to talk about her parents, she cut him off.

"I know all about what's just happened and about Dad not being well. Mum phoned me. Isn't there someone around claiming to be a nephew?"

"Unfortunately, that's all it turned out to be – a claim. He's a fraudster."

"So, you're left with nobody on your list!"

"Exactly – hence my call to you."

"Why me?"

Vos took a deep breath. Still, what was the worst that could happen? She'd never talk to him again. On the other hand…if he was right…

"I've been putting two and two together and hoping I make four," he said. "But I apologise profusely in advance if my arithmetic turns out to be completely wrong. I've been wondering if there was any likelihood that your father was Kurt."

"What!"

"Please, bear with me. I take it you know about Kurt and your mother…being engaged." Vos hoped to goodness that she did.

"Of course."

"Well given your date of birth, which I managed to find on a website, I wondered whether your mother might already have been pregnant with you when she left Kurt."

The phone went dead – then rang again immediately. It was Neumann telling him that their meeting with Elias Kirchner had been pushed back an hour.

A relief for Vos as it would give him time to put his feet up for a short while, once he got back to St Vith.

But he feared he might not hear again from Suzanne.

+ + +

They were in one of the interview rooms at the police station.

The man claiming to be Kirchner was annoyed. Why was there another meeting involving the police, when he should have been discussing the inheritance with Ahrendt?

Vos told him that all would shortly become clear.

"The thing is, we have a bit of a problem," he continued. Kirchner groaned. "Take a look at this photograph, which Mrs Emmerling kindly sent to me. No doubt you remember her."

Kirchner fiddled with his panama hat, twisting it this way and that, before placing it on the table. He blinked rapidly.

"How do you know about her?" Brusque almost rude.

"She was named as a witness on your parents' marriage certificate. Remember, you gave me a copy of it. I had a little chat with her and she sent me this group photo." Vos put it on the table in front of Kirchner.

"So, what's the purpose of showing me this?"

"Can you name the group members. I mean, it was taken a long time ago, but…".

Kirchner stared at the photo.

"They're not names I remember. We were students together.

Once that phase of our lives was over, we went our separate ways. I fail to see what this has got to do with either the inheritance or the kidnapping, which is what we're supposed to be focusing on here!"

"Can you at least point out which one of these young men is Elias?" Vos asked, exchanging a glance with Neumann.

"That's a very strange way of phrasing the question," Kirchner said. He pointed to the man who was second from the right.

"Interesting, because Mrs Emmerling told me that Elias is the man on the far left and that the man second from the right is you...Lothar."

For a moment it looked as if he was going to challenge Vos, to try and maintain the deception. But then his face crumpled, his shoulders slumped and as his head hit the table, it crushed the panama.

+ + +

Hunched over his computer, the screen and an angle-poise his only sources of light, Neumann was working late again.

Lothar Kramer had signed a confession. Given that he hadn't even managed to get as far as a meeting with the lawyer and that he'd suffered as a victim of the kidnappers, Neumann suspected he'd probably get off with probation.

Kramer hadn't been able to recall anything new about his abductors. In the end, when he'd departed, a thoroughly crushed man, Neumann had almost felt sorry for him.

Now there was paperwork to complete to expedite the charge against Kramer and those against the serial arsonist who had just been captured. His coffee had gone cold and he promised himself a top-up once he'd completed the first of the A17 forms.

It turned out that Dina Vermeulen didn't want to become a sailor, mainly because she'd never learned to swim. But she was keen to meet up with him once he'd reached Harlingen and stay on the boat for a night or two, as long as it was in the safe haven of the marina.

Neumann's brief moment of holiday day-dreaming was interrupted by a noise coming from the front of the building. He ignored the interruption and it went quiet. But a minute or two later there was a much louder sound. He decided to investigate and take the opportunity to refill his mug.

The night-duty officer was nowhere to be seen. Neumann suspected he'd gone outside for a smoke – which was of course strictly against regulations. As he was about to open the front door to take a look, the sound of hushed voices caught his attention. They were coming from an unlit corridor, where the lockers and the secure storage were located.

As the lightswitch at his end of the corridor didn't appear to work, he grabbed a torch from reception and made his way down towards the lockers. A hooded man suddenly leapt out from behind a filing cabinet, hurtled towards him and slammed him to one side. His shoulder took the full impact of the collision. A second man loomed out of the darkness. Despite the pain in his arm and shoulder, Neumann threw himself at the man. Both of them crashed to the floor.

Twenty Six

Suzanne had been very wary of the man on the phone who'd claimed to be a private investigator. His whole approach had the feel of a scam. But, ironically it was his boldness that had convinced her he might be genuine. And what he'd said about her parentage.

There'd been no attempt to raise such a delicate matter with any degree of sensitivity. He'd just come straight to the point. No shrinking violet, Suzanne had appreciated his boldness. Delicacy was not something people associated her with. Her reputation within the dance world was of someone who knew what she wanted and would push very hard to get it.

Since his call, she'd thought of little else, other than Kurt, her mother and Great Aunt Ada.

She'd visited Ada in Kinshasa a few times, liked and respected her. They had a certain unorthodoxy in common and both spoke their minds. The visit she could never forget about had happened nearly forty years ago. She'd been working in the animal sanctuary – a holiday job. On the last night of her stay, there was a third person at the dinner table. Her uncle Kurt. The only time she ever met him.

It wasn't as if there was any spark between them. Far from it. He was very dry and seemed full of resentment, although it hadn't been directed at her. But there was a strong facial resemblance. Not between him and her father but between him and her. She'd always thought it a little strange that she and her father looked so different. But then genetics sometimes worked that way.

Her aunt had spoken to her during the taxi ride to the airport the following morning. Of course, she'd set up the dinner with Kurt to see what resulted. For the first time in years, he'd spoken to Ada about his relationship with Miriam, how he thought they'd been made for each other, how his life had been shattered by the actions of his brother.

In the taxi, Ada had looked her straight in the face and whispered *from what he told me, you might be his daughter.*

On the flight home, she'd vowed raise the delicate matter with her mother. But somehow, it was never the right time and then she'd been away for months on end, travelling and dancing. And after that…well, she wasn't sure her parents would be able to handle questions about her paternity. So, she'd made herself forget about it.

But now, there was a reason to pursue it, the possibility that she might turn out to be Kurt's heir. At the age of nearly sixty she had no anxieties about who her biological father might have been. But she did have curiosity…and an interest in the money. From what her mother had said over the phone, Kurt's estate was very modest. But still … It was probably worth the cost of a return air fare to find out.

There was just about time to get there and back before the rehearsals for her new interpretation of *West Side Story* started in earnest.

Winston drove her to the airport. She'd wanted him to make the journey as well but, being in the middle of a particularly complex investigation, that hadn't been practical. His editor had been firmly against him taking leave.

+ + +

As a frequent flyer, she didn't feel unduly tired by the long flight and decided to drive straightaway from Brussels to the small town in the south east of the country where Kurt had lived and her parents were staying. She phoned her mother and broke the news of her arrival in the country, explaining that it was concern for her father's health that had motivated the journey.

She'd always got on better with Sebastien than with her mother – apart from during her stroppy teenage years when she'd 'hated' them both. But she felt they lacked principles and had been too cavalier in their approach to life. The way they'd jointly deceived Kurt was the prime example.

Her father would be devastated that the inheritance had slipped from his grasp. Over his lifetime, he'd been good at making money but even better at spending it. Which was the reason he was still working.

She needed only a brief stop on the outskirts of Liege for a coffee, a sandwich and a cigarette.

The final part of the journey seemed to be over in no time.

At the hotel reception, she was informed that her parents were out, but expected back within half an hour. An older man was evidently already in the queue waiting to see them.

He introduced himself as Harry Vos.

"I recognize you from photos on your website. Apologies for being so direct on the phone. I'm surprised, but very glad, you decided to make the trip."

They had a coffee together. She told him her story. He asked a few questions.

Although the conversation wasn't difficult, it felt very strange to him having a discussion about proof of paternity with a woman he'd only just met. He explained that a Dr Vermeulen, who'd carried out the autopsy on her uncle, still had some samples of his DNA which could be used for subsequent comparison with her own. Suzanne asked whether there might be any ethical problems involved, given Kurt was no longer with them.

"You'd need to ask the doctor," he said. "But I don't suppose it would be the first time this kind of request has been made."

Vos wondered how much more Sebastien would be able to take. Not a brother, therefore not the inheritor of Kurt's estate – and now, from what Suzanne had told him, maybe not even a father. It would be enough to drive a fit man crazy, let alone a man already struggling with his health.

When Miriam and Sebastien returned to the hotel, Vos said he'd leave the family to have a proper reunion, would spend some time in The Schloss and return later if someone could let him know when they were ready. The bar was conveniently adjacent and he felt a single glass of beer would be in order, enough to take the edge off his thirst without dulling his senses.

All too soon there was an empty glass in front of him. It had disappeared without him really noticing. Instead, the question of whether he'd been foolish to take on an additional job had dominated his thoughts. But then Jules Fontaine had been very persuasive and he'd wanted to do it for Kurt, who, much to his relief, had turned out to be one of the good guys after all.

He decided not to tell anyone what he'd be up to. The fewer people who knew, the better. There'd be the advantage of being completely unknown in the Brussels art world, set against the disadvantage of total ignorance of what went on there. He stretched back in his seat. The Schloss was a pleasant place to spend time, the staff friendly without being nosy and there was neither TV nor canned music to interrupt his train of thought.

All too soon however, he caught sight of Suzanne entering the bar. His R and R time was over. She collapsed into the chair opposite him. It hadn't gone well with her parents. There'd been a blazing row about the things that had never been said and no opportunity to move on to talk about practicalities.

"Well, let's see if I can help break the log-jam," he said,

hoping it didn't sound too blunt. He settled his bill and with rain beginning to fall, they walked quickly to the hotel.

Miriam was standing in the foyer, in tears.

"He's gone!" she cried out, grasping her daughter's arm.

"What do you mean gone, Mother?"

"What do you think I mean! Gone back home, said he couldn't take any more of it. Your decision to make a claim on Kurt's estate was the last straw."

"So why didn't you go with him?"

"I can't take any more of it either. I'm staying here. Apart from anything else, you'll need some help with your claim and I want to be here for you."

"Say what you mean, Mother. You're after a share of the money!"

Vos stood open-mouthed. He hadn't expected such a dreadful turn of events.

+ + +

Although Chief Inspector Neumann should have taken sick leave, he'd insisted on continuing to work with his arm in a sling. With too many other staff already off sick, his boss had readily agreed.

Although Neumann felt the theft of the diamonds had been a personal failure, the boss had reassured him it wasn't. On the contrary, his bravery had resulted in the capture of Zig Donici. They'd catch up with his brother Azov and the diamonds sooner or later. And even if they didn't – their owner wouldn't be missing them.

Neumann had spent a long time interrogating Zig. At the start he'd refused to say anything, confident his brother would soon be back to spring him. As time went on though, with no sign of Azov's return, he began to talk. Bits and pieces to start with, but gradually the floodgates opened. It wasn't the first time his older brother had abandoned him. He should have guessed it would happen again ...

Theirs had been a long journey: from the back streets of Chisinau to Antwerp's diamond quarter. But the brothers seemed to have remained hustlers at heart. They'd started trading in gems in the early nineties, whilst still in Moldova, soon after political change had swept through Eastern Europe. But they'd always wanted to fish in a bigger pond and it didn't get any bigger than Antwerp – the de-facto diamond capital of the world.

An opportunity had arisen quite by chance in 2010. Luc Torfs had been out of his depth on a questionable trading mission to Moscow. The brothers had happened to be on the scene, involved in a little trading of their own and had saved him from a brutal beating. He'd rewarded them with a route into Belgium.

Except things hadn't developed as they'd hoped. Torfs used the brothers as little more than lackeys and, where necessary, heavies. There were frequent promises of more, but nothing of serious money-making interest had ever materialised.

Which is why, having got to know by chance about the Baumer diamonds, they'd been so keen to get their hands on them. Azov had picked up enough of the discussion between Torfs and Baumer in the dealer's office to know that this was the chance they'd been waiting for. The gems had no paperwork and their owner was an old, frail man who, very conveniently, lived by himself. It hadn't been difficult to find his address in Torfs' records.

After Azov's initial recce of Baumer's house, parked up on his own in the stolen Datsun, the pair of them had arrived late at night in the same car. The back door to the property had provided very little resistance. They'd shaken Baumer awake in his armchair and made it clear that as long as he handed over the diamonds, there'd be no harm done. Looking petrified, he'd asked to go to the toilet. They checked him for a phone, followed him upstairs and stood guard outside the bathroom door.

Back downstairs, Baumer had sat firmly back in his armchair and announced he'd changed his mind and they weren't going to get their thieving hands on the diamonds. At this point, Zig confessed he'd lost it, grabbed a kitchen knife and started waving it around under Baumer's nose, which had produced an immediate response from the old man. He'd collapsed and lost consciousness. Zig was at pains to point out he hadn't actually laid a finger – or a knife blade – on Baumer.

Azov had checked for a pulse. There wasn't one. Theft was not a new experience to them. The prospect of being charged with murder certainly was. They'd panicked and fled the property. In the car on the way back to Antwerp they'd reconsidered. As far as they were aware, nobody had seen them at the house. Surely, given Baumer's age, a heart attack wouldn't be seen as unusual. All they'd need to do was wait a short while for the flurry of activity after his death to subside and then they could return to the house and carry out a thorough search.

Their second visit, in the Peugeot, had started well. There were some papers on the kitchen table about a nephew, the person who'd inherit no doubt. They'd made a note of his name and address and then started to search Baumer's place.

But then the seemingly empty house next door had turned out not to be – and they'd fled for a second time.

On their third visit to the St Vith area, in the Toyota, they'd paid the nephew a visit. He'd claimed to know nothing about the diamonds, so they'd carted him off to Charleroi to sweat the information out of him.

Eventually he'd admitted his uncle had told him about the diamonds. But he'd absolutely no idea where they were. So, they'd continued to grill him.

At that point there'd been the police raid on the metal works and their own just-in-time escape.

Neumann asked how they'd worked out where the diamonds were. At this point Zig's depression lifted long enough to allow a grin to creep across his face. Ah! That was Azov's brainwave. Why not phone the police and pose as a concerned diamond dealer, worried about the whereabouts of some valuable belongings of a recent client, who had unfortunately died?

The awful truth suddenly dawned on Neumann.

That's why Torfs had been adamant he'd never made a phone call to St Vith police station! He'd been telling the truth. Azov had been able to access the dealer's registration number and pose – all too effectively – as Torfs.

Having guessed from the phone call where the diamonds were, they'd talked it over and fuelled by too much plum vodka, had come up with the crazy idea of breaking into the police station to liberate the gems. Even the sober light of the following morning had failed to shake their conviction that the diamonds would be there waiting for them and that the raid was doable.

So, they'd made their late-evening visit to the station, overpowered the night-duty officer and forced him at knifepoint to open the safe. Azov had got away with the diamonds. Zig hadn't been so lucky and was now well aware that his brother wouldn't be returning to rescue him, any time soon. The bastard would disappear, sell the diamonds and use the cash to start his own business.

Neumann had heard enough.

Torfs would need to be interviewed again and the search for Azov stepped up.

To keep himself going he thought about his changed holiday plans. With his arm out of action for the foreseeable future, the boat would have to stay in dock. But the doctor had said she'd be keen to accompany him travelling overland to Harlingen. There they could watch the boats, maybe even stay on one in the marina for a couple of nights, as long as it remained moored.

+ + +

Jules Fontaine had told Vos the story of the mask.

It had been smuggled into the country by a freelance operator. Tipped off about a police raid, he'd been panicked into burying the object in his back garden. The police had turned up at his house the following day and arrested him for a string of offences. He'd died in custody two days later, not a suspicious death apparently, but the effects of a long-term condition that had finally finished him off. Only one other person had known about the mask – Kurt Baumer – who'd told Fontaine about it. They'd dug up the mask so that it could be repatriated through Circle 10. Since Kurt's own death, there'd been a change of plan. Before rehoming, it would be used to bait Claus Eyckmans.

Fontaine had showed Vos the mask. It really was a beauty and seemed almost alive and more than a little scary. She'd provided him with a plausible story to use regarding the mask's route of entry into the country.

Vos hadn't fancied the idea of working solo, or the prospect of trying to navigate by the seat of his pants through the very different world that Claus Eyckmans inhabited. So, he'd enlisted the help of his own art dealer, Ruud Okker. To Vos' surprise, it hadn't taken much persuading to get him involved. They'd cooked up a plan and used an intermediary to arrange an appointment with Eyckmans.

The Range Rover and the expensive but sober suits had been hired for the day to enable them to look the part. The vehicle slowed at the gates. The camera picked them up, the gates opened and they swept up the drive to the imposing country house.

The task was a real challenge for them both. They had to project the right mix of skills, show an awareness of the quality and value of the product, an ability to negotiate and the nous to know at what price to try and seal the deal. They also had to be able to provide convincing answers to the questions the purchaser would throw at them. Fontaine had coached them about how to answer a series of likely questions.

Things did not get off to a good start. Eyckmans was frosty, off-hand and Vos wondered if he had any real interest in purchasing the mask. He showed no emotion when Ruud unwrapped and revealed the artefact. But he was full of questions – how had the mask entered the country, what paperwork was available, how come the two of them were involved and finally what was their asking price. Vos responded.

"A very elderly uncle of mine brought the mask into the country. He'd spent years in the DRC and arranged for a number of pieces to be 'exported', shall we say. Unfortunately, he died before he could arrange a sale. I've inherited both the mask and the responsibility for arranging a sale."

"How do I know you're not just making this up?" Eyckmans cut in.

Ruud handed him a sheet of paper.

"That's a fair question," he said. "This is a list of items Mr Vos' uncle had a hand in bringing into the country. It's not my area of speciality, but given your own interests, Mr Eyckmans, you may be familiar with some of the items."

Fontaine had drawn up the list using information originally compiled by Kurt Baumer. It showed a number of artefacts that had been imported illegally and they were relying on Eyckmans' knowledge of this to establish their credentials.

"What was his name – your uncle?"

"You won't have come across him. He wasn't a dealer as such, more of a behind the scenes expert," Vos said.

"OK. What about the paper trail?"

Vos handed over half a dozen documents. He knew this was the weakest part of their pitch, but Fontaine had said that Eyckmans wouldn't be too worried if there were some gaps in the trail.

Eyckmans scanned the papers and sniffed.

"Hmm! Whoever's prepared these hasn't tried very hard! It'll cost me to complete the paperwork. You'll be aware your asking price will suffer as a result."

"We're realistic about what kind of price we'll be able to get," Ruud said. "But then Mr Vos is in no hurry to sell and we have other irons in the fire. A man called Cornelius is one."

Eyckmans flinched. Fontaine had told them about the endless competition between the two men.

"Wait here a while," Eyckmans said. "I need to make some calls."

"What do you reckon?" Ruud asked as soon as they'd been left alone.

Vos put his finger to his lips and pointed to the chandelier. He didn't know whether the room was bugged but it was the kind of thing that their host might have set up. Ruud got the message. They kept the conversation on safe ground, but threw in a few comments about Cornelius just to up the ante.

When Eyckmans returned, he seemed to have thawed a little and was followed into the room by a man holding a tray of drinks.

"Well then, gentlemen. Once we've agreed a suitable price we can drink to a deal. Naturally that won't actually be concluded until I'm satisfied the mask is the genuine article. An expert in the field is on his way. I take it you're not in a hurry?"

They said they weren't.

"No doubt you have a figure in mind. Which one of you deals with the money?"

"That's my province," Ruud said. "This is our proposal." He handed over a sheet of paper.

A sharp intake of breath from Eyckmans.

"I think you're living in cloud cuckoo land! I might begin to take you seriously at around half that figure."

"In that case, we won't waste any more of your time," Vos said rising from his seat. Ruud followed him, but they hadn't got more than halfway to the door before Eyckmans spoke again.

"No need for such an early departure. Maybe I was a little hasty. Sit down and we can talk some more."

Vos knew Ruud would have the same thought.

We're in here!

Twenty Seven

Vos was fully stretched out on the sofa at home in Heist, resting his knee, half his mind focused on a Venice guidebook, a plan for a holiday with Katerine slowly developing, the other half recapping recent events.

Dr Vermeulen had told Ahrendt that the tests she planned to carry out would show, with a very high degree of certainty, whether or not Kurt and Suzanne were father and daughter.

Although Vos was eagerly awaiting news of the outcome and the chance to wrap up the case, he couldn't help feeling sorry for the other two contestants in the succession stakes.

Despite his poor state of health, Sebastien, unable to cope with such challenging events, had disappeared. As far as his wife was aware, he was on his way back to South Africa. And fake EK had fallen at the final unexpected hurdle – the testimony of a witness who'd attended his mother's wedding.

Vos reflected on how well he and Ruud had done on the deal with Eyckmans, securing two thirds of their original asking price. But of course, the figure itself was not the important thing. The real purpose of the approach had been to hook their man. He'd enjoyed briefing Jules Fontaine about their success.

He flicked through the Venice guidebook again and was just nodding off when his phone rang. It was Elias Kirchner – the real one – calling from rural Cambodia. His father had managed to contact him.

He didn't have much time. A definite tone of condescension, reminiscent of the fake version of the man.

Vos explained about Lothar Kramer and the identity theft he'd almost perpetrated.

"That's typical Lothar. Always a chancer but I can't help liking him. As far as my uncle's estate is concerned, I want nothing to do with it. The man abandoned Mother and I in our hour of need. But thanks to a successful career as a commodities trader, I'm no longer in need. Having taken early retirement, the last thing I want to do is disturb my karma with thoughts about Kurt Baumer."

Not a word of thanks.

Vos decided he actually preferred the fake version.

+ + +

Magnus was thawing. At the start of their relationship, he'd been far too formal, clearly nervous and worried about doing the wrong thing. Dina was gradually unearthing a more playful side to him. Although it was definitely alcohol that unlocked this Magnus, she thought the amounts needed to trigger each appearance were getting smaller. A recent evening outing had provided a good example. It was him who'd suggested a midnight walk to the small fishing lake and him who'd 'borrowed' the rowing boat. *I need to requisition this for an official search* he'd told her before, taking an oar each and weaving their way across the water, they'd descended into fits of giggles. It was just a shame that afterwards he'd had to return to the police station *to try and catch up.*

Dr Vermeulen had met with Suzanne Ziegler prior to the DNA sample being taken, to discuss the implications of the test – whichever way the decision turned out.

Suzanne arrived spot on time for her appointment to get the test results and seemed in good spirits.

"Thank you for coming in," the doctor said. "I appreciate this isn't easy for you, so I'll come straight to the point. There's a 99% certainty that Kurt Baumer was your father."

Suzanne looked straight at Dr Vermeulen.

"Oh no! All these years I've pushed it to the back of my mind and never spoken to anyone about it. And now ... well ... I don't know what I feel. Numb, shocked, sad."

"Sad in what way?"

"Sad for Kurt, that he didn't know this decades ago. Sad for Sebastien and a little bit sad for myself."

"Well, I'm sorry you've had to go through this."

"I met Kurt once. My great aunt set it up. There was a definite physical resemblance, but I didn't feel any kind of connection. He probably resented me because of what Mum and Dad did to him and I couldn't really be surprised about such a reaction."

"This must all be very difficult for you. I'll contact Kurt's lawyer and let him know the results of the test – if that's alright with you."

"Yes – I'd be glad if you would."

"Are you sure you're OK? Is there anything else you'd like to know, or talk about?"

"No thanks. You've been very helpful and very professional. Now, all I need to do is work out how to rebuild a relationship with my parents!"

"I'm sure they'll gradually come round. After all, apart from deciding to request a test, you haven't been responsible for any of this. Will you stay here for a while or go straight back to South Africa?" Dr Vermeulen asked.

"I had planned to go straight back, but now, well, there'll be papers to sign and decisions to make so I'll probably have to stay on for a while."

Once Suzanne had left, Dr Vermeulen sat back in her chair. She looked at the details on the other piece of paper in front of her. She hadn't told anybody about the second DNA test which had been for her own personal reassurance.

It showed that there was absolutely no possibility that Sebastien could have been Suzanne's biological father.

+ + +

Part way through a TV documentary on climate change, Vos' phone rang. He muted the set and took the call expecting it to be his daughter Kim who'd promised to get in touch. But it was Doctor Vermeulen with news he'd hoped for but deep down hadn't thought likely. He'd found his heir.

Her call hadn't been restricted to news of Suzanne's paternity. She'd also told him the hard-to-believe story about Chief Inspector Neumann and the raid on the St Vith police station.

Twenty Eight

After a good night's sleep, Vos made an early start in the Berlingo on the short drive to Antwerp for a final meeting with Jules Fontaine.

The payment from Eyckmans had been lodged in a special account. Statements had been prepared and witnessed by a lawyer. Fontaine would be preparing a press release. Vos was very pleased about the way it had turned out. At first, he refused payment saying that he'd been more than happy to assist. But Fontaine insisted he accept it.

Just as he was about to leave, she told him there was something weighing on her mind. Did he have a few more minutes?

It was about Kurt Baumer.

"I'm afraid I haven't been entirely honest with you. Kurt's story is not quite as straightforward as I've made out. Your initial impression that he was on the wrong side of the fence was correct – at least in part. You see when we first came across him, he *was* one of the bad guys. Money was behind it. You may have gathered that he was hopeless with it and kept on needing more. As luck would have it, he met a man called Cornelius, the one I told you about, Eyckmans' competitor. They got talking. Cornelius had money and was willing to pay Kurt for his expert advice on Congolese artefacts – provided on a no-questions-asked basis. This began when Kurt retired, about twenty years ago. His pension pot had dwindled as a result of some very bad investment advice and he was desperate for cash. His job was to identify pieces that were in the DRC that could be exported illegally through various routes to end up in one or other of the private galleries run by Cornelius. Kurt's aunt, who needed money to keep her sanctuary going, was also in on the act."

Vos thought about the typewriter-produced memos he'd found which had led him to conclude that Kurt was involved in dodgy dealing.

"So how come he ended up switching sides and working for Circle 10?"

"About ten years ago, we found out what he was up to. As you know, part of our job is to expose such illegal importation. However, we were so impressed by the extent of his knowledge that we gave him a choice. *Come and join us or we'll turn you in!* Which was really no choice at all. He told Cornelius he was getting too old for the game and we kept his new role for us a secret. He told me later how glad he was that we'd rescued him from the *path of sin*. Not that he was at all religious, but the guilt had been getting to him. Given what a help you've been to us I thought you should know about this – but please keep it to yourself."

+ + +

It was a short walk back to the Berlingo. He now had a much more rounded picture of Kurt Baumer, warts and all. Somehow the previous portrait Fontaine had painted had always seemed a bit too good to be true. And the involvement of Aunt Ada? Maybe that was one possible explanation for the appearance of the diamonds. Had they been paid in gems for their illicit work, or in cash that had been converted to diamonds? Vos reckoned he'd probably never find out.

As he reached his car, he was surprised to see Kela on the far pavement, walking quickly in the direction of Fontaine's office. Why wasn't she already in hiding? About to call out, he noticed a man a few metres behind, clearly tailing her.

It didn't look good. She had to be warned. Would her phone be on? The last thing he wanted was to be routed to voicemail.

She answered.

"Kela, it's Harry Vos. You're being followed. Don't turn round! Just carry on walking. Completely by chance, I'm on the opposite side of the street from you both."

"Harry – I don't believe it! Do you know about the gang? Has Jules told you?"

"I know enough. Are you on your way to her place?"

"Yes. It must be a man called Skip. What does he look like?" Vos described him. "Yes – that's him. Shit, I thought I got rid of him yesterday."

"You carry on," Vos said. "I'll intercept him. He won't know me from Adam."

"No – wait, Harry, he can be very dangerous!"

"Thanks for the warning."

Vos crossed the road and increased his pace until he was just behind the man.

"Oi – baldie! Why are you following that woman?" he said in a low voice.

The man turned.

"Fuck off, old man, before I lose my temper!"

"I know all about you, Skip. You're following her. That's why I'm following you."

For a moment, Skip looked totally confused. But he recovered quickly, scowled and swung a large fist towards Vos' chin.

He probably hadn't given any thought to the possibility that the 'old man' might retaliate. But Vos had been a promising boxer in his youth. And the recent sparring sessions at the local gym had turned out to be a much-needed refresher.

Of course, Skip didn't know any of this. His punch only half-connected.

In response, Vos didn't go for anything fancy, just a straight right into the stomach. With his opponent doubled over, Vos used the moment to slip his wallet into Skip's pocket.

As a crowd gathered round, Vos shouted out – *stole my bloody wallet, didn't he* – before reaching into the man's pocket and retrieving the 'stolen' item. Much to his surprise, the police arrived within minutes of his call. They took statements from him and a couple of witnesses. When Skip attempted to escape, they arrested him. To his relief, having already given a statement, Vos wasn't required to visit the police station.

He phoned Kela to give her the good news. She retraced her steps to meet him.

"Thank you so much, Harry," she said. "Where did you learn to punch like that?"

"It's a long story which belongs in the past. But it has come in useful now and then. Is there somewhere safe you can go to?"

"Once I've seen Jules. Something very important came up. Then I'll be off – a long way from here!"

+ + +

After the confrontation with Skip, Vos had gone to the hospital more as a precaution than anything else. But he also wanted to be able to tell Katerine how sensible he'd been getting things checked out– even if it hadn't been particularly sensible to tackle Skip on his own in the first place. Still, it had all worked out fine. Having the element of surprise was half the battle.

It was a long drive back to St Vith – and a relief that he wouldn't have to do the journey again. During his brief stop at the motorway services, Vos read the article in the online edition of

Liege's La Meuse about the police station raid carried out by the two brothers from Moldova. Neumann had forwarded the link.

He stared at the photo of Azov, who was apparently on the run.

He'd seen him somewhere before.

Twenty Nine

In Kurt's house for the final time, Vos completed his report for Ahrendt, attached his invoice, which included details of hours worked and expenses incurred and emailed it to the lawyer. It hadn't been easy to separate out the hours that could genuinely be attributed to his official heir hunter role and the time he'd spent pursuing his own special interests in relation to Kurt's dealing and diamond activities.

There was no more searching to do. An heir had been found. He wanted to leave the house neat and tidy – even though that wasn't how he'd found it. The place felt very different than that first day he'd let himself in through the front door – lighter, airier and much more spacious.

What would Suzanne do with the house? Presumably it would be sold. A new neighbour for Marc. And what about the Rekord? Perhaps he should ask her whether he could buy it. Ryck's comment came to mind. Would it be a sensible vehicle for him to own and would he take care of it well enough? Well, there'd be no harm in asking her.

He filled the refuse bin in the shed with bagged rubbish and wheeled it out of the side gate ready for collection. About to close the shed door he noticed a small box in the space behind where the bin had been. The box contained a phone.

A very unsmart phone. No code required to gain entry. He quickly established it was Kurt's, but was then disappointed to find only a handful of texts in the inbox, all from the same DRC number. He recognised the code. Two of them had been sent after Kurt's death wanting to know why he hadn't responded to earlier queries. Rather than making a call, Vos sent a text and asked the recipient to respond. He pocketed the phone.

Having spent so much time in Kurt's house he felt almost reluctant to leave it behind. After locking up for the final time he walked next door to drop the keys off with Marc.

Over a coffee, they discussed Kurt's heir.

"She called in yesterday," Marc said. "Offered me first refusal on Kurt's house!"

"It wouldn't be of much interest to you, would it? I thought you were considering a move to an apartment."

"I am. And it could be right here."

"I don't understand," Vos said.

"Nor did I. It was Suzanne's suggestion. *Why not buy the house, convert the two into apartments, live in the lower one yourself, which would be nice and easy to get around and sell the upper one?*"

"Could you afford to do that?" Vos asked, thinking it sounded a particularly expensive solution to his friend's housing needs.

"That's just what I'm looking into. But it's an attractive idea. And I might even be able to persuade Astrid to move in with me."

+ + +

A long goodbye with Marc, was followed by a short drive to St Vith and a short walk to the deli. Just as he was selecting the ingredients for his bespoke sandwich ... out of nowhere ... a sudden vision of Torfs' office ... the man who'd brought in the dealer's diary ... a man who looked just like Azov Donici.

Vos phoned his son and asked him to check the online photo. Eddie agreed. The diamond thief was definitely the same man who'd appeared briefly in the dealer's office.

Had Torfs been in on the whole scam? A call to Neumann to let him know.

Sitting on a bench in Rathausplatz and soaking up the sun, he tucked into his lunch, trying to stop bits of salad from tumbling out of the well-filled sandwich. To complicate matters further, Kurt's phone rang. After some juggling, he managed to answer it.

"Kurt? Where the hell have you been?" The caller spoke in French.

"I'm sorry. This isn't Kurt, but I'm a good friend of his. Please don't hang up. I'm afraid I have some bad news. Are you still there?"

"Yes I am. Don't tell me the old boy's dead!"

"He is, I regret to say. It happened a few weeks ago, but I've only just found his phone. You were wanting his response on some queries. Maybe I can help."

"Well, I'm really sorry he's gone. He wasn't the easiest guy to get along with but he sure knew a lot. What exactly was your relationship with him?"

Vos explained he lived next door and had helped Kurt out over the past few years, trusting that the caller had never actually met or spoken to Marc. He'd been tidying up when he'd come across the phone.

The caller asked some questions about Kurt, which Vos was able to answer. He felt he'd established his credentials.

"Look – this might be a complete shot in the dark – but would your texts have anything to do with diamonds?" There was a pause at the other end of the line.

"You do know him well! Where are they now?"

"The police have them," Vos lied.

"Look, the reason I was so keen to speak to Kurt was that I've finally tracked down the origin of the damned things. It had been bugging Kurt for months. The good news is they're legit. I've found the paperwork." Had it not been for his bad knee, Vos would have danced a jig around the bench. "I assume you'll know who Kurt's lawyer is. Give me his contact details and I'll send him the necessary."

Vos gave him Ahrendt's email address.

"Just out of curiosity, what was their origin? I'd been led to believe they'd something to do with Kurt's aunt and had a bit of a question mark over them?"

"They did. Originally, they belonged to a friend of Ada's and he gave them to her for safe-keeping. I was his lawyer and he asked me to sort out the paperwork. I've only just managed to do that, but can confirm they're definitely legit. Unfortunately, my client died before I'd completed my work. His will said the diamonds were to be passed on to Ada. I think they had a bit of a thing going. So now it'll be up to Ada's lawyer and Ahrendt to sort out what happens to them."

Even though, with the diamonds in Azov's pocket, this was all a bit academic, Vos was pleased that the mystery of their origin had been cleared up. With both phone conversation and sandwich finished, he made his way over to the police station.

Chief Inspector Neumann seemed almost genial, but then it was his last day at work before going on holiday. Vos asked him where he'd be going. A trip to the sea without actually going on the sea. With Dr Vermeulen he added, reddening only a little.

"So, it was the daughter who inherited."

"Much to everyone's surprise!" Vos said. "I do feel for Sebastien. But really, he should have known right from the start that it would be very difficult to substantiate his claim. Whether the rift between him and Suzanne will ever be healed, who knows."

"And what about Miriam? Had she known all along about Kurt being the father?"

"According to Suzanne, her mother hadn't known for sure, but had felt he might be."

"You must be pleased with the way things have turned out. An heir found and Kirchner foiled."

"I'm very pleased. But what really rankles – as I'm sure it does with you – is Azov getting away scot-free with the abduction, the threats to Kurt Baumer which probably led to his heart attack, the attacks on you and your colleague, not to mention the theft of the bloody diamonds. I don't suppose there's any news about him." The chief inspector sighed.

"It's a matter of great regret to me that he escaped our clutches. The diamonds should never have been kept here. We don't have anywhere near the right level of security. I tried to get them transferred elsewhere, but nobody higher up the chain was interested enough in what they saw as a dead smuggler's ill-gotten gains. That's all changed because of the attack on officers and the theft. Finding Azov is now a high priority. I suspect that's mainly because he made us look bad. They've drafted someone in from Liege to head up the search. If Azov's still in the country, we've probably got a good chance of finding him. But my guess is that he'll have left Belgium behind. And if we locate him somewhere else, we might well have problems with extradition."

"It would awful if he got away with it," Vos said. "But I might be able to help. You sent me that link to the press article, which included a photo of Azov. I knew straight away I'd seen him somewhere before."

"Really – where was that?" Neumann asked.

"It took me a while to realise, but he was in Torfs' office when I visited. To my mind that suggests the dealer was in on it. What are the chances of him being brought in for questioning?"

"That's a very useful lead. I'll set the wheels in motion. With my holiday just about to start, I'll have to leave it to others. But before you go, Harry, I'd like to thank you for your input into all this. When we first met, I had some reservations about you and there's always a problem drawing a line between the official bit of any investigation and the unofficial. But I think we got it about right."

The two men shook hands and Vos wished the policeman a happy holiday.

His final port of call in St Vith was the bed and breakfast, where Helga received his grateful thanks, a bouquet, a bottle of fizz and a kiss on both cheeks.

+ + +

He arrived back in Heist the day before Katerine was due home.

His phone rang just as he was about to get into the shower. Although it was *number unknown*, he took the call.

"Vos – please don't hang up." Jos Webers! Surely, he wasn't going to start hassling again. Keep calm, play it neutral.

"Hello. How's the hip?"

"I've had a replacement. All happened much quicker than I thought. Brittle bones – runs in the family unfortunately. Listen there's something I need to tell you." Here we go, thought Vos.

"It's been preying on my mind. I left something in your toilet cistern – the one upstairs."

Vos couldn't stand the idea that the man knew all about the inside of his house. He wondered what kind of object was in the cistern. A mini-explosive device that could be triggered by Webers' phone perhaps. He tried to stop his imagination running riot.

"What is it?" he asked, his anger mounting.

"I'm afraid it's a bag of cocaine. Not much – I'm not that generous – but enough to cause you problems. The plan was to tell the police about it. But I've had a rethink. I still reckon you're an annoying bastard, but the way you and your pal helped me and the fact that you haven't grassed me up to the cops, well I can't forget that, which means I can't go through with my plan. You're officially off the hook. I trust our paths will never cross again. Goodbye."

A few minutes later and Webers' little gift had been flushed away.

Vos had one more outstanding task.

Neumann had already left on his holiday and Vos had been unable to find a way through the bureaucracy of the Antwerp force to find out whether they'd re-interviewed Luc Torfs. He was just a civilian and it was none of his business. In the end he'd managed to speak to Neumann's deputy in St Vith who'd told him that an interview had taken place but he'd not been informed of the outcome.

Vos decided to take matters into his own hands. It took all his powers of persuasion to get Torfs to agree to meet him again.

Arriving early, he had to wait a while before the dealer was free. The receptionist hadn't been there on his previous visit. She seemed pleasant enough and they chatted intermittently about the weather, holidays and Antwerp traffic.

When he was shown into Torfs' office it was clear the dealer was edgy.

"I understand you were interviewed by the police about Azov Donici." Vos had to assume they would have asked about the Moldovan.

"Who?"

"Come on! The man who worked for you until he absconded recently. I saw him in this very office the last time I was here. This man," he said showing Torfs a copy of the photo from the online article. "You'll know that he phoned the police in St Vith posing as you, to get information about Kurt Baumer's diamonds. Even used your registration number. Now I don't know what the police are doing about this but unless you start co-operating with me, I'll need to release some details about your activities to the people who regulate you dealers."

Torfs squirmed in his seat. Vos could imagine him weighing up the options. Ignore the PI who might well just be bluffing, or get him off his back by telling him what he knew about the thug who used to work for him.

"Alright! I admit that he and his brother carried out certain tasks for me. But I had absolutely nothing to do with their idiotic raid on the police station. Why on earth would I risk my hard-won reputation by having any connection with a stunt like that?"

"What sort of work did they do for you?"

"Odd jobs, courier services, protection against some of my more unusual clients. You'd be amazed how some diamond owners turn out to be barely civilised. But they were not involved in any way with the buying or selling of precious gems."

"And that phone call?" Vos asked.

"I've already told the police that wasn't me. It's a matter of great regret, firstly that Azov was somehow able to access my dealer registration number and secondly that the pair of them used confidential client information to attempt a robbery. Azov is very much the rough diamond – if you'll pardon the expression. I've no knowledge of where he is now, but based on what I know about him, I'm almost certain he will have taken his ill-gotten gains and headed home. And by that – I mean Moldova."

"What about other details? If the police are to have a chance of finding him, it would be helpful to know of any relatives, and maybe even an address back home."

"Relatives – let me think. He used to refer to his mother occasionally, lives in the capital in an old folks home as far as I can remember. I presume she shares a surname with them, so that could be a start."

"And what about if he hasn't managed to make it back home yet? The police were quick to circulate his details to airports and stations. If he was still holed up here, any idea where that might be?"

"Not really. Look I didn't have anything to do with them outside of working hours. So, there's very little I know about them."

"And yet, Zig told the police that you were the reason they came to this country in the first place," Vos said. "Something to do with them saving you from a beating – or worse – in Moscow."

"There is some truth in that. Look I knew where they lived, here in the city, but the police told me they'd already checked that out. Apart from that, they had one or two close friends and he mentioned seeing a woman. But I don't have any names or addresses. Besides, it's much more likely Azov has already left the country."

A woman, Vos thought. How close might they have been? Would he have wanted to leave her behind?

On the way out, he asked the receptionist about Azov. She wrinkled her nose. Not her favourite man. Had she ever heard him mention a girlfriend? Yes, she'd even come into the office once recently. Very good looking. Any chance you remember her name? First name was Natalia. No mention of a last name. And any idea where she lived? No. But they'd mentioned going to BH – wherever that was.

+ + +

A quiet afternoon drink in Eddie's bar after some shopping for a welcome home present for Katerine. His son joined him.

"I've just been having a chat with our friend Luc Torfs."

"You should have told me you were going there. It's not safe talking to people like him on your own. What were you after?" Vos felt suitably admonished. He could be more than a little careless with his personal safety.

Vos explained about Azov Donici.

"The receptionist there mentioned his girlfriend who had some sort of connection with a place she referred to as BH. Ring any bells?"

"No, I don't think so. Can I get you another, Dad?"

"Yes thanks. Just an orange juice please. Don't want to be too late back. There's a bit of tidying up to do."

Eddie returned with two glasses of orange.

"I've just remembered about BH," Eddie said. "We did a school project on the place. It's got more boundaries than people. Well almost. Baarle-Hertog! Twenty two Belgian enclaves completely surround by the Netherlands – and the answer to a popular pub quiz question. Want to nip across there now? I'll drive. Won't take much more than an hour. Unless of course that tidying up really can't wait."

"Are you sure? It might well turn out to be a wild goose chase!"

"Who cares. It'll be good to get out of the city."

At Turnhout they took the N119 to Baarle-Hertog. Vos realised all they had to go on was a woman's first name but he was banking on Natalia not being a common name within the enclave.

They asked around at a few cafés, without success. Eddie suggested trying some of the firework shops of which there were several owing to the Belgian laws on sale being more lenient than the Dutch. One of the proprietors knew a Natalia. First left and second right. Number 27. Watch your step with her, they were told. Bit of a temper.

27 was a small mid-terrace house. A woman answered the door.

"Azov in, by any chance," Vos asked, making a few assumptions and thinking there was no point in beating about the bush. She bridled immediately.

"Don't talk to me about him!"

"Gone back to Moldova, has he?"

"And left me with all his debts. Who the fuck are you anyway?"

"Azov and his brother paid a visit to my good friend Kurt Baumer who ended up dead. Not only that but Azov's now got Kurt's diamonds, which probably explains why he's buggered off home."

"Sorry about your friend. Of course, I didn't know about any of this. You from the police?"

"No, as I said, I'm just a friend of Kurt's. Has he gone to his mother's?"

"Don't make me laugh. She died years ago, abandoned by him and his brother. No, he'll be with his ex."

"Do you have a name and an address by any chance?"

"Is there anything you don't want? She's Valentina, don't know her last name, or her address. But she lives in Chisinau, works at the zoo. That's all I know."

"Thanks for your help. I'm sorry, there is just one more thing." A long theatrical sigh. "Would it be possible to use your toilet? You see I have this condition … old age you know."

"Jesus. You're a pain. Very well, but you'll need to get a move on. I've got things to do. Follow me!"

Vos was led through the kitchen to an outdoor toilet in the back yard. There was a gradual realisation that she was standing guard outside as he performed.

He was bundled out of the house as soon as he'd finished.

"Hell hath no fury …" Vos said to his son as they sat in the car.

"Bet she can look after herself," Eddie replied. "Did you spot anything useful on your visit to the toilet?"

"Nothing!"

"So, what'll happen next?"

"You know about Neumann the chief inspector in St Vith?" Eddie nodded. "Well, he's on holiday just now so I'll tell his deputy about Azov's ex, he'll pass it on to the chief inspector in Liege who's handling the investigation and he'll pass it on to the Interpol bureau in Chisinau. Apparently, they've already issued an international alert. Let's just hope that the news gets through OK and that Natalia's information's reliable."

"OK. Just one thing though, Dad. She didn't convince me with that story about Azov's ex. I mean, if she was an ex, would he really still be in contact with her in Moldova after ten years of living in Antwerp? That's how long you said he'd been here, wasn't it?"

"Yes, you're right. I hadn't thought of that. What do you reckon then? That he might still be in the country?"

"More than that. I think he might be shacked up in that house with Natalia, waiting for the hue and cry to die down."

"What makes you say that?"

"Well, while you were out back, I took the chance to have a look at the cars parked nearest to her house – just to see if any of them gave any clue as to Azov's presence. That old red BMW," Eddie said pointing to the vehicle. "In the tray by the gear stick there's a ring. A man's ring. Unusual coiled snake design which I've seen before – on Azov's finger in Torfs' office that day. Doesn't prove he's in the house but it would be worth checking. The police, I mean – not us."

"So, you fancy yourself as an eagle-eyed investigator eh? Well spotted! I'll phone Neumann's deputy and see if he can go through the channels to get a squad out here ASAP. Are you OK for time? It would be good to stay here just in case Azov *is* in the house and decides to do a runner."

"No problem. I'll give Sibilla a ring and let her know what's going on."

The calls were made.

They were parked on the roadside, in a line of cars, about 15 metres from Natalia's house and with a good view of the front door.

"Is there a risk he'll get out via the back yard," Eddie asked.

"There's no way out, just a big brick wall."

Keeping one eye on the nearby doorway, Vos found he was enjoying the unexpected opportunity for a conversation with his son. Eddie said he'd been thinking about selling the bar, moving out to Heist and setting up a new online business. Vos had no idea these plans had been cooking and was very pleased at the prospect of his son and family living close by, if a little worried about the chances of success for a new online business.

His phone rang. The message had got through and Antwerp had alerted a specialist team in Turnhout. They were on their way, ETA ten minutes. *Whatever you do, don't go near the house.* Vos wasn't tempted.

A few minutes later, Azov burst through the front door of Natalia's house and jumped into the BMW. After a nod from his father, Eddie started up the Subaru and followed the red car at a distance. His father phoned the mobile number he'd been given, to tell the Turnhout team about Azov's movements and give them details of the car. He kept the line open. Having crossed the border into the Netherlands within minutes, they passed through Chaam. Eddie said it looked as if the Moldovan was heading for Breda – and maybe Amsterdam and Schipol beyond. The Turnhout officer told Vos that they were liaising with their Dutch colleagues.

It all happened very quickly. An Audi overtook the Subaru at speed and tailgated the BMW. A Volvo with Dutch plates pulled out from a side road just in front of Azov, forcing him to pull off the road. Three men leapt from each of the unmarked police vehicles and swooped on the BMW, weapons drawn.

Azov was overpowered.

+ + +

By the time he got back to Heist, Vos didn't feel much like tidying up. He collapsed on the sofa and fell asleep immediately. Two hours later he was woken by a call from Jules Fontaine and was very pleased to hear that the case against her had been suddenly dropped. Wheels had moved within wheels. Circle 10 hadn't been exposed. They could carry on working. Her cover blown, Kela wouldn't be returning to the DRC. But there was a chance of a new role for her, negotiating the return of artefacts from Belgian museums to the DRC. And Claus Eyckmans would be facing charges of illegally importing just such artefacts. Despite the strength of evidence against him, Fontaine wasn't confident about the outcome of the trial. The art establishment might have good reason to close ranks.

Ryck arrived to re-home Barto. Feeling like some early evening air, Vos joined them for a walk around the block, his nephew eager to hear all about the events of the day.

Having waved Ryck off, Barto asleep at his feet, Vos felt one way or another he'd earned a beer or two. One of Kurt's Afro-Jazz albums was spinning on the deck. Suzanne had told him to take the lot. It wasn't her sort of music. And he'd made a bid for the Opel Rekord. Not perhaps a sensible move but he just couldn't resist.

A call from Katerine. Back earlier than expected. She'd be home within the hour.

Only then did Vos realise just how much he'd missed her over the past few weeks.

Thirty

A fortnight had flown by.

The four days in Venice had been everything they'd hoped for.

The garden had got some much-needed attention.

And Barto had never been fitter.

When Katerine told her husband there was a Sunday surprise lined up for him, he pulled a face and said he didn't like surprises.

On the day, she drove him to Eddie's bar. There was a sign at the foot of the stairs inside saying the function room was booked for a private party. She led him up the stairs and pushed open the double doors. Tables were set, food was being brought in by staff and the corner bar was in operation.

A large banner on one wall read – Happy 70th Birthday Harry!

"Hang about!" Vos said. "My birthday was last Sunday. You took me out for a meal in Dorsoduro – remember?"

"I know that, you old grump," Katerine said. "But it just so happens that nobody else was able to join us for that meal. Whereas everyone can make it today. So here we all are!"

Vos looked around the room. She was right – they were all there: Eddie, Sibilla and the two boys, Kim, Anders and little Marika, Josina and her boyfriend, Ryck, Magda, Sun and Freddie, his brother Pieter, Jan Wouters smiling broadly – and was that really Uncle Albert in the far corner? There were friends as well as relatives sitting at the tables, all wishing him a happy birthday.

He decided, after all, that he liked the idea of a party and moved around the room greeting everyone in turn.

It was a buffet rather than a sit-down meal which suited him fine as he'd never been one for formality. However, he decided a little bit of formality, a short speech, would do no harm. Once the food was finished, he clinked a knife against a glass to get his guests' attention.

"Well, it really is nice seeing everyone here today and very convenient for me to have you all in one place. I must thank Katerine. She knows me too well to have asked my opinion about a party. As a card-carrying old misery guts, I'd have said I didn't want any fuss and would have just taken her and Barto out for a walk instead!

As some of you may know, I've just finished one of my little investigations, trying to find out whether a man called Kurt Baumer, who died recently, had any living relatives. As things turned out, there were three possibles. But on further expert investigation, I managed to narrow it down to just one. And I wouldn't have got there had it not been for Josina's magic online family-tracing skills. So, in the end Kurt wasn't the end of his line.

But it is the end of the line for me. Nothing to do with my health I hasten to add, but in relation to my sometime private investigator status. Yes, I've decided to put away my notebook and hang up my magnifying glass. When I started out several years ago, I never expected the variety, the stimulation and, from time to time, the danger that has come my way. I've met some very interesting people, some of whom have become friends and some of whom … haven't.

So, even though I've really enjoyed my time as a sleuth, I've recently come to realise that there are other things I'd prefer to be doing, like spending more time with Katerine, my children and the growing band of grandchildren! It's about time I tried full-time retirement. Which also means I'll have more time to come round and bother you lot. Thank you one and all for coming today.

And now I'm going to give my wife a first retirement kiss."

+ + +

As Katerine drove them home, he checked his phone. There was a text from Chief Inspector Neumann.

Thanks for all your help Harry. It turned out Azov still had the diamonds and they've now been recovered and passed on to their rightful new owner! Maybe she'll share some of her good fortune with her mother and father.

Acknowledgements

Many thanks to Emma for editing, Gabrielle and Paul for reading and Neil for providing the St Vith map which kick-started the story.

By the
Same Author

Shoreline

Harry Vos, a retired man in his 60s and a part time private investigator, is shocked to find a body on a beach on the Belgian coast.

Unable to get a signal on his phone, he hurries to a local bar to contact the police.

On his return, he discovers the body has disappeared and finds he has some explaining to do once the police arrive.

They regard him as a time-waster.

Harry decides to try and find out what has happened and his investigation leads him into the murky and dangerous waters of people-smuggling

Redline

A man's body has been found on a riverbank near Charleroi in Belgium.

The police make no progress in identifying him, until private investigator Harry Vos gets himself involved.

Harry is drawn into the very contrasting worlds of tattooing and land deals for nuclear waste and fracking sites.

Working with Edith, a former partner of the dead man, he delves more deeply into the case.

They find themselves under serious threat from a powerful company.

Matador

For exclusive discounts on Matador titles,
sign up to our occasional newsletter at
troubador.co.uk/bookshop